THE LOST DOOR

STEEN JONES

In every world,
[signature]

Copyright © 2018 by Steen Jones
Front Cover Design: Copyright © 2018 Brittney Kaefer

All rights reserved. This book or any portion thereof may not be reproduced or used in any manner whatsoever without the express written permission of the publisher except for the use of brief quotations in a book review.

Printed in the United States of America
First Printing, 2018

ISBN 9781985695580

Steen Jones
steen@thedoorkeepertrilogy.com

www.thedoorkeepertrilogy.com

*This book is dedicated to Andy, my best friend.
I love you times 3.*

THE LOST DOOR

THE PROLOGUE.

Eden

The gentle sway of the bed rocked us to sleep, while a steady breeze provided the perfect temperature, despite the hot suns of mid-afternoon. I woke up finding a foot tangled in the white sheets, my dark, bare skin peaking out here and there. The subtle fluttering of butterflies tickled in my stomach again, like I felt before we'd fallen asleep. Squinting for a moment, I allowed my eyes to adjust to the two suns reflections glistening off the shallow sea, flowing just a couple feet below me. I rolled over and sat up, covering my chest, looking out at the vast beauty before me. The expansive turquoise sea was only interrupted by a fruit orchard springing up from its sand and the occasional blue swan flying low, skimming the ever-lapping water.

My new husband lay next to me, breathing in and out slowly, enjoying his well-deserved nap. His usually paler skin was tan and freckly on his nose, forehead, and shoulders from our time here. Laying on his stomach, his back rose and fell with each breath, and I smiled noticing a little of his left buttocks exposed. Not able to resist myself I popped him on the butt, then almost fell out of the rope swing bed when he startled awake.

"What? What is it?" James pushed himself up quickly before he remembered we were in bed. I grabbed his arm before I fell off and laughed.

"Nothing, everything is fine. I just couldn't resist."

"Couldn't resist, huh? Well, resist this!" He growled and grabbed me, pinning me underneath him.

We relaxed into each other's arms, laughing and settling into another comfortable cuddling position. We'd been here a week already, and in a few days, our honeymoon would be over. But I knew our new lives were just beginning. As we drifted off into another lazy nap, a picture of the little curly, chocolate haired little boy with round cheeks flashed in my mind, and the odd sensation of the butterflies fluttered my stomach once more.

Later that day, we finally climbed off the bed swing and up the ladder into the treehouse. My mother had been raised in this house, preparing to become Queen, and it had remained abandoned and uncared for since. My Aunt Mae cleaned it up and gifted it to me and James to use as a vacation/secondary home while visiting Caelum. The house was built around a gargantuan magnolia tree. A large studio apartment, Swiss family Robinson style. There was a main living area with a small kitchenette and a large, ornately carved, wooden bed. The restroom facilities were basic at best, but sufficed. My favorite feature was the wall of windows, twenty feet high and twenty-four feet wide, over looking the suns setting. It was constructed from discarded windows from the bigger islands, different sizes and shapes. Every night, James and I lounged in the oversized bed, drinking wine, and watching the two suns disappear into the horizon. High above the tin roof were two additional seating areas, only accessible with a rope ladder. A pulley system allowed us to hoist our meals up to the top deck and eat in the top of the tree.

That night perched up in Ava's tree, we ate dinner and talked about our future and the adventures we would share together. It was heavenly—just dreaming, imagining, and planning our life. Our surrogate horses, Nox and Cocoa, slowly made their way toward the treehouse as they did most nights, so we could ride and explore other parts of Caelum. We decided to visit the lake surrounded by mountains that Marek, my brother, and I had both dreamt about. As I took a bite of dinner, the nervous tension in my stomach twisted once again. I must have made a weird face because James asked me what was wrong.

I simply smiled and looked up at him.

"Nothing's wrong. I just . . ."

I couldn't find the words.

"What?" he asked, the crease in his brow deepening.

"I . . . I just think that earlier . . ."

"Earlier? Yeah, I thoroughly enjoyed earlier."

"Yeah, well." I laughed uncomfortably. Then I finally brought myself to say it.

"I think we might have made a baby."

THE BEGINNING.

Eden

I leaned against the doorframe and watched her sleep, as I did most nights the past few months. Her lips slightly parted as she dreamed. I knew she was dreaming, the tiny scratches developing on her arms were a dead giveaway. Focusing, I closed my eyes to enter her subconscious. She was with Lolli, climbing on a limb perched over a field of budding Serenbes. Lolli giggled, flying next to her as they maneuvered up the tree. I should have known. It was one of her recurring dreams. As she climbed higher and higher, Lolli warned her to be careful. Gabby's foot slipped for just a second, long enough for a small branch to swipe the right side of her face.

I opened my eyes already knowing what would be there, the small fresh scrape on my daughter's right cheek.

I first noticed it almost two years ago, right after her sixteenth birthday. Gabby hadn't yet realized that her dreams and her physical body were connected. Thankfully, there hadn't been anything too traumatic to make the connection.

The worst one was a nightmare she had a few months ago, when she dreamt she was swimming and accidentally inhaled some water. Gabby woke to coughing up water in the bed. She just assumed she tried to drink water in her sleep, and I let her think it. Gabby sleep walked a lot, so it was a reasonable assumption. I understood time was running out, and soon I would have to tell her the truth, but tonight, I just wanted her to stay my little girl. My little girl that didn't know that her dreams weren't harmless, that other worlds beyond this one existed, and that one day she would rule one of them.

The next morning, standing out on the front porch, I slowly sipped my coffee. A perfect chill hung in the air, despite the heat predicted for later in the afternoon. Early spring gave North Georgia a beautiful balance on most days. Leaning against the wooden pole, I eyed the mist hovering over the lake across the road. The flocks of geese, my neighbors for almost eighteen years, were unusually quiet this morning. The screen door squeaked open and shut behind me. My husband wrapped his arms around me and kissed the top of my head.

"You're up early this morning. How did you sleep?"

"Alright, I kept a part of my subconscious on Gabby."

James followed my gaze out to the lake, not needing to reply. We both already knew what that meant.

"Good morning." Gabby shut the screen door behind her and yawned. "JJ is awake. I went ahead and gave him cereal." She plopped down on one of the rocking chairs with a bowl of her own.

"Thanks, hon."

"Good morning, family!" Marek burst through the door and startled every one of us. Only wearing pajama pants, I noticed a new black tattoo crawled off his shoulder and down his right side over his rib cage.

"Geez, Uncle Marek, it's too early," Gabby whined.

"Gabbs, I only get to see you a couple times a year—cut me some slack." My brother rolled his light green eyes dramatically to tease her. She just smiled sarcastically through a mouthful of cereal. We chit chatted about our plans for the day, and not long after, Gabby went in to get ready for school.

After she left, Marek's voice fell from jovial to concerned within seconds.

"She dreamt again last night. There's a scratch on her cheek."

"I know," I sighed.

Marek was silent for a beat. "You know, she is looking more and more like the vision we had of her in Caelum. Eden, I know you don't want to hear this, but it's time. You need to tell her. It's dangerous to keep letting her dream without telling her she can control it."

"You're right. We discussed it before you got here." I nodded at James. "We decided to tell her in three weeks."

My brother exhaled in relief. "Good. That's around her eighteenth birthday?"

"Yes. She will have gotten what we all wanted for her, a normal childhood. Gabbs will be old enough to make an informed decision about her future."

"But it's not really much of a choice is it?" James spoke up.

"Of course it is." I turned to him. "Timing will play a huge factor in her decision. This will happen on *her* timeline. I'm making sure of that."

"We all will," Marek reassured me. "Are you still planning to give her *The Door Keeper*?"

"Yes, I feel like it's the best way for her to hear the whole story."

Marek referred to the book I had put together, transcribing of all of my journals from the first year of learning who my birth mother truly was, a Door Keeper from another world, called Caelum. It included the journals I kept in Italy, about meeting Rosalina, one of my mother's friends, and about Ava herself and my family. The book detailed the truth about my mother's death, more specifically how and why she died. I also included the journals I kept during our travels to Palus, the dangers we encountered there, and how it led to me falling in love with James. The story of meeting my brother, Marek. Not to mention our trip to Caelum, the birthplace of our family and the family drama that finally led to peace between our worlds. I decided to end the book with our wedding. The rest I could tell her over time. Overall, the transcribed book contained ten different journals, and I hoped it would be a good start to the lifelong conversations that would surely follow.

Although, this wasn't the first book I'd put together for the purpose of introducing my kids to our family's linage. A year after our son, JJ, was born, I wrote and illustrated a children's book about Terra Arborum and some of my adventures with the butterflairies. Terra Arborum was the first world I ever entered through the door on James' property off Arnold Mill Road, a door I drove by for years without ever knowing where it led. The door he was charged with protecting and the reason we met. That world meant so much to me, and it was important for me to document it for my children.

Gabby read *Lolli's World* to JJ most nights. She loved making the cute voices of Lolli and Vi, and every time she growled, mimicking Strix's voice, her little brother laughed in delight. I only had a handful of copies made because I was nervous about the truth being out in the world, but it was wonderful to be able to share a part of myself with my kids, even if it was under the guise of children's fiction.

Most of the dreams Gabby had been having lately included people and places I included in *Lolli's World*. I wasn't sure if Gabby would be thrilled or terrified to soon realize that her favorite children's book was actually a real place, and not just one she visited in a book or in her dreams.

Knowing I needed to get JJ ready for school, I went back inside to find him perched on the couch with his tablet and my cell phone, both playing different videos. He sat positioned like a bird on a branch, with his knees bent and pointed out and his butt resting on his heels.

"Good morning, bubby."

"Good morning, Momma!" he answered emphatically, his voice echoing through the room. JJ always spoke as though an exclamation point followed. "It's great to see you!"

I laughed and leaned down to kiss him on the head. "It's great to see you too."

Our son had list of scripts in his head he used when he wasn't sure what else to say. Most times, his "great to see you" followed any period of separation, even if it was just to sleep. Although, it never failed to make me feel good to hear him say it.

"Gabby made my cereal!" He beamed and pointed to his empty bowl.

"I see that. That was nice."

"Yes, very sweet and kind for my sister."

"You mean, 'my sister is very sweet and kind,'" I corrected him.

"Whoa, whoa, whoa, let me try again. 'My sister is very sweet and kind.'" He beamed when he realized he said it right.

We were still working with him on his sentence structure. Often times, he knew what he wanted to say, but struggled with putting it all together correctly. His speech delays had made for a difficult seven years, but over the last two, we had made great strides with his communication. When he was five years old, he only had about five words he could say. We'd come a long way since then.

"Why don't you go put on your clothes and brush your teeth? It's time for school."

"Not yet!" he countered. "How many minutes?"

I knew that was his way of asking for more time, and considering he used his words instead of pitching a fit, I gladly obliged.

"Ok, you can play for five more minutes. Then at 7:20 you need to go brush your teeth and get dressed, okay?"

"Okay!" He smiled. "Thank you Momma. 7:20 I go brush my teeth. Go to school at 7:30, in the car."

"That's right, thanks bud."

I ran upstairs to get myself ready and passed by Gabby's room as she curled her hair. She called out, "Hey Mom? Can I stay over at Emmie's tonight? She's having the girls over after we go shopping."

"D didn't say anything about that." I stopped at her opened door.

"Em just asked her last night. We had already planned on dress shopping anyway, so we just wanted to make a night of it. Talk to her about it today. She'll vouch!" The newly released curl bounced perfectly along side the others. Her beautiful chocolate hair hung loose and long down to the middle of her back. The lighter streaks around her face highlighted her dark skin, and her pale blue eyes inspected a few pieces of hair that had moved out of place.

"I don't remember you saying anything about dress shopping."

"Yeah, we've got to get our prom dresses before all the good ones are gone. But don't worry, I'm driving." She gave me a knowing look. I never trusted Emmie's driving.

"I forgot prom was coming up." I sighed. "Do you think Brian will ask you?"

"Eh. Even if he does, I'm not sure I'd want to go with him. He's nice—he's just not very exciting." She shrugged her shoulders. "This is my last prom, I'd rather just go with my friends than with someone boring." My daughter dated a lot, but always lost interest after a few weeks. Her relationships never seemed to progress past a couple dinners and a movie, which reminded me of myself before James.

"Well, at least let him down gently if he does ask. You can stay over at Emmie's tonight. Just be safe okay? When you're driving tonight and when you're with the girls after. Seriously, no crazy gymnastics stunts. Y'all need to be more careful. Trust me, you don't want to have a broken arm your senior year."

"Sounds like you've had experience." She raised her eyebrows.

"Yes, I told you that story."

She looked back at me blankly.

"Well, I don't have time to tell it to you now—just trust me. Learn from my mistakes."

"Since when do teenagers learn from their parents' mistakes?" She laughed.

I exhaled over-dramatically. "Oh, how I wish you'd be the first."

Sure enough, at 7:20 on the dot, JJ's footsteps barreled up the stairs and into the bathroom. With that little man, the clock was King.

THE TURN.

Eden

Later that afternoon, Marek and I scavenged a friend's barn for discarded windows up in a northern town, when my phone rang.

"Hey Charlie."

"Hey, you got a minute?"

"Sure, we're just looking for windows for the renovation."

"Yeah, I tried my brother, but I guess he's busy at the gallery cause he didn't answer his phone."

"Is everything alright?" I asked, suddenly worried.

"Um, yeah, I think so." His voice didn't seem to agree. "I was just reviewing the recordings from last night and saw something a little unusual. I think you guys should see it."

"Okay, it'll take us a bit to get back down to Woodstock. We're up in Jasper."

"No problem. I'll text James and see if he can get here in an hour. See ya then."

"Alright, thanks, Charlie." I stuck the phone back in my pocket and looked at my brother. "We have to head back. Apparently there's something we need to see."

"Hope it's something fun. We haven't had anything scandalous in awhile." A boyish grin crept onto his face.

"Yeah." I rolled my eyes at my brother. "Cause raising two kids, renovating the gallery, and normal Door Keeping responsibilities aren't enough."

My brother shook his head. "Don't act like you don't love every minute of your life."

"Oh, I do, absolutely." We jumped in the truck we borrowed from Danielle, and I cranked the engine. "But just because you are a lone bachelor, who apparently needs constant adventure to stay stimulated, doesn't mean I want my life any more complicated than it already is."

"Yeah, I know. How are things going with JJ?"

"Much better. I think we are finally beginning to understand how to teach him new things. Everything shifted last year. It almost felt like we unlocked something in this brain."

"I can't believe how much more he's talking since the last time I visited." Marek looked out the window, and then added to reassure me, "You did the right thing."

To this world, my son was autistic. He was diagnosed at the age of three, but we hesitated with it because we knew the truth. His brain wasn't wired for this world, it was hardwired for all the others. James and I realized it almost immediately, with the way he inspected every little thing and how he reacted to noises. He obsessed with tiny details and yet ignored the most basic things. As far as we all knew, JJ is the first child born from two different Door Keeper linages, definitely the only one from two different worlds of Door Keepers. As it is, most Door Keepers have special abilities depending on the world they are from, and JJ is a product from both sides.

But in order to move forward with his education, it was best to get him diagnosed as Autistic, so this world would know what to do with him. It was tough, for all of us. Even understanding that JJ was different and accepting that truth, having your child diagnosed with such a label brought challenges. I'd never get used to explaining his behaviors to random people in the grocery store when they cut their eyes rudely at me. Or seeing the anger and hurt flooding Gabby's eyes when someone said something to us at restaurants if JJ had a fit.

After several difficult years of violent tantrums and zero communication, James and I decided to try a different approach. Since we knew his brain struggled to compute with this world, we decided to try a different one. About a year and a half ago, we took him to Terra Arborum. Once we got him above the cloud cover, it was an immediate transformation. His eyes focused and zeroed in on every single flower he saw. He would point at one and grunt or squeal, and I would tell him it's name. With every flower and every flying animal, his words and ability to communicate got better and better. He blew us away when he met Lolli and could almost speak their language better than ours. Something about the sing-song higher pitch noises were easier for him. That first week back after visiting Terra Arborum was the easiest week I'd ever had with him up until that point. His behaviors subsided, he was calmer, and more patient when he couldn't communicate what he wanted or needed.

Since then, either James or I took him for a visit at least every other week, more often if we had the availability. It was therapy for him. Even the different oxygen levels seemed to help unlock different parts of his brain. I felt consistently torn, not telling Gabby the truth yet, but JJ's progress has helped me deal with it. JJ talks about Terra Arborum all of the time, but Gabby just thinks he is talking about the book and using his imagination. She loves her little brother so much, and I know she wants what is best for him as much as any of us, but I can't help but think she will feel betrayed when she finds out JJ has already crossed worlds.

Marek broke my train of thought. "I can't wait to take him home."

"I've thought of that too." I smiled. "If Terra Arborum was that good for him, imagine him being in Caelum. I feel like it will be soon. I've been having dreams of us all there together, and he can't be much older than he is now."

"Next time you have one, throw it over to me. I'd love to see it."

"Psh, it doesn't work that way," I teased.

"Come on, I know for a fact it does. Seriously, I expect to wake up tomorrow with a beautiful mental image of my niece and nephew with me in Caelum."

"Why wait?" I pulled the memory from deep within. JJ's light brown curls bounced around his face, his matching brown eyes wide, pupils reduced to pins. His laughter carried over the shallow seas as he ran, splashing, trying to escape his daddy's chase. Both he and James wore long flowing fabric, pulled up and tucked between their legs, so they could run freely. JJ's skin color was a perfect balance between his father's and mine. Marek and I sat on the bed swing under the treehouse watching them play. Gabby laid behind us, propped up reading a book. The suns were hot, and a steady breeze blew, cooling us under our Caelun home.

As I recounted the dream/future memory, my right palm began to tingle. I took my hand off the steering wheel and placed it on my brother's shoulder.

Knowing he currently saw what I had just replayed, I waited while he went silent for a second before shaking his head. "Wow." He exhaled. "I'll never get used to that."

"You asked for it." I placed my hand back on the wheel.

"That sure is an amazing gift."

"Most days it is. But honestly, I miss dreamless sleep. It happens so rare now, that when it does, I don't want to wake up. It's hard to rest when your brain never stops replaying things, even the good things."

I had spent the last seven years honing my gift and pushing it to test its limits. But it seems once the gates were opened, it was difficult to turn it off. Decades of dreams filled my subconscious, and it took me the last couple years to train my mind to fully relax without an influx of imagery.

"How is James handling all of this?" Marek pressed. I could always count on my brother to check in and see how my heart felt.

"We're actually doing great. It was rough for a while, figuring out how to help JJ, dealing with keeping secrets, and doing what we do. He was so used to it, but it took me some time to adjust. He was patient with me, though. We decided early on to make decisions together and to work hard on prioritizing our marriage. Take a mental note big brother, marriage is a daily decision you have to make. Everyday you have to choose the other person. It's tougher some days and easier the next, but it's always worth it."

"Geez, you ever think about doing a marriage seminar?" he joked, and then with a more serious tone he added, "It just seems easier to be alone."

I shook my head and looked over at him. "You sound like me before I met James. Trust me, it just means you haven't met the right one yet. When you do, easy won't seem to matter as much."

"Lest I remind you, little sister, I am older than you. Why do you always think you know best?"

"Because I've popped out two babies. I'm a mom, and everyone knows that moms *always* know best." I smiled, only half kidding.

* * * * *

Within the hour we pulled into James' old house. Charlie and his dad currently lived there, sharing the Door Keeper responsibilities. Jay had been such an important part of our lives for so long now, it's hard to imagine that he missed so much of Charlie's childhood. He was a very active grandfather, despite having been in a Caelum prison for fifteen years and frequently took JJ on trips to Terra Arborum when James or I couldn't go.

Marek and I walked upstairs to the surveillance room to find James, Charlie, and their father all huddled over a computer monitor. Charlie was just a few inches shorter than James, with a much leaner build than his older brother. His hair was cut much shorter than James', but their faces became more identical every day.

"What's going on?" I spoke up.

We were met with three blank stares.

"We're not sure." Charlie stood and offered his chair. "I reviewed last night's recording from Brazil, and there was a lapse in footage. Take a look."

He hit the back button on the keyboard twice, and the door in Brazil from the inside of the beach cabin filled the screen. There was a slight flash across the video, and then it was back to normal. Normal, except for the smudges on the floor at the door's base.

"Wait, what happened?" Marek asked.

"We don't know." Jay shrugged. "The camera went out for less than a minute, based on the time clock. We checked the rest of the footage, and there was nothing out of the ordinary."

"What is that?" I pointed to the smudges in front of the door.

"We have no idea. Could be dirt or animal poop for all we know," Charlie answered.

"Do we have any idea what could have caused the break in the feed?" I questioned, starting to feel a bit nervous, considering our past with Palus.

Jay turned to face us, leaning against the computer desk. "No. We need to check the source. I think one of us should go check the house and the cameras onsite to look for damage."

Marek's cell phone rang, making everyone in the room jump. He looked over at me, mouthed, "Gio," and walked towards the door. After he left the room, we all turned our attention back to the Palus door on the monitor.

Jay continued, "Well, of course Charlie or I could go. This is definitely our responsibility. But considering your past with Palus, perhaps one of you two should go." He nodded between James and I.

"I agree with Dad." Charlie looked expectantly at us.

My mind flashed to trudging the Palun jungle as my gut involuntarily plunged remembering our narrow escape from the Sloths that inhabited those lands. I let out a breath and shook it from my mind.

Not taking my eyes off the door on the screen in front of me, I answered before James could. "Well babe, we are a few days behind at the gallery. You should stay. I can handle this."

"Are you sure? I know you don't like to be away." I felt my husband's eyes on me.

"Yeah, but it's easier to explain why I'm traveling to the kids. A friend from Tokyo reached out the other day about her upcoming gallery opening. I can say I'm going to visit her and buy some art for Wall Polish. No worries. I'll bet some beach bum just broke in and messed with our cameras and got scared off. It should only take me a few days to check and fix anything that's been damaged."

Once we landed on final details of the trip and got everything worked out, I walked outside to find Marek hanging up with Gio, Earth's Door Maker. He made and maintained all of the doors and keys leading to other worlds on Earth. His home base was in Italy, in the same city as the door to Caelum. Not only had he been the officiant at our wedding, but he had also become a close friend to us over the years. Marek looked at me with pursed lips and a furrowed brow.

"I have to head back to Caelum. Dad contacted Gio to call me. There are reports of a disturbance on an island a few hundred miles away from home, close to the door leading to Iskrem."

Staring at my brother, a growing sense of dread took root in my stomach. "I'm heading to Brazil to check on the door to Palus. I wouldn't say anything to anyone about this yet. We don't need everyone to panic for nothing."

"What are the chances that these aren't related?" he asked, already knowing the answer.

"I'd say about the same as the chances of you finding a wife within the next century." I countered without fake amusement.

THE WARNING.

Eden

"Take me with you." Danielle whined, covered head to toe in dust.

"If only." I sighed, lifting the other end of the table. "It would be way more fun with you."

"Of course it would. Everything is more fun with me."

"Then why isn't *this* fun?" I countered. The large wooden table creaked and groaned as we hauled it to the other side of room.

"Because manual labor is manual labor. Even Superman has his limitations."

"So working hard is your kryptonite?"

"Exactly. See, you so get me." Her face softened and relaxed as we lowered the table. "Seriously, I can't believe you are leaving me to deal with this mess."

"James is staying. I'm leaving the muscle, and after lifting that table, I'd say that's more important." We hoisted ourselves to sit on the table.

"True. This renovation will be worth it though. That window wall was a brilliant idea." D grinned at me. "I'm so glad you thought of it. The natural light will transform this whole space. Not to mention the amazing view of downtown." We over looked the restaurants and rooftop patios where people enjoyed their meals and drinks.

"Hey, are the girls staying at your place after shopping tonight?"

"Yeah, sorry I didn't text you. Emmie asked me late last night."

"That's fine. I can't believe our girls are seniors," I sighed.

"I know. I'm feeling it more now, the pressure and anxiety of having to let go. I really don't want to. I mean, take prom. Do you know how hard it was for me to agree to that?"

"Come on, D. Prom is hardly anything to freak over."

"Sure, prom itself isn't, but their plans for the rest of the weekend are." Her eyebrows met in the middle of her forehead.

"What plans?" My eyes narrowed.

"What do you mean 'what plans?' I agreed because you agreed!" Her voice raised an octave.

"I didn't agree to anything," I said slowly.

"Our girls are so dead," she growled.

* * * * *

I arrived home to find Gabby and James in the kitchen talking while James cooked dinner. I decided to ease into the conversation I had with D earlier that day in hopes Gabby would come clean about her plans. I broke the news to her and JJ that I'd be going out of town for a business trip the next day. Gabby was only mildly interested. "Tokyo, huh? Make sure you bring me back something cool for my birthday." She over-dramatically winked at me.

"What? Your birthday is coming up?" James teased, spatula in hand.

"Dad! This is no joking matter. I only turn eighteen once." Her eyebrows rose as she glared at him.

"Don't I know it." He smiled and turned down the burner on the stove. It only took Gabby about a year after James and I married to transition to calling him, *Dad*. They had the sweetest relationship, and one I was extremely grateful for. Especially if my daughter was about to become severely mad at me.

"Are you eating with us tonight or with the girls?"

"We're gonna grab something before we shop, but thanks though. Mom, I won't be home tomorrow until after your flight. I'll miss ya. Love you!" She kissed me on the cheek and walked toward the kitchen door.

"Um, Gabbs, real quick, speaking of prom—have you and Emmie decided what your plans are yet?" I asked a bit too slyly.

"Ah, not really. I mean, we have some ideas, but nothing concrete." She cut her eyes to the door, anxious to leave.

"Oh, so you're not planning on staying at the Clark's lake cabin for the weekend with all the other couples?"

"I'm sorry, what?" James spun to face us.

"Listen, it's no big deal . . . " she started.

"Nope, you don't get to roll your eyes and tell me it's no big deal." I crossed my arms.

"What? It's not! I'm almost eighteen."

"The big deal is that you lied to Danielle and attempted to manipulate us into agreeing. The big deal is that you didn't tell me the truth."

"I didn't lie. Emmie did! And technically, I didn't lie to you. I haven't even brought it up to you yet!"

"You aren't getting around this on a technicality!" I retorted. "And you are definitely not staying overnight at a lake cabin with girls and guys after prom."

"Mom!" Gabby cried. "All of my friends are going. Everyone else's parents said it was okay!"

"Well, sweetie we aren't like all the other parents," James said calmly.

"Obviously." She sniffed.

"Don't you take that tone. We've tried to teach you from the beginning to come to us and tell us the truth. That we will always be fair and considerate if you simply come to us first. So why didn't you this time?"

"Because I knew you wouldn't let me." A tear slid down her cheek.

"Well, you were right, and I'm sorry," I said simply.

"No you're not!" Anger flooded her cheeks. "You don't trust me? You don't think I'm capable of making good decisions on my own?"

"Of course we do." James walked over to her and grabbed her hands. "But you have your whole life to make decisions, and you are going to have to make more important ones than you ever thought possible. We are just trying to help you with them until we can't anymore."

"That sounds lame." She rolled her eyes.

James let out a bark of laughter. "Trust me, I wish sometimes someone else could make all my decisions for me."

"Mom, please trust me to make my own choices," she pleaded.

"Whether you believe me or not, I am sorry. But no, not yet."

"You are so unfair." Gabby glared at me through tears.

"Maybe, but I'm doing what I think is best. You can be mad at me if you want," I said softly.

"Good, because I totally am." We stared at each other for a long minute. "Hope you have a great trip," she said sarcastically, then grabbed her purse and left.

"Well, that went well." James sighed and went back to cooking.

I walked up and hugged him from behind. "Sorry I didn't give you a heads up before I confronted her."

"It wouldn't have changed anything. We're on the same page."

"I'm glad, cause that definitely makes dealing with the teen angst easier."

James chuckled. "At least we're in it together."

"In every world." I buried my face in his back.

We spent the evening eating dinner and watching a movie with JJ. Then of course promptly at eight o'clock, he informed us it was time for bed. We asked him if he wanted to stay up late and finish the movie, but "8 o'clock is bedtime." After we recited the poem we have every night since Gabby was little, James and I cuddled up on the couch with some wine and a movie that wasn't animated.

Not far into the movie, James reached over and brushed my now longer and completely silver hair off my shoulder. After tucking it behind my ear, he leaned over and kissed my neck.

"I'm gonna miss you when you're gone."

A girlish giggle slipped out as his closely cropped beard tickled my neck. "I'm only going to be gone a couple of days."

"I know, but you're so pretty to look at," he said softly.

"Hey, before you go into your deep, husky, sexy voice, I need to tell you something."

He sat up and turned his body to face mine. "Okay."

"Marek didn't leave today to help Gio. He left because our Dad called and asked him to come home. There was a disturbance around one of the doors in Caelum."

James' face turned from playful to serious within seconds. "That's not good."

"No, and I didn't say anything because I didn't want everyone to worry."

"I should go with you to Brazil."

"See, this is exactly why I didn't say anything. We made a pact years ago that we wouldn't do this, unnecessarily risk both of us at the same time. We have two kids to think about."

"Eden, if these two incidents are connected, you and Marek may be walking into a trap."

"Everything has been quiet for years. We have no reason to think the worst."

James got up and walked towards the window. "That's what worries me. It's been so quiet, no disturbances, no attempts at crossing worlds, no wars. What happened with us in Palus—there should have been consequences, extreme ones at that. Samuel was right, it should have resulted in unrest at the very least."

I stood up and tucked myself under his shoulder. "So let me get this straight. You're frustrated that our little visit to Palus *didn't* result in a multi-world war?"

"No, I'm just waiting for it to come back and bite us in the ass." James rubbed the inside of my arm. A couple years after JJ was born, I had one of my mother's notes she left for me in Caelum tattooed onto my forearm.

Eden, you will build the bridge.

"I'm not sure your bridge building days are over." His eyes moved from the tattoo up to my face. "I trust you, Eden. Just be careful, and we will monitor you the whole time you are there, okay?"

"Fair enough." I nodded.

He turned around and placed his hand under my chin, looking deep into my gray eyes. He kissed me gently, and then let his right hand drift down to my shoulder, tracing the flowers tattooed there.

"We've been through a lot in this world over the past seven years with JJ. And I know that with Gabby turning eighteen and learning the truth, we might be in for a lot more in all of the other worlds pretty soon. We have to be careful and stick together. I know you don't need my protection, but that doesn't stop me from wanting to keep you safe."

"I love it when you talk Door Keeper to me. Now can you just repeat all of that, but in your deep, husky, sexy voice?" I said coyly.

"What, *this* one?" His voice deepened, and his eyes sparkled. He swooped me up in his arms and carried me upstairs.

THE BEST FRIEND.

Gabby

It was bad enough getting reamed by my own parents, but having to listen to Aunt Danielle felt ten times worse.

"You couldn't have dealt with this before I came over?" I whispered to Emmie.

"I can't help that your parents got over it faster than mine." She shot back.

"I swear, you two better be listening to what I'm saying." Danielle glared down at us. "How could you be so manipulative?"

"I'm sorry, Aunt D." I gave my best apology face.

"Oh, don't you look at me with those ridiculous blue eyes. They haven't worked on me since you guys hit puberty."

"Mom, don't be mad at Gabbs. It really was my idea."

"I'm sure it was, but it doesn't excuse you." She pointed her perfected manicured nail at me. "I'm very disappointed with both of you. And don't you think for a second that I'm allowing you to go to the lake house after prom."

"Mom, you already promised!" Emmie squeaked.

"Yes, it sucks when someone you trust goes back on her word, doesn't it?"

"Mom, this is so unfair!"

"Unfair? Really? You're lucky I'm not grounding you right now! I think I probably should." She let the words hang in the air.

Emmie deflated next to me. "No, Mom, please. I'm sorry. I shouldn't have lied."

"That's the first thing you've said today that doesn't make me want to strangle you."

"Listen, I'm sorry about prom, but can I please still go dress shopping tonight with my friends?" she begged. "No lake house after prom. Gabbs and I will just do something else."

Danielle softened. "Gabby, your mother knows you're over here and is okay with y'all going out tonight?"

"Yes ma'am, you can text her if you want." I nodded, anxious to get out of the house.

"No, despite all of this, I still somehow trust you." She looked back and forth between us. "The only reason I'm not canceling tonight is because you have all the girls coming over here, but as soon as they leave in the morning, you are grounded, Missy."

"But Mom, Spring Break is in a couple of weeks! How long?" Emmie groaned.

"Until I feel like it."

"Mom," she whined.

"Emmie." Aunt D cocked one eyebrow, challenging her.

"Yes ma'am," Emmie resigned. "I am really sorry. We'll be home tonight before eleven."

"Make it ten."

"Yes ma'am." My best friend and I said in unison.

* * * * *

"That was brutal," I said as we climbed into my car, cranking the engine. "Thanks for sticking up for me. I totally threw you under the bus with my parents."

Emmie snorted. "Of course you did."

"It *was* your idea." I pointed out. She stuck her tongue out at me.

"Well as I recall, you thought it was genius." Emmie hung her arm outside of the jeep. My dad had given me his old one for my seventeenth birthday. I had been trying to save up money to buy one, but at the rate I was going, I would have been twenty-five before I could afford one that wouldn't break down after driving a mile.

"Well, as I recall it was three in the morning, and I was in a pizza coma so apparently wasn't in my right mind."

Emmie shrugged. "It was worth a shot."

"Yeah, but now you're grounded."

"I would have gotten grounded from something else anyway. At least this could have led to us having a legendary weekend."

"What, watching everyone get drunk and wake up with regrets?" I smirked.

"Um, yes!" Emmie's laugh rang through the air.

"You are so warped."

The lingering warm air whirled around us as we drove down the interstate. I loved driving this car, and driving at dusk just as the sun was beginning to set was always my favorite. The light was soft, throwing long shadows across the highway, as pop songs blared from the radio. Even with my fight earlier with my parents, my spirits were high. It was a Friday night, I was with my best friend, I was just a few credits short of graduation, and my eighteenth birthday was just three weeks away.

"Gabbs, our whole lives we've had a reputation as the 'good girls.' If we have any chance of changing that before we graduate, we've got to do something soon. Prom weekend was our best shot."

"Since when do you care about our 'good girl' image?"

"Since Caleb said he wouldn't ask me to Prom because I was a 'prude.'" She used air quotes as she sang the word prude.

"Well Caleb is an idiot! You are so not a prude."

"True, he is. But if I can't have Charlie, then I've got to find someone." She shrugged.

"Geez, girl. Enough about Charlie. You've had a thing for him forever."

"I can't help it. He's so hot."

"Ew! That's my Uncle you're talking about."

"Well, he's not your blood Uncle, so it's not that gross. Plus, how can I think about high school boys when you have such a good-looking, mature *man* hanging around all the time." She pretended to faint.

I rolled my eyes.

She was right about guys our own age, though. I fumed, thinking about how ridiculous the boys at our school were. The last three guys I dated were only interested in how far they could go with me. As much as I didn't want to admit it, I knew our reputation preceded us everywhere we went. The few boys I dated that were sweet and never pressured me, were insanely dull.

"We've drank before. That's not prudish," I reminded her.

"Gabbs, drinking beer mixed with Dr. Pepper at your grandparent's beach house does *not* count."

I almost choked on my laughter. "That was seriously the worst idea ever!"

"Totally. It was the most disgusting thing I've ever tasted. We should have known something was wrong when the foam hardened." She snorted, holding her stomach.

"Yeah, maybe I'm proving the point rather than discrediting it."

"Ya think?"

We drove the rest of the way to the restaurant in silence listening to the radio. As we parked and hopped out, walking toward the rest of our friends waiting for us at Pure, our favorite Mexican Cantina, Emmie grabbed my hand. "Thanks Gabbs, you always know how to cheer me up."

THE DRESS.

Gabby

Downtown Woodstock was bustling, even for normal Friday night standards. From the rooftop of Pure, we heard the music of the concert from the new amphitheater down the road. People wandered from shop to shop, talking and laughing with one another. White lights strung from building to building gave the illusion that all of Main Street was connected. And on this beautiful spring evening, as my friends walked among the masses, it felt that way.

Every dress boutique brought another friend finding the perfect dress. I was the only one who hadn't found one yet. Emmie picked a vibrant, red, off the shoulder dress that accented her large chest and curvy hips. She would look like a vintage bombshell with her blond hair pinned back and her red lips. I on the other hand, had tried on at least twenty dresses and looked like a boy playing dress up. My hair, still in a messy bun on the top of my head from driving the jeep, didn't help.

We finally made our way into Spirited, always one of my mom's favorite stores. The clothes were more of a bohemian style and totally went with her artistic vibes. I had pretty much resigned myself to giving up when Emmie called from the back.

"Gabbs! Look at this."

I walked back and gazed at one of the most beautiful colored dresses I'd ever seen. She held it up against me.

"It matches your eyes perfectly." She gasped. The rest of our friends ooo'ed and aah'ed.

"Really? It's such a pretty color."

"Hello, have you never seen your own eyes? They're amazing." She grinned at me. "You've got to try this on."

"It looks a little plain besides the color." I hesitated.

"Oh, just do it. Trust me."

I pulled the curtain back to the dressing room and stripped off my clothes. Only panties would work under this number. The soft material draped perfectly, and as I wrapped the braided rope around my midsection and tied it off, I felt a pang of familiarity.

I walked out to gasps and hands covering their mouths. My friend Eleanor approached me, turning me to face the mirror and pulling my hair out of my rubber band, causing my top bun to spill chocolate hair everywhere. She quickly whisked it over to the side and loosely braided it, laying it over my shoulder.

"There," she beamed. "Perfection."

The color of the dress did indeed match my eyes, a light grayish blue, the color popping over my dark skin. The simple draping and braided accents combined with my hair braided to the side made me look Grecian. I couldn't tear my eyes from my reflection, and then Emmie's appeared next to me.

"It looks so much like the one your mother wore at her wedding. I think she would love it."

I smiled, realizing that was why it felt so familiar. "I do too. It's definitely the one."

Emmie put her arm through mine. "I'll tell you one thing, we may be 'good girls,' but we sure ain't gonna look the part on prom night."

"Caleb is gonna feel like such an ass when he sees you in that red dress."

"They all will." She smiled deviously. "Come on, let's go get some coffee at Copper Coin and make some different plans for after the dance."

* * * * *

"White Mocha!" the barista yelled over the chatter of the coffee shop.

"Hey Brian." I smiled at the boy holding out my drink order. His sandy brown hair fell in his eyes as he turned his head to notice me.

"Oh hey, Gabby. Are you the white mocha?"

"I am."

"I forgot you like your coffee sweet." He blushed. "You out with your friends tonight?"

"Yeah, just dress shopping." I took the coffee, immediately regretting my choice of words. A look of interest filled his face.

"For prom?"

Oh no. I did not want to give him the opportunity to ask me. I couldn't reject him here at his work. I was trapped and searched for an escape.

"Hey Gabby!" Brian's boss barged over, slapping him on the back. "Can you tell your mom to finish the renovation already? All the construction is driving me and my customers crazy."

"Well Steve, you can't have it both ways. If you want the best view in Woodstock over your coffee shop, you got to let her finish. Trust me, it'll be worth it." I turned to leave. "Well, I better get back to my friends."

"Wait," Brian ran around the glass case and I cringed. He wiped his hands on a hand towel nervously as he approached. "Um, I was wondering who you're going to prom with . . ."

"Oh." I glanced at all my friends sitting at a table outside, eyeing us through the glass. "Actually, we are all planning on going together. You know, kind of a single solidarity type of thing." I strung all my words together, nervously.

Disappointment flooded his face. "Yeah, sure I get it. Not a bad idea." He regained half a smile. "Maybe I'll suggest that to my friends." He moved to return to work but paused. "Save me a dance at least?"

"Yeah, that would be great." I said genuinely. He was a super nice guy, just not one I could see myself in a relationship with.

Relief hit me the same time as the night air. Brian was the only guy I'd dated recently that I thought would ask me to prom, so now I was at least in the clear.

"Did you let him down gently?" Emmie drawled.

"Yeah, I just blamed you guys."

The girls threw their napkins in my direction.

"Alright, alright!" I yelled, blocking one from hitting me in the face. "We have some serious business to take care of. We have the dresses, we have the dance, now how can we make this the most legendary night of our lives?"

THE TRUTH.

Eden

It'd been years since I had stood in front of the coral door of the small beach house in Brazil. I pulled out the regular house key, took a deep breath, and opened the door. I had texted James to let him know I had arrived, so I knew they were recording and watching live to make sure nothing crazy happened.

Everything looked completely normal. I walked over to the door that lead to Palus, a handmade, worn, wooden door with wrought iron embellishments in all four corners. Reaching out and touching the large circular pattern of metal in the center, I marveled at the beautiful craftsmanship. Leaning down to the smudge on the floor, I inspected the dried mud, once wet but now hard and caked. As I rubbed my finger over it, a picture of James covered in Palus mud from head to toe resurfaced from my memory bank. Huh. As I studied it, it seemed to disappear under the door. Some animal must of tried to scrape under it unsuccessfully. I stood up and checked the rest of the house. Nothing was out of place, and there was no indication of forced entry at the windows, or anywhere for that matter. I thought about the animal that could have left the mud by the door and where it could have come in. I walked into the bathroom and bedroom; everything checked out. I texted James that everything looked fine, and that I was going to eat some lunch, then start checking the surveillance equipment to make sure everything worked properly.

The quicker we figured out what happened with the cameras, the sooner everyone would relax.

After a quick sandwich, I checked the wiring for the cameras in the house and on the exterior. Everything was hooked up and working solidly. I reset the system, hoping that would fix any glitches. I called James after I'd completed everything I'd come to do.

"So, everything looks fine?" He picked up the phone without a greeting.

"Yeah, it's weird, but I don't see anything wrong."

"Tell me about the smudge on the floor."

"Well, it's definitely mud and has dried. It's hard and caked into the carpet. Some animal must have gotten in your mother's garden then found a way in. It looks like it tried to scratch under the door..."

I paused for a moment, remembering how the mud from Palus had dried on me during our last traipse through its jungle. I shook it off and continued, "I think I should stick around for the next day or so to see if whatever it is tries to come into the house again. We can't keep having this scare. I'd rather figure out what it could be when I'm down here, so we don't have to worry about it any more."

"Okay, that sounds good. We'll keep an eye on you. Charlie has tonight's shift, then I'll be here tomorrow after I drop JJ off at school. Call me if you need anything, alright?"

"You got it. Love you, babe."

"Love you, too. Talk tomorrow."

* * * * *

I relaxed on the back deck watching the waves crash over one another, fighting to reach the shore first. The moon was full and cast a beautiful white glow over the surface of the ocean. It was so quiet out here, the only other lights were miles down the stretch of beach. I thought back to the first time I'd come here with James, the moment before we left for Palus, when I knew I loved him, but refused to admit it to myself. This house, this door, changed the course of my life. Because Jay and Charlie shared Door Keeper responsibilities, James and I hadn't been back here since our last visit.

It was crazy to think we entered the door to Palus to find information about his father's disappearance and presumed death, only to find him alive months later in Caelum. Even though the trip to Palus itself didn't yield any results and resulted in our own capture and narrow escape, it did force me to admit my feelings for James. Which of course led to our marriage and to having JJ. I would always be grateful for this place for that reason alone, but it did more than that. Crossing worlds caused my brother to find me, reuniting me with my family and Caelum and ultimately James with his own father. So much came from that dangerous trip to Palus so many years ago. I reached up and traced the scar that ran through my eyebrow and down next to my eye. The scar left from the fight of my life, from a giant ground sloth's claw.

Thinking about all of this made me miss my family. I definitely felt bad for how I left things with Gabby. I didn't like being gone as it was, but being angry at each other made it all worse. I decided to check in with their dreams. James was dreamless, so I threw him some memories from our honeymoon. JJ dreamt about being in a Pixar movie. Seeing his face animated through his eyes made me smile. Gabby was in a nightmare being chased by some creepy gangsters on motorcycles, so I quickly threw her into Caelum, the motorcycles dissipated into fruit trees. It was strangely sweet, watching her realize she was no longer in danger and look around in awe at her surroundings. She leaned down and felt the water lapping at her feet. I couldn't wait for her to experience the real thing. Finally, realizing how tired I was from the day's travels, I walked inside, locking the door behind me, and climbed into bed.

My mind quickly relaxed, and my breathing steadied as I drifted off into a deep sleep.

Not soon after falling asleep, rough male voices began growling at each other . . .

Quick we only have one minute before the cameras turn back on.

If we can get her while she sleeps, she won't be able to fight and leave any evidence.

Stop being so loud, you idiot.

Stop yelling at me—the cameras are off.

There are no cameras in the bedroom, this is our best shot.

Hurry. . .

Get her and let's get out.

Wrap her up so she can't knock anything over. We don't have time to put anything back.

Giant claws landed on me, heavy and pushing me into the bed before I could even struggle. The huge talons tore into my flesh through the thin bed sheet and my T-shirt. The smell of mud and wet fur filled my nostrils, the putrid breath of his snout next to my face.

No.

I've smelled it before.

God, no.

One claw was clamped over my mouth, unable to make a noise other than the panic rising from my flailing body. They wrapped the sheet over me around my arms and legs preventing me from grabbing anything or fighting. I was lifted from the bed and carried towards the door to Palus. It was wide open. Oh my God, this can't be happening.

I jolted awake, sweating.

The Paluns. They were coming. Their stench already filled the room.

I quickly kicked the sheet off of me, knowing not being wrapped up was my only chance to leave behind evidence of my abduction. The weight and the pain of their claws hit me immediately. Knowing their main objective was to get me out of the house as fast and cleanly as possible, I attempted to make the biggest mess I could. I struggled under their mass strength to no avail. Even without the sheet, they managed to get me out of bed without disrupting the furniture around us. It didn't matter anyway, there were no cameras in the bedroom. My only chance was the main living area, the one with the door. I strained and tried to pull my arms free. This was my only opportunity. I had to do something.

With every twist and attempt to free my arms or legs, the giant sloth's talons dug into me deeper. Pain tore through my body, only the adrenaline kept me alert and aware. They were ready for this and were prepared for my struggle. Two sloths held me, but I quickly realized they both couldn't fit through the door at the same time. I had only one shot, so I faked fainting and went limp. Their iron grips around me loosened ever so slightly, and I hoped the plan might work. I had to leave something behind, something to alert James to what happened. One of the sloths let go of me, so the other could carry me through. As he slid sideways to pass through the opened door into Palus, I lunged out and dug my hands into the doorframe, attempting to scrape my nails along the wood. What felt like hot needles being shoved into my fingernails shot down my fingers, and I knew I had made a mark. It was all I could do before a blunt force hit my head, fading the world around me into darkness.

THE ABDUCTION.

Eden

I stood on the beach, my toes digging into the sand, the sun warming my face. I noticed a large lighthouse towering into the sky like one of the large mountains in Caelum. The ocean crashed against the lighthouse like it was angry that it had intruded its rush to shore. I'd never seen a lighthouse out in the ocean before, but there it stood about a hundred feet from shore, withstanding the constant beating of the giant waves. The pounding surf sent water splashing half way up the height of the lighthouse. Unmoving it sat, stubborn and unwilling to give to the ocean's wishes.

Suddenly, finding myself in JJ's room, I looked down to see him fast asleep in his bed. His lips were squished, pushed against his pillow. His breathing was slow and deep. I wanted so desperately to reach down and brush my fingers through his hair; but I couldn't move. I tried to enter his dreams, but wasn't able enter his thoughts either. The room melted away and turned into my father's house in Caelum.

She sat in the courtyard, her back to me. But the long, beautiful braided lavender hair told me it was my mother. She was painting a picture of the shallow seas at the suns-set. I recognized it as one of the paintings she had left with a message for me. She stopped, looked over her shoulder as though she felt my presence, and then placed her brush down. Standing, Mom flipped the large canvas over and picked up a different brush. After dipping it in paint, she wrote on the bottom corner.

Eden, you will build the bridge.

She glanced back over her shoulder, showing me only her profile. She smiled and nodded, as if making sure I understood she knew I was there.

I came to, my head feeling light and fuzzy. I tried opening my eyes, but my vision was blurry and made me queasy. I felt drunk and hung-over, but I didn't remember drinking anything. My face was frozen, pressed against something hard. A stone floor. I attempted to move my hands to wipe the drool, but they were tied behind my back. What the hell? What happened? Where was I? Realization hit me like a mountain of bricks. The sloths took me. Did James know what happened? Did I make enough of a mark on the doorframe to signal them? I tried to sit up to see where I was, but instead I almost threw up.

"I would just lay there for now." A soft voice said from the other side of the room, hoarse and barely audible. I slowly opened my eyes, attempting to focus, but had trouble. My eyelids ached under the pressure and a white blur sat across from me.

"And do not try to use your subconscious. It is useless. You have no control over your dreams, or your ability to contact others in theirs. You might as well just take this time to rest." He spoke slowly and very pointedly, like he was bored.

Panic ripped through me. How did this person know about my gifts? Who was he? Why did I feel so terrible?

"What . . . you do . . . to me?" my voice slurred.

"There is this beautiful plant where I am from. If you ingest it, it slows down the functions in your body, like a temporary paralysis, even one's brain. We use it when animals are hurt, so they don't hurt themselves further. Today, you are that animal," he said matter of factly.

His nonchalant tone made me angry. I was not an animal. But I had to attempt to get more information.

"Where . . . you . . . from?" It was all I could muster.

"Shhhh. No more questions."

"Where am I?"

"Now, you see, that is another question." The man sounded put out. The white blur grew closer. "Enough. It is time to sleep, you poor, wounded animal."

Anger, confusion, and fear muddled my thoughts and words as I tried to speak.

"Who . . . " was all I got out before the pin pricked my arm and warmth spread through my body.

I lost track of time, having no sense of where I was or how long I'd been where ever I was. I would wake up every now and again in different places, only the feel of the floors or walls around me to tell me I had moved. I couldn't control my dreams, they just fluctuated between past events and nightmares. Gabby and I had fought. I had to make it right. Anytime I tried to contact anyone in the subconscious realm or throw a dream, my thoughts would fuzz, like a connection was lost.

Finally, I awoke with a little more clarity, wrapped in a large blanket under some trees with snow falling in sheets around me. My lungs burned breathing in the frigid air, the moisture of my exhale almost freezing instantly as it hit the air. Feeling warmth behind me, I turned to see I was propped against a huge animal. After closer inspection, and the steady rise and fall of its body, I realized the oversized buck was asleep. I'd never seen a stag so large and could only assume I was still drugged and hallucinating, but soon realized that wasn't the case when my captor's voice disrupted the sound of the quiet snowfall.

"Ah. You have decided to join us." His voice seemed to carry a bit more authority than before, which did nothing to ease the growing dread coursing through me.

My throat was scratchy and dry. "I don't feel like it was my decision."

I tried to at least muster courage in my words, but my hoarse voice betrayed me.

"You need water." I was unsure if he meant it as a statement or question. He lifted a warm cup of liquid to my face, and it spilled into my mouth before I could stop it. It tasted like pure water, thankfully. I took the moment to look at the man's face. His skin was the whitest I'd ever seen, the texture of it thick and rough, like what I would imagine an elephant's hide if it were bleached white. My heart raced when my eyes landed on his eyes, large, black disks filled with malice. An involuntary shudder rippled through me as he studied my face with a smirk.

Not knowing what else to do, I attempted to contact James with a dream, but there must have been enough drugs in me still to keep me prisoner in my own mind.

As if reading my thoughts the man answered me. "We had to lower your dosage, so you can travel with us, but do not worry. We found a good balance to keep you awake and still unable to contact your family."

"How thoughtful, you ass," I said smugly, again, faking my courage. This monster somehow knew my secrets and about my family, which only fed my worst nightmares.

The man bore his eerie, coal black eyes into mine, unwavering. Out of nowhere, his fist punched me right in the cheek. Exploding pain radiated across my entire face. The stag flinched behind me. As I attempted to bring my face back to his in defiance, I noticed a half dozen sloths appearing around us. They were covered in snow, and as they moved, the snow broke off, exposing their presence. Remembering how their talons tore into me, and the pain from the abduction, I cowered into the warm stag behind me.

"I would be mindful of your words considering I am not alone." He drew his face within a foot of mine. My thoughts swam, trying to understand what was happening and who this man was.

"I see that." I eyed the sloths approaching us under the tree. "How?"

"You mean, how are they here?" he whispered, his rank breath hitting my face.

He turned and looked at the huge beasts walking toward us, leaving large gashes in the otherwise gorgeous blanket of snow on the ground. My body ached and hurt, and the frigid temperatures disguised whether my teeth chattered from the cold or fear.

"They are not the only ones tired of the world they were condemned to. We decided to work together." He paused and looked back into my eyes. "I assume you know where we are. You are such a bright Door Keeper," he mocked.

"Iskrem." I remembered my brother telling me about Iskrem's cold and ice.

"Ah, yes!" His smile exposed his stained teeth. "I knew you were a smart one. Well, you need to get some rest. We have a long journey ahead of us."

"Who are you? Why did you take me?" I pressed. I had to know why he took me, how he knew everything about me, and what he wanted. If my family was in danger, I had to find a way to save them. My brain swam with pain and questions, frustrations and terror; I couldn't grasp any clarity or answers regardless of how hard I tried.

"That is no matter. Soon, we will have gotten what we need from you, builder of bridges." He smirked down at me condescendingly and turned to leave.

"And what is that?" My voice shook.

He stopped and turned, his eyes churning with hate.

"To burn every one of them to the ground."

THE STAG.

Eden

One of the sloths pulled me along after wrapping my body in a large animal skin and hood, towing me with a rope attached from my wrists to his belt. The snow fell down thick around us, but somehow we remained sheltered under a couple of small oak trees. We walked for hours before we stopped to rest again.

I fell to my knees after the sloth tied my rope loosely around one of the low hanging branches of a tree close by. Sitting still in the cold, I began to lose feeling in my extremities, and the shooting pains steadily grew, inching inward from the places where numbness resided. Feeling so scared and afraid, my state of mind became more fragile. I couldn't lose control over my body as well. I wanted to cry but knew I shouldn't exert any more energy than necessary. Trying to steady my breathing and calm myself, I mentally pulled all the warmth I could to my heart—resolved to stay strong, despite the unknown. I knew the importance of it. Even though I was not able to use my subconscious gifts, I attempted to gain as much information as I could about what was happening and my surrounding. It was my only chance of escape. Even if James and Charlie saw what I left behind, they think I'm in Palus. They have no idea I'm in Iskrem.

My mind raced to Marek? Did he fall into a trap too? Where was he? How was Gabby feeling? What would happen to her if something happened to me? I fought the overwhelming sense of hopelessness, when a voice interrupted my thoughts.

"Rest, my child."

I looked up and was face to face with the stag I'd seen earlier. His eyes were a chestnut brown and were so close my own reflection mirrored in them. Tears were frozen down my face.

"Sit with me and warm your weary bones."

It was at that moment I realized why the trees protected us as we walked. The oak trees grew as the buck's antlers. Upon closer inspection, I saw what appeared as bone growing out of his large head transitioned into a hard wood, then branched out as regular trees. He had been walking behind me, so the trees provided a constant canopy as we moved. In fact, my rope was attached to one his lower branches. The huge animal sat down slowly and gestured with his nose for me to sit nestled in the nook his shoulder and stomach provided.

"Thank you." I joined him, his fur soft and his presence peaceful. My spirits instantly lifted.

"You should rest while you have the chance. The journey ahead is long." As the giant stag spoke, his trees above rustled gently. I relaxed my body into his thick fur, allowing the warmth to thaw me from the inside out. Almost simultaneously, I found myself in my uncontrollable dream world.

Despite the inundation of imagery while sleeping, I awoke feeling more rested than I could remember since being taken. My mind was still not my own, but a peace resided where fear had taken hold. Within minutes, the sloth had me up and moving.

I snuck a peek at my new friend behind me when I could. He didn't say anything as we walked, and somehow I knew not to ask any questions with sloths within earshot. With every step in the deep snow, my appreciation for the giant stag grew. Not only had he provided me with a peaceful nap but relief from the elements. Every time we stopped for a break, the huge buck invited me to nestle under his protection and the warmth of his fur. The sloths seemed to ignore him and keep their distance when they could, which allowed me yet another reprieve. Other than his first invitation, he hadn't spoken a word and surprised me when he finally did.

"My name is Taran."

Somehow his voice sounded exactly like I'd imagine a giant deer with trees as antlers would sound: deep, grounded, and ancient.

"Hello Taran, my name is Eden."

A slight smile crossed his wild lips.

"Eden. Like the first woman of your world."

"Ironic, I know." I shivered and managed the first grin since leaving my world.

"You must go to sleep. I will stay with you as long as I can to give you rest and comfort, but I'm afraid our time together is soon coming to an end."

"Why?"

"I know you have no reason to, Eden, but you must trust me. Rest dear one, while you can." He closed his eyes slowly as to signal me to do the same. Somehow it worked, and my eyes closed, my body grateful, and I allowed myself to doze off.

Something about his voice, his reassuring presence in the midst of such a frozen wasteland, allowed parts of me to unwind that I had no idea were even tense. All the worries, fears, and anxieties I had about my family, Gabby, and Marek melted away. His large heart beat steadily underneath me, and I relaxed into him, no longer feeling the cold.

I finally woke up to my hand tangled in his fur and his glassy eyes looking down at me.

"How do you feel?" His ancient voice vibrated his chest.

I yawned. "So much better, thank you, Taran."

"I wanted to give you one last rest, for you will need it for what is to come. I do not have long, dear one. Once he realizes I am sympathetic to you, he will end my life." Panic rose within me.

How could anyone hurt this magnificent creature? He continued softly, "Aslak is one of this world's Door Keepers. His alliance began with the Paluns a couple of years ago. Once he heard about what happened with you in Palus, he reached out to them."

"How do you know about that?" I whispered.

"All will be explained. Although it took Aslak awhile to earn the sloth's trust, they are now working together to cross into other lands. Aslak only has access to three of the thirteen doors, that's why they need you. We believe he is planning to use you for leverage, knowing how important you are."

"I don't understand. I am just the daughter of Caelum's Door Keeper. I'm no one important," I urged.

"Eden, the path you have been on for years may not seem important, but everything that happens from here on out would not be possible without it. You should know, their plan to capture your brother failed. He escaped back to Caelum."

Relief filled me as he spoke the last sentence. They didn't have Marek. He was safe.

"They are taking you to the Apex to . . . "

"Tsk Tsk, Taran."

I jolted up hearing the seemingly bored voice speak up from behind us.

"You betray me so easily, for nothing but a ridiculous legend." He looked completely disinterested in what he said.

"You betrayed us first Aslak, and we both know the legends. You know who she is and what she is capable of." Taran looked at me as he spoke. "You are as scared of her as you should be."

Legend? What legend?

"Scared? Hardly. Stop playing her protector. It doesn't suit you." He looked at his long, curled fingernails. "We both know the Stags are indifferent, neutral in the wars of the worlds. You don't care about any of our fates anymore than I care about this fragile woman's."

I didn't like the direction of the conversation. Aslak's nonchalance was unnerving. An unshakable fear that something bad was about to happen to my new friend grew in the pit of my stomach. Sensing my emotions, Taran spoke to me once more, his eyes not moving from mine. "Find my brethren, they will lead you where you need to go." He bowed his head ever so gently, the snow falling from the branches of his trees.

The cold ring of Aslak's sword unsheathing rang in my ears. Every inch of me screamed in horror as he sliced through Taran's body, blood spattering across the blank white canvas of the snow around us.

"*No!*" I screamed. "No . . . " I crumbled next to the stag's now lifeless body. The creak of his trees echoed as they fell, and finally crashed as they hit the ground, their life source dying. "No," I whispered.

Everything Taran had given me, peace, rest, shelter, all felt like it was dying with him. I cradled his nose in my lap and rubbed his cheek as he took his final breaths. I looked up to the monster that could murder such an amazing animal so heartlessly. I wanted to kill him as he glared down at me with his cold, black eyes. Or at least wanted to enter his mind and twist it until he lived in a permanent nightmare for the remainder of his pathetic life.

"You only have yourself to blame," Aslak said as he walked away. "Heed my warning, Door Keeper. The more you fight me, the more will die."

THE MOMENT.

Eden.

I didn't want to leave Taran's body. He had willingly sacrificed himself to give me the truth. He had helped me and been there for me when I was alone and scared. My mind raced back to Squash and the similar sacrifice he had made. Why did the people who help me always seem to end up dead? Was this the fate I brought to those around me? My Mother, Squash, and now Taran. I couldn't take it—seeing such a beautiful, majestic animal, lying lifeless in the white snow. With his trees now fallen on the ground, the snow began to accumulate on all things still. His blood, still warm, was spilled at my feet. Snow landed on the puddles of blood, each flake slowly dissolving into the deep blackish red liquid. Within minutes, Taran and every trace of him would be covered by the precipitation, frozen in this damn arctic tundra. My heart broke. He had walked behind me, sheltering me for days, without saying a word. He would still be alive if he had just stayed quiet. The air hung with silence as the sloth untied my rope from his downed tree and tugged, forcing me to leave Taran behind.

Without the protection of Taran's trees, the snow completely covered my hood and coat. I turned back one last time before I was out of sight, and my friend was now only visible as a lumpy snow bank, as the falling snow covered his body and his trees. His death would not be for nothing.

An ember of anger burned in my chest. As it grew, I allowed it to encompass my thoughts. Aslak would not get away with taking me, whatever he was planning, or his brutal murder of one he had sworn to protect. He would not succeed in leveraging his position given to him for selfish ambition. He did not deserve the title of Door Keeper and would regret the day he decided to turn on his calling.

I imagined Gabby's and JJ's faces. Then James' face. My family's faces in Caelum, and every one of my father's subjects. I pictured Charlie, my adopted parents, Jay, Danielle, and Emmie. My sweet Rosalina's face. I recounted Squash and Taran. Then Lolli, Vi, and Strix. I saw my mother's face.

These are the people I fought for.

These are the people who make my life matter.

These people deserved my protection, and that is what they were going to get.

As the fury and anger burned within, the stabbing pains subsided in my extremities and slowly worked their way out of my body. I was gaining control. That empowering awareness spread throughout my core. Resolving to strengthen myself physically first, I would attempt to reach out subconsciously as soon as I was strong enough. Even with his death, Taran was providing me what I needed to survive.

We walked for several hours, my strength and clarity growing with every step. The snow fell heavier and thicker as the day progressed. I continued to breath in and out as deeply and slowly as I could, despite the frigid temperatures, and tried to concentrate on every muscle in my body staying warm and alert. I knew the mental exercises were working, and spent every moment staying as lucid as possible.

Without warning, I sensed someone encroaching in my mind. I turned around to see if the sloth walking behind me was too close, but he was about ten feet behind me, dragging his claws as he walked. I stopped walking and closed my eyes, my breath catching as I felt it again, this time more intense and much closer. My eyes shot open and wondered what it was. What was here?

Who was here?

No . . . yet, I could feel her presence.

But that was impossible.

No, it wasn't, not the way she dreamt.

I turned slowly, completely terrified as to what I would see.

My every fear was realized as I saw her, standing in the middle of the blizzard swirling around us, in her tank top and flannel pajama pants, arms wrapped around herself, her long hair blowing and already coated in snow.

"No! No baby, wake up. You've got to wake up!" I tried to run towards her, but my captor yanked me back, causing me to fall backwards. At least I knew the sloths couldn't see Gabby, but they would soon smell her. I refocused every ounce of my energy to get to my daughter. I jumped up and yelled, "Get Marek, tell him I'm in Iskrem, and they are taking me to the Apex. The Apex, Gabbs. Don't forget!"

She looked so confused. I was afraid she couldn't hear me. What was she doing here? She was in an incredible amount of danger and didn't even know it.

Her voice sounded like music to my ears floating over the rush of the wind.

"Mom! What is happening? Are you okay? Tell me what to do!" She looked like she was crying.

Baby, no, please don't cry. I couldn't control my own tears, my heart full of grief and frustration over the past week, and now fear for my daughter. I wanted to say I was sorry, that I wasn't mad at her. That I loved her.

"Just tell Marek and please stay home. Take care of JJ. I love you, baby. Now, wake up!" I begged her. Pain radiated through my head as a claw hit me across the face, catching me off guard, since I had totally been focused on Gabby and unaware the sloth had moved next to me. I fell flat on my back, the only thing in my vision was snowflakes falling on my face in slow motion, growing larger and larger until they finally hit my eyes.

"Mom!" Her warm hand cupped my cheek.

Oh Gabby, please wake up. You are going to get hurt. You have no idea how much danger you are in. Any moment the sloth will smell you and know you are here. I looked up, and her face looked like an angel carved from ice. Snowflakes resting on her eyelashes and her cheeks flushed from the cold; she was so beautiful.

I channeled every ounce of energy I had left and did the only thing I dared to.

"Wake up sweetie." I slapped her as hard as I could muster.

THE SEARCH.

Gabby.

Charlie stared at me wide eyed. I reached up and touched the side of my face where my mom had slapped me. It still stung. I brushed the frozen tears from my cheek.

"We have to call Uncle Marek. I know where Mom is." Panic rose up in me, remembering the giant beast that hit my mother. I jumped off the couch. "We have to call him, Charlie. She's somewhere in Iskrem, and those huge sloth things have her."

"Wait," Charlie looked puzzled. "How is that possible? The sloths live in Palus."

"I don't care where they live. That's what I saw! One of those giant things hit her!" We didn't have time for this. I had to get my Uncle.

"This doesn't make sense." Charlie's face mirrored my rising sense of terror. "If Paluns crossed worlds, they would have had to have help—this isn't good." He leapt up, seemingly ready for action. "But what do we do? We haven't heard from my brother or Marek in days."

"We. Call. Marek," I said through gritted teeth.

"It's not that simple, Gabbs. We don't have a cell phone that crosses worlds," he responded in an equally agitated tone. We both felt helpless, and neither of us liked it.

"I'll call Gio and see how quickly he can get a message to him."

"We don't have time for that!" I knew I wasn't helping the situation, but I couldn't believe there wasn't an easier way. "Charlie, wait! We *do* have a cell phone that crosses worlds."

He looked at me like I'd lost my mind.

"Me."

"I'm not sure it works that way."

"But it just did!" An ounce of hope was fueled by my realization. "All I had to do was think about Mom, and I went right to her. I should be able to do the same with Marek."

"I guess it couldn't hurt to try. Here, lie down, and I'll go call Gio. Either way, he needs to know what's happening."

I laid back down on the couch and tried to calm myself. I was so amped up there was no way I could go to sleep right now. I thought back to the book my mom had written for me. Her journals, the first hand experience of everything she went through when she first discovered the truth. Most of her dreams happened when she slept, but there was that one time . . .

That time she showed my grandfather the future, where I had become Queen.

Holy crap.

Since Charlie had given me *The Door Keeper* last night, I hadn't even had time to process that if everything in the book were true, then I would become Queen of a place I'd never been, and never even knew existed until today.

Come on Gabby, pull yourself together. One thing at a time. The first thing I needed to do was contact Marek, so we could make a plan. There will be plenty of time to deal with all of this. If I didn't find Mom, I may never get a chance to hug her, say I was sorry, thank her, and ask her the zillions of questions that were beginning to form in my mind.

This whole time she had been protecting me, teaching me, trying to prepare me.

I had to focus. I reopened the book and tore through the pages until I found what I was looking for.

"I closed my eyes and asked for what I needed. I'm not sure who I was asking, but I felt it bubble deep from within me, until it rose to the surface. I could feel it as it moved down my arms towards my hands."

So I did as she did that day, pulling her gifts from the subconscious while awake. I closed my eyes and asked to see Marek. I focused on it coming from within. When doing gymnastics as a kid, my mom used to tell me to visualize myself completing the tumble, seeing it happen before I attempted it. So I tried to use that now. I envisioned my Uncle and imagined standing in front of him. Goose bumps floated down the back of my neck, and spread down my arms toward my hands. I did what felt natural, placing my fingers on my temples. I closed my eyes and everything melted away.

Warmth instantly spread through my body. My skin tingled, and I instinctively raised my face towards the suns. The intense heat and water licking at my ankles told me exactly where I was. I recognized it from Mom's description—Caelum. Although, I couldn't see anything it was so bright. Splashing and a sudden man's outburst followed by the loud neighing of a horse right in front of me, almost scaring me to death. I flinched, not having any idea what was happening or where the commotion came from. My eyes started to adjust, and a huge black mass materialized in front of me, breathing hard. A dark figure moved down from above it.

"Gabby?"

"Uncle Marek!" I moved towards the voice and the slowly focusing blur in front of me. We embraced, and as we pulled apart my eyesight fully adjusted.

"What in the hell are you doing here?"

I spoke so fast, he didn't have a chance to interject. "I found Mom. She's been taken. She is in Iskrem, and the sloths have her. She told me to tell you they are taking her to the Apex. You have to do something. She's in trouble!"

"How did you talk to her?"

"I asked to see her and fell asleep. I went in my dreams."

"Damn it!" He looked seriously upset. "Are you okay?"

"Of course I'm okay. Mom is the one in trouble!"

"You don't understand. Here, climb up on Nox. We have to get you into some shade. You're going to burn."

"Burn? This is just a dream."

"No, it's not Gabbs, not for you. Now come on!" he ordered, and his tone told me I shouldn't argue.

We rode for a few minutes until we came to a giant oak tree growing straight out from the water. Simply the most incredible thing I'd ever seen. It was one thing to read about it but a whole other thing to witness it. We rode up underneath it's generous shade, and I slid off the horse, my skin already sensitive.

"I don't understand. Why are you upset? What did you mean it's not just a dream for me?"

"The only people that know are me, your dad, and your mom. We didn't tell anyone else, because we weren't sure of the extent. Gabby, your dreams just aren't in your subconscious. You are physically present as well."

"What? How is that possible?" He had to be mistaken.

"We have no idea. But your mother noticed it a few weeks after your sixteenth birthday. You woke up with fresh scrapes on your knees one morning, so that night she monitored your dreams. She watched you for days before she saw the next sign. You hit your arm and woke up with a bruise, same spot as in the dream."

"Are you being serious right now?" With everything I had learned over the past twenty-four hours, this still shocked me.

"Completely."

"So when I was talking to my mom . . ."

"You were in fact there and could have gotten hurt."

"That's why she was yelling at me to wake up—why she slapped me."

"We don't know the extent of your abilities yet. If one of the sloths grabbed you, took you, or worse, we have no idea what would happen to you."

"Oh my God." My mind raced back to unexplained bruises, bumps, and scrapes the past couple years. I always wrote them off as me just being careless.

"Yeah, I know." My uncle finally seemed to relax before he continued, "Um, Gabby?"

"Yes?" I had completely zoned out. I was realizing that this was my home. This is where my grandmother was born and raised and where Mom should have been. This was the world I was to rule one day. A giant, bluish, turquoise swan floated a few feet from us, completely unaware of the drama unfolding right next to him. We were standing in the middle of a world of shallow oceans and giant, blue, swan birds. It was too much to take in in such a short amount of time.

"How did you know how to find your mom, or how to come see me?"

I looked at my Uncle, already suspecting he knew the answer. "Dad is missing. He went after Mom a few days ago. Charlie got scared and gave me her book."

He looked up into the tree and took a deep breath.

"Oh." Then he looked back down with a mixture of pity and relief. "Well, then I guess you have some questions."

"Yes, yes I do. About two and a half billion. But before we get to those, can we figure out a plan to find and save my parents?"

"Of course, now tell me everything you saw from start to finish."

THE PLAN.

Gabby

I recounted everything I witnessed in the dream as best as I could remember. Down to the sloth's fur, Mom's wind burnt skin, and everything she said.

"Okay, the Palun's aren't the smartest of the bunch, so they must have had help crossing worlds." The crease between his brows deepened.

"That's what Charlie said."

"The question is who? Who would help them? And why Iskrem?"

"That doesn't matter right now. We've got to get her out of there!" I was losing patience.

"Sorry, it doesn't matter now, but it will later. And if I know Eden she is gathering as much information as she can. I wonder why she isn't the one reaching out to us. Did you get a look at her eyes by any chance?"

"They were red and swollen, like she had been crying a lot. They looked darker than usual, and she definitely looked tired." I tried to shake the mental image of Mom looking so rough. I'd never seen her look like that.

"Dark? I bet her eyes were dilated. They've drugged her. That's why she's not reaching out. She can't."

"What do you mean?"

"If they drugged her, she can't control her subconscious. How did they know about her gifts?" Marek paced, looking even more upset.

"What do we do?" His worrying made me more uneasy.

"It's up to us. If you can break her out of Apex, then I can get to her and bring her home. There is a door to Iskrem in Norway that would be my closest option. I have never met your Door Keeper to that world, but I'm sure Gio can connect us. But even once I get there, it might take me a couple of days to get to her at the Apex. Our best bet is to tell her to go to the Tree of Light, and I can meet her there. That won't take me as long to get to."

"Okay, but how am I supposed to break her away from those giant sloths?" I recalled their size and menacing weapons.

"The Apex is an old military base. Chances are that she's in a cell with one guard, max. So you'll just need to get her out of the cell and make sure she gets out of the facility. I guarantee she will already have a plan. Your mom is smart. Just follow her lead."

"Alright, so we get her out and to the Tree of Light, whatever the heck *that* is. Then she'll meet up with you and come home?"

"Gabbs, we aren't going home. We both walked into very strategic traps. Thankfully mine was poorly executed, or I wouldn't be here. There is something happening across the worlds, and we have to get to the bottom of it. We are going to Italy, where we'll meet with Gio and figure out what is happening. You need to find your dad and get him there. If something crazy has happened, and he's been captured too, just send Charlie after him. The important thing is for you to get JJ and bring him to Sorrento. I will find your mother and meet you there."

"Uncle Marek, I'm scared." Tears filled my eyes.

My Uncle bore his wild, light green eyes into mine and put his hands on my shoulders.

"Gabbs, you have known the truth for less than twenty four hours, and you have already visited two different worlds that you didn't even know existed. Without even crossing through a door. Eden is in danger, and you have no idea where James is. I'm asking you to knowingly walk into a very dangerous situation for the first time in your life. You have every right to be scared. But I promise you this, you come from a lineage of some of the strongest and bravest women these worlds have ever seen. You were made to do this—your mother and mine made sure of it." He kissed me on the forehead and jumped back on his horse.

"Now wake up, and go find your dad!" He galloped straight towards me, and I jolted awake.

THE SWAMP.

Gabby

When I woke up, Charlie was nowhere to be seen. I jumped off the couch and heard him talking outside on the porch. Rain pounded the tin roof, and the heavy spring downpour weighed heavy on my already unsettled mood. Charlie turned around when the screen door closed and breathed a sigh of relief after seeing I was in one piece. He lifted one finger and spoke into the phone.

"Gio, let me call you back. Gabby is awake."

"Wait," I interjected. "Tell him to contact Iskrem's Door Keeper in Norway. Marek is going to need him."

Charlie relayed the message and hung up the phone.

"Dang, what happened to your skin?! It's like you've been on the world's shortest vacation." His brows furrowed like my dad's. "Did you see Marek?"

"Yeah, it's crazy there. Have you ever been to Caelum?"

"Unfortunately not. I've asked, but they always shoot me down. I pretty much sit at the kiddie table." He joked, attempting to mask his irritation.

"Well, the adults need these kiddie's help, so I guess we are at the adult table now." I recounted my conversation with Marek.

"Okay, wow." His face contorted when I got to the part about my body being connected to my dreams. "So somehow your body actually goes to these places? Like, you're physically there?"

"I guess. We really didn't have time to get into the physics of it. If they even understand it."

Charlie shook his head. "This is crazy. Like seriously nuts."

"Tell me about it. I'm going to have to be much more careful when I dream."

"For sure." Charlie nodded and opened the door for me back into the house.

"Alright, first I need to find Dad and make sure he's safe."

"I'm going to keep an eye on you. If I see injuries appear, I'm waking you up."

"Not a bad idea."

I laid back down, not believing I was about to do this again. Everything in me already felt so emotionally drained and unsure. I hoped I had the strength. As if knowing what I was feeling, Charlie put his hand on my shoulder.

"Niester, you are doing amazing. You've known the truth for all of a few hours, and you've already accomplished more than I have in over ten years. I'm really proud of you."

I was unable to stop the smile spreading across my face at his using our old pet names for each other. Shortly after my parents married, Charlie and I combined our weird family dynamic/relationship into nicknames, combining niece and sister, and brother and uncle. But we hadn't used them in years. "Thanks, Bruncle. How do you always know what I need to hear?"

"You have your gifts, and I have mine." He shrugged. "Maybe not as glamorous as yours, but they come in handy. Now go do what you do and find my brother."

I closed my eyes and pictured my dad's face. His brown wavy hair with gray sprinkled around his temples. His warm brown eyes with small creases forming in their corners. His easy laugh when he teased me and his furrowed brow when he was frustrated. His large shoulders and the feeling of being wrapped in his bear hug.

I needed to find him. The now familiar tingle crept down my neck and towards my hands. Lifting my fingers to my temples, this world melted away once again.

The sound of the rapids startled me, and the greenish yellow haze of my surroundings, made me feel uneasy. I slowly sank, the mud squishing between my toes.

"Gabbs!" A giant swamp thing called my name. If his voice hadn't been so familiar, I would have run away screaming. But instead, I lunged toward the blob of mud and wrapped my arms around it.

"Dad!"

"Oh my God! Baby girl, what are you doing here?! Are you okay?" He pulled back, cupping my face in his hands. The only part of him I recognized was his chocolate eyes.

"I'm alright. Wigging out just a bit."

"Is your mother okay? Where is she?"

"I've seen her and know where she is. Are you safe?"

"Yes, I've been following a trail from the door, but I lost it yesterday. What happened to your skin?"

"Um, I went to see Uncle Marek after finding Mom to come up with plan."

"You went to Caelum?" His eyes widened.

"Not exactly. I went in a dream."

"Gabby—"

"I know, Dad. Marek told me. I'm being more careful now."

My dad's face softened, and he slowly nodded as realization hit him. "Charlie gave you *The Door Keeper*. I thought he might after I didn't come right back. Thank heavens he did. We need you, sweetie."

"Apparently." The corners of my mouth tilted up despite my fear. "Listen Dad, you've got to get back. Mom isn't here. She's in Iskrem. It's a long story. Charlie can fill you in. You need to get to Sorrento, and we will meet up there. Uncle Marek and I are helping Mom escape."

"Escape? Why is she is Iskrem? Gabby, what happened?" His entire body tensed at the word "escape."

I didn't want to lie to him, and he deserved to know the truth. I knew how much he loved my mother.

"She's been drugged. That's why she hasn't been able to communicate with us. The sloths have her, and she didn't look good. But Dad, if I've learned nothing else from that book, it's that Mom is strong. She's going to be fine." I was trying to convince him as much as myself.

"Yes, she is." He wiped his forehead and took a deep breath. "How is JJ doing?"

"He's fine. He's at school and has been staying with Grandpa. He has no idea that anything is wrong. Uncle Marek told me to bring him to Sorrento."

"Good. Take care of your brother. I love you, and please be careful."

I hugged him one last time. "I promise I will, Dad. I love you too."

THE REALIZATION.

Eden

Something deep within me realized I was dreaming, but I was still unable to control what happened next or direct my subconscious. I was simply a spectator—just as I was before I knew I could control my dreams. Before I learned the truth about where I came from. Before my life changed forever.

My daughter stood before me, regal in her dress and posture. She looked like the Queen I knew she would be. However, she was unaware I was there watching whatever unfolded. I took immediate relief in knowing she was alive, realizing I witnessed her future. Her future as Caelum's Queen. With a crown of Elisium flowers woven through her long, loose hair and an intricately embroidered white dress with gold trim, she stood on the edge of a cliff overlooking the shallow seas. The same cliff I'd changed the course of our family by showing her grandfather her future and securing peace between our worlds. She stood with her eyes pooling with tears, unwilling to let them fall.

Why are you sad, baby?

Suddenly, I was back walking on the same beach as before, following footprints stretched out before me. The large lighthouse in the middle of the sea was being pummeled by the ocean, furious it would interrupt it's trip to shore. I glanced up at the light, perched high above the surf, thinking a shadow flashed of something up there, or someone.

As if expecting the sudden change in scenery, I sat down on JJ's bed, watching him dream. I knew he was dreaming because his facial expression subtly changed. Breathing in slow and steady, I reached out my hand and placed it on his head, twirling my fingers in his hair. He was so special. I was sure of it. He would play a very large part in whatever was to come. Then, as though she whispered from within me, I heard Ava's voice, "*You will need her, and you will need him. They will make you stronger, and you will need all of that strength for what is to come. None of it is possible if we stay. I'm so sorry. I love you, sweetheart. I promise you, I will always be with you. You will never be alone.*"

Upon waking, I left my eyes closed. The tears fell anyway. She had said those words in the dream I had years ago, that I needed her and him. She was talking about JJ. She understood that if I had been raised in Caelum, I wouldn't have Gabby or him. And she knew I needed them both. Tears formed in my closed eyes, burning with the realization of truth. My thoughts drifted back to Gabby.

Gabby.

I sat up too quickly and paid for it. My head swam in pain, and the sting of a new cut above my scarred eye made me wince. She had been here, in Iskrem, looking for me. But why and how?

The book.

I had no idea how long I'd been missing since I spent so much of it knocked out or drugged, but I knew it had to have been around a week, more or less. If James came after me and was now missing too, Charlie would know his best chance of finding me was Gabby.

He gave her the book.

The truth hit me with a force that knocked the breath from my lungs. She knew everything—where I came from, her biological grandparents, how I met James, and all of the danger we encountered. And I'm not there to guide her or answer her millions of questions. I'm not there to comfort her if she is confused or scared. *Of course* she was confused and scared. Her life just got turned upside down. I wanted so badly to hug her and whisper that I would explain everything in greater detail. I couldn't imagine how she must be feeling, now knowing the truth about the past eight years. But I never told Charlie how Gabby's gift was different than mine. He wouldn't know the danger she was in every time she traveled in the dream world.

I attempted to throw myself into my daughter's mind, but the constant dull ache in my head keep me from reaching her. The only thing I could do was to try to get as comfortable as possible and take an inventory of my injuries. I looked around, seeing that I was in a ten foot by ten-foot stone cell. There was nothing except the three gray walls and one wall of bars. Up above my head was a small horizontal rectangular window, so I stood slowly, pushing through the pain in my head. Finally, standing on my toes, the swirling snow blew furiously in every direction. I couldn't tell for sure, because of the white out, but I believe we had arrived at the Apex. Gio had told me stories over the years of many of the different world's histories and old wars. Iskrem had barely survived a war with a neighboring world over a century ago, and the Apex was an old base used as a fortress. It was located high up on a mountain, providing the perfect defense against attack.

I eased back down, trying to collect my thoughts. What do I know for sure?

Marek wasn't captured—that was important. I was afraid James was missing. Giving Gabby the book was a last resort, not one James would have done unless he had no other options. His first reaction would be to come after me. So it's safe to assume Charlie hasn't heard from him either, hence him going to Gabby. Gabby knows the truth and now knows where I am, so hopefully she will get the message to Marek.

My brain began to hurt. I had to get these drugs out of my system and get a clear head. I refused to continue to feel so hopeless and useless. I realized what ever was in my system was in my blood, so the only thing to do was allow time take it's course. I crossed my legs and started meditating, breathing in and out slowly.

Gabby knew everything. I'd waited so long to have so many conversations with her, and now I can't.

I opened my eyes. The guard outside my cell wasn't visible, but I smelled him. I didn't see where the lock to the bars were, but knew one must exist. Nothing was on the floor but dirt and a few small pebbles. I pulled the fur that was still around me up tighter around my body. My thoughts drifted to Taran, and I as I rubbed my hands through the fur that surrounded me, the absence of warmth behind the fur filled me with sorrow.

The cell was cold, and I decided that it would do my body and spirit good to get my blood pumping. So I stretched and held some yoga poses, not wanting to draw too much attention to myself with any noise. The longer I went unnoticed, the better.

After about thirty minutes of exercise, my mood improved dramatically. Even the illusion of having some sort of control over what was happening to me was empowering after feeling helpless for so long.

A tingle ran down my spine, not my own, but an outside force. Gabby was on her way. God, please keep her safe. She slowly appeared in front of me as a mist rolling in from nowhere. She wore complete winter garb—boots, coat, scarf, and earmuffs. Marek must have told her the truth about her gifts. My girl learned quickly.

"Mom!" She fell into my arms, my throat choked with unshed tears after smelling the familiar scents of home.

"Gabbs. It's okay, baby." I whispered stroking her hair. "We've got to be quiet. We don't want them to know you are here."

She answered, her voice softer. "Are you alright?"

"Yes, I'm feeling better. I don't know the last time they checked on me, so I don't know how long we have."

"I understand." She composed herself and sat up. "Mom, I'm so sorry. I shouldn't have lied to you about Prom, and I'm sorry for what I said. I didn't mean it."

"Oh honey, me too. It's okay, we'll talk about that later. We'll have plenty of time to work all of that out." I placed my hands on either side of her tear stained cheeks. Our argument about prom felt a lifetime ago.

"Okay," she sniffed. "Marek told me I needed to help you get out of here and for you to meet him at the Tree of Light. Do you know where that is?"

"No, but I think I know some friends who do. Have you found your dad?"

"Yes, he's okay. He was following your trail in Palus but obviously lost it. He's heading back to meet up with us."

My entire body relaxed once I knew he was safe, albeit it only lasted for a moment. "Where is JJ? How is he?"

"He's good. He's with Grandpa. Everyone is safe, Mom."

"Not everyone." I wiped away the last tear on her face with my thumb, missing the sweet chubby cheeks no longer there. "I'm assuming Marek told you about how dangerous it is for you to dream."

"He did. I got a little sun burned in Caelum." She looked at me sheepishly, like she did when we was ten, confessing a wrongdoing.

I closed my eyes, willing my own tears away. "You were in Caelum?" My heart hurt that I couldn't be with her there for her first time but softly chuckled to soften the mood. "You should have seen your Dad when he got back from his first trip. His skin peeled for weeks."

"It's good to see you smile."

"I'm sorry this is happening, sweetie. This is not the way I wanted you to find out the truth."

"It's okay. I'm looking forward to hearing all about it," she answered as if sensing my sadness that I wasn't there for her. I pushed some hair away from her pale blue eyes. Once so unassuming, now they'd seen more than even I could comprehend at that moment.

She continued, "Once you find Marek, y'all are going to meet the rest of us in Sorrento. We're going to see Gio to figure out what is happening."

"Ok, before you leave for Italy, you need to tell Charlie to go see Strix. Tell him we can't trust all the Door Keepers, and he needs to secure the doors from inside Terra Arborum the best he can until we can sort everything out. I'm sorry, I don't have time to tell you more."

"Of course, I'll tell him. Oh, man . . . Strix is real." Her eyes grew, and she exhaled in disbelief. "All these years, I've been reading *Lolli's World*, and it's real."

I let her have a moment to process, simply happy to have her sitting across from me.

"Okay, sorry. So, how do we get you out of here?"

"Do you remember in *The Door Keeper* when I put my Aunt Vera into the nightmare? We have the ability to throw other people into a dream state, even while they are awake. It's like a trance of sorts. You can make them see whatever you want them to. You just need to walk me out, ready to put any person who stands in our way, into a dream state. Once they wake up from it, I'll be long gone."

My daughter looked back at me with desperation in her eyes.

"Mom, I'm so tired. I've been dreaming off and on for hours. I don't know if I can do it."

"Oh, hon." I embraced her once more. "We've asked so much of you. It's okay. It'll take everyone a few days to get where they need to go. Why don't you rest and come back in twenty-four hours. Relax your mind—music and a couple good meals will help. I'm gonna be fine. Go pack, get your brother ready, and tell

Charlie to go see Strix. I'll see you tomorrow. I promise, I'll still be here."

"Mom, what if something happens to you?"

"Nothing will happen. I've seen too much of our future. But if we are going to pull this off, you need to be strong and well rested. Trust me, this will drain your energy. When you are ready, I'll be here waiting." I attempted a reassuring smile.

"Okay." She hesitated. "I'll be back soon, I promise."

"I know. I love you, Gabby."

"I love you too, Mom."

And just as mystically as she appeared, she disintegrated, and I was once again alone, feeling the full weight of what lay ahead.

THE CLOSE CALL.

Eden

The waiting was harder than I had anticipated. Being cut off from everyone I love, unable to help or change the dire circumstances we all seemed to be in. Every expectation I had about telling Gabby the truth had vanished. There wasn't time to explain, or story tell, or answer questions. She was just thrown into the deep end without instructions or directions.

Time felt like my enemy, purposefully tormenting me. Suddenly, the longer I was left alone, the wearier I became. I tried to sleep but the dull ache of hunger never receded. I didn't know what Aslak's plan was, or why he needed me, but he wasn't drugging me anymore. The only thing keeping me from reaching out to my family was knowing everyone was on the same page and moving into position. But why would Aslak allow me access to my mind after all this time?

Unsure how much time had passed, I finally heard the clumsy dragging of the sloth approach my cell. He opened the bars and crouched low, grabbing my hands and tying them together with a thick, rough rope. Then, after placing a noosed rope around my neck, he tugged it giving me no choice but to follow. The rough braided material scratched my neck, making me once again feel like an imprisoned animal, reigniting my hatred and rage towards Aslak, who was obviously determined to strip me of my humanity. I still had the blanket wrapped around me, which was fortunate considering it became colder with every step we took. We trudged through tunnel after tunnel, only the sound of the sloths heavy breathing and the occasional echo of doors closing in the distance. A white light became visible in the distance and cold air rushed through the tunnel. We were going outside.

Unsure what was happening, I called out to Gabby in my mind, giving her a warning that I was being moved.

The frigid air hit me hard, cutting through every fiber of my being. I suddenly lost control over my body as my muscles spasmed. The sloth took me out and shoved me down within a circle of the huge creatures. The snow pierced my bare feet like knives, sending shooting pains up my legs. On my knees, I forced my face up as the circle parted and Aslak entered. His long white hair almost invisible in the blizzard surrounding us. His face smug, he crouched down in front of me, taking hold of the rope tied around my neck. I noticed my key hanging from a large chain swinging under his stained smile. This leathery monster had my key.

"I am certain that by now, your family knows where you are."

The deep shivers roaring through my body prevented me from answering.

"Would you mind, my dear, letting them know what is about to happen? It would make my job so much easier." He pursed his lips together and tilted his head.

Once again, I couldn't speak.

"Oh, you do not know what is about to happen?" he mused. "Well, I assure you, Eden, your death will play the perfect role in what happens next. Now, would you please let you tell your family that I am about to kill you? It is very important that they know." He was talking so nonchalantly, he could have been talking about cooking me breakfast.

He stood up and walked around me in circles, as though he were being kind in giving me enough time. I attempted to throw my captor into a nightmare and save my self, but as soon as he felt me encroaching his mind, he yanked on the noose practically blacking me out. With no physical strength, and pain ripping through me, I did the only thing he wouldn't see coming.

Gabby, we don't have anymore time. It has to be now. Hurry! Be ready!

I yelled as loud as I could muster within my own head.

Gabby!

He stopped behind me, ripped the blanket off of me, fully exposing my skin to the raging and angry snow whirling around us. As he unsheathed his sword, the sloths around me banging their over-grown claws on the snow and grunting in unison. My mind raced back to Palus, when James and I had been captured, and the Paluns called for our blood, just as they did now.

James, I love you. Take care of Gabby and JJ.

Maybe I was wrong. Maybe this was the part I was supposed to play all along. Maybe the bridge I would build would be my death. Maybe . . .

As I opened my eyes, she appeared about two feet in front of me, face filled with horror at the scene that surrounded her. She stood immediately, her hands spread, palms faced out, fingers wide. A look of furious determination quickly replaced the fear.

My capturer gasped and whispered behind me. "Well, that was unexpected."

Relief coursed through me as every one of our enemies fell into the white snow, completely asleep. Gabby grabbed the blanket and wrapped it around me.

"Mom! We've got to go!" She had to yell over the growing storm.

"My my f-feet, too c-c-cold." I stuttered.

She ran over and grabbed the boots off of Aslak and helped me put them on. Grabbing under my arms, she helped me stand.

"I'll help you get off the mountain, then I'll need to go back. Our flight leaves in a few hours."

"Wait!" I barely heard my own voice over the howl of the wind. I limped over and yanked my key from the unconscious body lying behind me, hand still clutching his sword. For a moment, I imagined killing him with his own sword for what he did to Taran, for what he was about to do to me. For a brief moment.

I turned and nodded at Gabby as every part of my body shook violently. We walked together in silence until we found a path that led down the mountain. As we carefully made our way down the steep inclines, the blood pumping through my heart and into my limbs warmed me, and the wind eventually decreased as we slowly made our way down. We had almost reached the bottom before she spoke up.

"That was too close."

"Yes, it was." My voice steadied. "But now I know what he wanted, and we can use it against him."

"I don't want to leave you, Mom." Her voice shook and her breath caught on my name.

"Honey, it's okay." I nodded ahead of us. "I won't be alone." Her eyes followed my gaze down the path to the base of the mountain.

"Holy crap! What is that?" Her entire body straightened when she saw him.

"A friend. He'll help me get to Tree of Light."

"But *what* is it?"

I smiled, realizing I was finally able to experience her new discoveries, her wonder at it all. "It's a very old deer, that happens to have trees for antlers."

"Oh. Sure. Makes sense." She looked at me, and we burst out laughing for the first time since being reunited.

As we approached the Stag, he ever so slightly bowed his head. "You must be Eden of Earth and Caelum."

"And it talks?" Gabby raised her eyebrows.

"It? My young one, I was born before your mountains were raised from the depth of your seas."

"Um, I'm sorry. I've just never talked to a deer before." Gabby looked uncomfortable.

"You must be Taran's friend. I'm so sorry about his death."

"Taran knew the risks of protecting you. The Stags are loyal to you now. My name is Teik. Come, we must leave this place."

"Thank you." Gabby bowed her head, looking unsure what else to do. "For taking care of my mother."

"The time will come, young one, when you will be the one taking care of us. Your rule will extend far beyond Caelum. The Stags have seen it. Peace to you until I see you again, Queen Gabrielle."

His words hung ominously in the air. Complete shock rang through me, unsure what he was talking about. I glanced over my shoulder at my daughter, whose jaw seemed to have dislocated.

"Um—and peace to you, sir," she stammered, looking nervous about Teik's words. I leaned over and hugged her, whispering, "Don't worry, we will both just take one day at a time. No one is Queen yet, and it is not even an option until you are good and ready."

"Yeah, one day at a time seems to be enough as it is." She pulled away. "I'll see you in Sorrento. JJ can't wait to see you. He asks about you everyday."

My hope was rekindled and it spread warming my still cold extremities. "Tell him I miss him and can't wait to give him a big hug. I love you, honey. See you again soon."

"I love you too, Mom. Be safe."

I didn't wait for her to vanish before I turned to Teik. Although, as I climbed on his back, I looked over my shoulder to see the now empty space where she once stood.

THE STAGS.

Eden

"Your daughter still has much to learn." Teik finally said after miles of silence.

"We both do," I mused, much more relaxed. I laid, cuddled up, on Teik's back, allowing his warmth to course through me. I stared up into his giant tree antlers, slow moving through the gray overcast sky above.

"That is true. You did not immerse yourself in the worlds as one might have expected after learning the truth."

"My mother gave her life so that I would be raised on Earth. I wanted to be patient and allow Gabby the same opportunity."

"You think living on Earth is an opportunity?"

"Certain aspects of it, yes. Of course, compared to other worlds, there are drawbacks. The deer aren't quite as friendly, for one."

I couldn't see Teik's face, but I hoped he smiled.

"But truthfully, I trusted Ava that this was what needed to be done," I added a moment later.

"I understand. A mother's wishes are hard to ignore."

"Teik, will you tell me about Iskrem?"

"Where shall I start?"

"How about the Tree of Light?"

"Of course. As you shall soon see, the Tree of Light is unique to all of the worlds. Our closest light source is over a billion miles away, according to how you measure distance. Hence, our perpetual freezing temperatures. The Tree of Light gives us animals and living things warmth and energy from under ground, using it's root system."

"How does that work?"

"If I could explain it to you in words you could understand, then it would not be so special now, would it?" He paused. "The main thing to realize is that while on Earth, your life giving source is the sun in your sky, ours flows through the ground, traveling through the roots and vines growing in our soil connecting most of our living things." Teik spoke slowly, as if to allow me time to process.

"So the Tree of Light is your life source?"

"Simplified, yes. Our ancestors tell tales of our land before the Tree of Light. A barren wasteland of ice and darkness. Nothing was able to grow or live, until a distant traveler found this world, and planted a handful of sunlight from another world. After centuries of growing, the Tree provided what this world needed for plants and wildlife to grow and survive. We call the celestial, Numen, for divine power. She was our life bringer."

"She?" I smiled.

"Of course. In most worlds, women are the bringers of life."

"So who and what types of life live here?"

"All manner of animals, some more intelligent than others. The Stags have been alive here the longest, our trees grow from the seeds from the Tree of Light. We ate them when we were fawns, and as our antlers grew, they continued growing into trees. We are the protectors of the lesser animals, providing what the tree supplies for us—warmth, energy, and life."

"I notice that your antlers begin as bone, like most, but then then give way to the wooden trunks. It's incredible." I touched the part of his antler where it turned into wood.

"The bone is the base that allows us to carry the weight. It is much denser than your bone and difficult if not impossible to break. Our wood fuses with our bone to keep it strong and able to withstand the elements."

"Amazing," I breathed. "So, if Aslak is the Door Keeper, then there must be people that live here."

"The closest things we have to humans are the Hiems, which is Aslak's race. They were nomads from another world and slowly evolved to handle the harsh conditions. Over the years, their skin toughened to that of wild animals, and their eyes dilated to a point of no return. They are mostly a peaceful race, content to remain secluded and isolated. The Stags know for certain that Aslak acts alone, but the rest of Iskrem is not convinced. His murder of Taran has recently spurned a deep fear and hatred for the Hiems, despite us trying to reassure them he doesn't represent his tribe."

As our conversation progressed, I began to understand Teik's worry. If there was another war within Iskrem, it could have dire consequences that reached beyond its borders. Maybe that is what Aslak wanted all along.

"How big is Iskrem?" I asked to change the subject.

"We are very small compared to your other worlds. I personally have seen it in its entirety. It only took me seven hundred and fifty years to travel."

"Only seven hundred and fifty, huh?" I laughed. "You must be tired."

"You forget dear one—I have a constant source of energy."

"I was joking, Teik."

"Oh yes. I forgot you humans like to joke."

"How do you know so much about humans and Caeluns?" I was super curious about this one.

"Because we are connected to the Tree of Light, our energy is connected as well. The Tree's energy pulses through many worlds, interconnected by the same energy forces that create the portals from one world to the next. It seems as though, whatever Sun Numen used to create the Tree of Light, is shared by multiple worlds. Or it is possible she took pieces of Suns from different worlds and combined them together for the Tree. We are unsure of how it originated. Regardless, sometimes we get glimpses into those other worlds, small pieces of information. Although, Earth's obsession with technology has created quite an energy surge, and we get more from there than any other world."

"You mean to tell me that all of the worlds are connected through the Tree of Light?"

"Not exactly. Imagine every snowflake you see falling right now is energy flowing from every world in and through each other, and we placed one small empty pail on the ground. How ever much it could collect at a time would be a good representation of how much energy we intercept as it flows. So while it is very insignificant in its totality, it is still enough to give us an insight into other worlds."

"That is incredible," I exhaled in disbelief.

My head reeled with all of this new information. I acknowledged the idea forming deep in the recesses of my mind. Iskrem was far more important in what was happening than I would have ever thought. If the tree is connected, however small, to the other worlds, no wonder Aslak wanted to create chaos here.

As we made our way through the vast frozen tundra, I noticed animals stopping and peering at us as we walked slowly through the ever-accumulating snow. Many smaller animals that reminded me of hamsters or lemurs huddled together and stared. A pack of large white and gray wolves stopped, and bowed low as Teik and I passed. I spoke up when we were alone again.

"Why didn't those wolves attack? We're the perfect prey."

"We are respected here, and no one's prey. Hiems and animals understand that Stags are connected to the tree. The tree is our life force, no one would dare harm it. No one of course, except Aslak."

After seeing what he was capable of, murdering Taran in cold blood, I had no doubt that he wouldn't be willing to harm the Tree. After everything Teik had told me about the Stags and the Tree, I held a deep sense of obligation to keep them safe.

We kept walking for hours with periodic rests. At one point we stopped by a deep, raging river flowing down off of a glacier. It's water was the freshest and most pure water I'd ever tasted.

We crossed the river over a oversized tree that had fallen across. I nervously looked down as the rushing water carried with it large chunks of ice that had broken from the glacier above. The tree trunk was unstable and wobbled under the stag's large hooves. After stabilizing and about half way across, Teik's footing slipped. I was mesmerized watching the rushing water below us and wasn't holding on at the moment. Terror raced through me, plunging my heart into my stomach as the icy water rushed towards me at lightening speed.

My feet hit the water and instantly went numb in the frigid temps, and as the water reached my waist, my hands hit against a tree branch. Somehow, despite the panic and chaos, I grabbed on before becoming completely submerged in the rushing water.

"Hold on Eden!" Teik's deep voice boomed.

Slowly, the tree rose, pulling me from the raging river.

"Don't let go."

I couldn't respond with words, only a grunt in understanding. My entire lower half had no feeling besides the angry needle pricks up and down my legs. The tree I clutched for dear life moved slowly toward the shore, gently laying me down on the white powdery snow.

"We must hurry, the Tree of Light is not far. You won't last long without it." Teik lowered himself, so I could roll back onto his back. My teeth almost broke on each other they chattered so hard.

"Up ahead, we are almost there," my ride murmured.

I raised my shivering head to a glow emanating from the top of the hill stretched out before us. A few trees obstructed the view completely, but the most beautiful warm light reflected off of the snow covering the ground and trees surrounding it. The closer we came to the source, the more the light danced, flickering in constant movement.

Once we came into full view of the Tree of Light, my frozen body relaxed in silent reverence on Teik's back. I was incredibly aware that we were in the presence of something mystic, something beautiful, something rare. It wasn't like looking into the sun. My eyes didn't strain or hurt to gaze into it's luminous glow. In fact, it drew me in, like looking into a fire. The massive tree itself looked like any other, but the similarities stopped there. Each leaf on the tree was a small ball of light, illuminating in every direction. As we approached I found myself getting lost, immersed in the warmth and life radiating from it—welcoming in such harsh conditions.

Beckoning me in from the cold to warm, rest, and be healed.

THE TREE OF LIGHT.

Eden

Teik lowered his own head, so he was able to walk me under the branches and let me slide off, landing right at the base of the tree. My face lifted up into the millions of tiny candle flames burning above me. Each one glistening apart from the other. My body warming and drying by the minute. Looking over at my new friend, the golden light danced on his warm brown fur. He backed down from under the tree and laid down, relaxing instantly. Instinctively, I sat against the tree trunk. Every worry, fear, and anxiety melted away, leaving only peace in it's place. Every ounce of pain, sadness, and mourning dissipated, leaving only joy where the darkness once resided. I noticed an amazing sense of body awareness, every extremity that had been enveloped in cold, was now warm. A tingle grew and stretched through my limbs, and somehow I understood that my injuries had healed, and any remnants of the drugs had left me. My mind felt sharp and alert.

Feeling one hundred percent for the first time, in perhaps years, I stood and approached one of the lower hanging branches. The leaves of light were small, about the size of quarters, with a pulsing whiter light at the base of the leaf where it attached to the branch; it seemed to be where the warmer light of the leaf itself originated.

The wind picked up around me, whistling through the tree, swaying the branches causing the most beautiful light show flickering across the surrounding snow-white canvas. A couple of the light leaves fell off the branch and landed softly in the snow. The leaf fizzled and slowly snuffed out in the frozen precipitation, nothing remaining behind. Knowing I had some time to wait for Marek, I walked back over, sat once again against the trunk, and dozed off to sleep.

We held hands, making our way down the beach, enjoying the waves crashing over our feet as we walked side by side. I looked down at my sweet little man. His hair wet from playing in the ocean, his smile unusually large. He always loved the ocean. "Big waves crashing!" he always exclaimed whenever anyone mentioned the beach. That was truly one of my favorite things about JJ, his excitement over everything, small or large.

"I love you, Momma." He smiled up at me. *Oh, how I love you too sweetheart.*

"This is my favorite," he added looking out at the water. "It's the best day ever!"

He let go of my hand and ran out ahead of me, leaving footprints in the sand, his stride growing longer the further from me he went. Noticing the lighthouse in the water in the distance, I called out to JJ to be safe.

As the water lapped at my feet, my eyes lowered to see I was no longer at the beach, but standing in the middle of the shallow sea in Caelum. I recognized where I was immediately, turning my gaze to see her, standing on the cliff, looking out over me towards the horizon. Her hair blew out behind her with the Elisium flowers woven throughout. I materialized next to her, as you can only do in a dream. My daughter held a piece of paper in her hands and fought back tears as she read whatever was written. Her dress was gorgeous and one of the more elaborate Caelum dresses I had ever seen, white with gold trim from top to bottom.

Why are you so sad, sweetie? You look so beautiful . . .

I reached over and tucked a piece of hair behind her ear, and her tears began to flow.

I woke up to the sound of a branch breaking in the distance. I jumped up, anxious to see my brother. Walking out from underneath the tree's cover, my body froze when the largest wolf I'd ever seen emerged from the tree line, carrying a man on it's back, his skin thick, tough, and white as snow, with eyes pitch black. He wasn't Aslak, this man's hair was long, white, and dreaded.

Teik arrived next to me, and I instantly relaxed, remembering he'd told me Aslak was acting alone. Still, with my guard up, I approached the stranger, exposed under the heavy snow. The wolf stopped, it's light gray eyes boring into mine and lowered his head. The man slid off it's back in a fluid, easy motion, his feet hitting the ground as silent as the falling snow. The wind opened his fur cloak, exposing his bare, white, leathery, upper body. His eyes never left mine as he approached, stopping just a couple feet in front of me.

"My name is Xander, and I have come to pledge my allegiance to you." He knelt before me, bowing low. Curiously and a bit uncomfortable with the formality, I lowered myself to be eye level with him.

"Well Xander, thank you. But may I ask, why?" Raising his face towards mine, I noticed a hint of something familiar, a sliver of silver around the perimeter of his dark pupils. He glanced towards my shoulder, despite it still being covered by the blanket. He seemed young, maybe his early or mid twenties at most. I stood, and he followed my lead.

"The Hiems know that Aslak has betrayed his Door Keeper lineage and betrayed his people. I represent them and am here to make you sure understand that we do not stand with him nor condone his actions."

"I promise you, no one will hold your people accountable for Aslak's actions."

"Thank you, Eden from Caelum."

"How does everyone know who I am?" I raised my eyebrows, looking from the young Hiem in front of me back to Teik.

We were interrupted by the sound of rustling in the tree line. Before I could blink, Xander threw his arm out, pushing me behind him, and swung a large wooden handled double-sided axe that he pulled from thin air to attack whatever was coming. My brother emerged slowly with his own weapon drawn.

"Eden!" He lowered his sword when he recognized that the Hiem seemed to be protecting me. "Are you alright?"

Xander lowered his guard, and I ran to embrace my brother.

"Yes, I'm fine. Better than fine now, believe it or not. Thanks for coming."

"Yeah, you know how much I hate Iskrem." He shivered and looked around at the unusual scene. "Although, all of this does look interesting." He grinned. We crossed back towards the solemn Hiem standing next to his wolf.

"Marek, this is Xander. Xander, this is my brother Marek."

Xander's entire posture shifted, and he once again bowed low.

"Marek, warrior of Caelum. It is an honor to meet you."

"The pleasure is mine. Now, come on, stand back up, you're making me uncomfortable."

Xander rose in silence, staring reverently between us both.

"Marek, this is Teik. He was the one who brought me here." They nodded at each other in greeting.

"Not to break up this weird little party, but we've got to go Eden. We have a full day's trek till we get to the door to Norway."

"Wait, please, before you go. I have a gift for you." Xander spoke as he untied something from the wolf's back. He held out a large piece of a knotted branch, about five feet long.

"Taran," The stag whispered behind me.

"Yes." Xander bowed his head reverently towards the stag. "This is one of Taran's trunks. The energy that flowed through him at the time of his death remains in his trees. It is a rare gift and will bring you health and good fortune. It is lightweight, but denser than any other natural grown material. It will be a sign for any other worlds that you represent Iskrem and the Hiems. Please, he would want you to have it." He handed it to me.

"Thank you, Xander. I appreciate your thoughtfulness. This means so much." My eyes stung with moisture. Just holding it filled me with the peace and warmth Taran had provided for me before he died.

I walked over to Teik and hugged his neck, not caring about protocol. "Thank you Teik, for everything."

"Being in possession of a Stag's tree is of the highest honors. We rarely die and when living, never part with a live branch. I know my friend's sacrifice will be worth what it cost." His voice broke at the end.

"I promise you I will do everything in my power to honor him." I smiled and turned towards my brother. Heading for the tree line, I stopped abruptly. Glancing back towards the Tree, I took in it's breathtaking light for one last time. I noticed Xander's face, looking soft in the incandescent light as he waited for us to leave.

"Xander," I called out, "Why don't you come with us?"

"What?" My brother's head jerked in my direction.

"I gave you the branch. You will represent us in other worlds."

"Here is the thing. This," I said, gesturing to the tree. "This is your life. You know everything there is to know about the Tree of Light. And we are going to need that knowledge and to understand everything we can about it if we are going to protect the tree and stop Aslak."

"Eden, I'm not sure this is a good idea. Look at him." Marek spoke softly and eyed me carefully.

"I'm trusting my gut. He has more to lose than anyone with the Paluns being here."

"Fair enough, but he's going to be hard to smuggle into Norway looking like that." He shrugged. I rolled my eyes and looked back at the Hiem watching us argue.

"I have never been outside of Iskrem; this is my home," Xander said simply.

"All the more reason to do what is necessary to protect it. You told me you represent the Hiems. I'm simply asking is that you represent them in my world. There is a counsel convening representing several different lands. You would be a welcomed ally."

He nodded as though understanding, and walked over to Teik, whispering in his ear. Teik backed away, bowing as low as his trees would allow, then turned and left. The wolf followed behind the giant stag into the trees and disappeared.

"Very well, Eden and Marek of Caelum. I will accompany you to the land you call, Norway."

THE NORTH PORTAL.

Eden

It took us many hours to get to the door that lead from Iskrem to Earth. Marek took the opportunity to fill me in on his failed abduction. Hearing his side of what happened made me even more thankful he didn't get kidnapped as well.

"The idea behind the trap was smart, but because I was with you and knew about the disturbance at the door to Palus, it didn't work. It was actually the only thing that saved me. The door to Iskrem is several days ride from our home, so by the time I knew we were both walking into a trap, it was too late to warn you. In fact, when Gabby found me, I was riding straight to the door to Italy to warn Gio."

Marek trudged next to me through the snow, Xander falling behind us.

"When I arrived at the door, there were fresh marks and scrapes on the cliff face surrounding it. Had to have been made by a large animal. Of course, hindsight it was the Paluns. But I had no way of knowing that at the time. There were also scratches at the base of the door, like something tried to claw it's way under. At that point, I was fully on guard, considering what we saw on the monitors back in Georgia.

"I had my weapon pulled when I opened the door to check for a breach. Three steps in and I fell into a giant hole covered by a snowdrift. Thankfully, I had this." My brother nodded towards the long spear and axe combo he currently held. "I held it over my head sideways, and it was wide enough to catch me and stop me from falling in. I swung out of the hole and ran back through the door, locking it immediately. They knew I was coming and dug the hole early enough for the snow to cover it over. I'm just glad I went in weapon drawn, or I might still be there."

We walked the rest of the way in silence. The weather was brutal, and it took most of the strength I'd gained from the Tree of Light to make the journey. When we reached a small tunnel that led underground, my relief for the shelter was palpable. Marek lead the way with a lit torch, and Xander followed behind me. The three of us crouched low and sank deeper and deeper under the mountain the tunnel ran through. After about thirty minutes of trudging through damp darkness, we came upon a tall narrow door in the wall. Upon closer inspection, there were carvings on the cave wall on either side of the portal. They looked like two slender deer-like animals on either side, seemingly guarding the door. A giant winding snake wound around the opening and tangled with the deer. I couldn't help but think about the Stags and the evil that was threatening Iskrem.

Marek switched the torch to his other hand and pulled out his key. Inserting it, he turned the key multiple times to line up the bits with the locking mechanism. I took notice of Xander watching on, solemnly. Once we heard the clicks of the locks, Marek turned, looking over his shoulder at us.

"You ready? I'll warn both of you—this Door Keeper is a little feisty."

Xander nodded slightly.

"Nothing I'm sure we can't handle," I said, amused.

"Don't say I didn't warn you." My brother smiled. "Xander, I'd pull up your hood. It should be early morning, but we don't want to freak out any tourists."

"Tourists? Why would we see tourists?" My stomach flip-flopped.

"You'll see."

And with that, he opened the door. A loud creak echoed through the cave. Early morning sun flooded every nook and cranny. Xander flinched, pulling his hood lower. Marek walked through first, Xander followed, and I passed through last, making sure to close the door behind me.

We stood in the middle of an old cemetery. Early morning fog hovered, creating an eerie gloom. Behind us, sat an ancient church, built from a dark wood and looked like it could have been handcrafted by the Vikings themselves. Steep pitches and ornate steeples rose from various rooflines. The door we had walked through mirrored the other side, the same carvings on either side of the door.

"Follow me. We will go see her to get the rest of our supplies." Marek walked around the side of church, and I finally understood why we might bump into tourists. Beyond the beautiful ornate church and the cemetery, encircled by a three-foot stonewall, lay one of the most fantastic views I'd ever seen, in any world. The warm light of early morning sun bounced off the steep cliff faces that dove straight into the icy blue waters in the valley. Snow capped mountains rose beyond the cliffs, and the last remnants of glaciers slowly melted into the fjord below.

"Where are we?" I said in awe.

"We just walked through what is known as the North Portal. This is the Urnes Stave Church and that . . . " Marek nodded towards the fjord. " . . . is the Lustrafjorden."

"Gesundheit," I quipped, my eyes still fastened on the fjord.

"That's German, fool. Show some respect! " A raspy, thickly accented voice shot out from inside the church.

"I told you she was feisty. Come on. She beckons."

I let Marek and Xander go first, unwilling to leave the beauty sprawled out before me.

"We need her, too. *Jentunge*, get your ass in here," she yelled.

Reluctantly, I turned and stepped into the church, seeing bags packed and sitting on the wooden pews. The dark wooden architecture continued on the inside of the old church. Xander sat on one of the pews with his hood drawn low, and Marek was gesturing, talking to one of the smallest women I'd ever seen.

The woman in her mid to late fifties looked up at me, her blond hair braided around her head. "My name is Wilhelmina Von Stron. But you can call me Wanda."

I peered down at the tiny woman wearing a canvas dress and matching smock and a permanent scowl with plenty of frown lines to match.

"Hello, Wanda, I'm Eden, and this is . . . "

"I don't need introductions." She raised her hands and stopped me. "I can't have you three here when guests arrive. This *Dökkálfar* would blow my cover to pieces if anyone saw him. I'm not sure you thought this through, Girlie." Her arms were crossed and her face conveyed every bit of her irritation.

"Dökkálfar? Girlie?" I raised my eyebrows and looked at my brother, who could barely contain himself. "Do you know who we are?"

"Don't know, and don't care. Gio told me to give you supplies and safe passage for two, and I've fulfilled my end of the bargain. If you walk down to the village, there is a boat tied up for you to take to the Sogndal airport. It's a good thing he arranged for it because you can't be in public with *him*." She threw her thumb towards Xander. "A private plane is waiting to take you to Naples. Should be room for all three of you. Everything is under Gio's name." She picked up the bags and shoved them at us and handed me a set of keys that I assumed were for the boat.

"Wanda, how long have you been a Door Keeper?" I tried to be polite.

"No. No time for talking. You need to get this monster out of here."

"His name is Xander, *Wanda*. It would do you good to show respect to those from other worlds." I was already tired of this lady's rotten attitude.

Wanda stopped walking away and turned back towards us.

"Listen, Eden. You want my life story? I am the only girl of seven siblings, that's right, six brothers. I have been married twice, both fisherman, both died at sea. I may be small, but I am tough as iron and have been keeping this door for over thirty years. I do not like strangers and especially do not like them in my sacred spaces. So you will excuse me if I do not have patience when my door is used to transport fugitives!" She pointed annoyingly again at Xander.

"I am not a fugitive," Xander spoke up from under his hood.

"Forget it, Xander. Wanda is clearly upset at us being here." I rolled my eyes and turned my attention to the tiny, angry Door Keeper. "Thank you for the supplies, and we will be out of your way immediately."

"Next time I will not be so nice." She crossed her arms over her chest.

Marek's body shook with silent laughter, unable to contain his amusement any longer.

I yelled over my shoulder, "By the way Wanda, I'd bar the North Portal up, or the next visitors you have from Iskrem may not take your insults so well."

THE PLANE.

Eden

Once we reached a cruising altitude on the plane, I called my family. The kids were already airborne on their way to Naples with Charlie, and James had already arrived a few hours earlier on a direct flight from Brazil. It would be evening once everyone got to Italy, so we decided to meet at St. Francis, since the church would be cleared of people by then.

I hung up the phone, relieved that everyone was safe and on their way, grateful that we would soon be reunited and together as a family again. I glanced at Xander sitting across from me, stoically looking out the window, and clutching the armrests. With his white, thick, almost leathery skin, and dark coal eyes, it was hard not to see Aslak. I shivered at the flood of horrid memories that monster forever tattooed in my mind.

"You doing alright?" I tried to turn my mind and attention to the man in front of me, not the man who kidnapped me.

He tore his gaze from the window. The silver color around his eyes had grown larger and more pronounced. He nodded slowly. "This is unlike anything I have encountered before."

I smiled apologetically. "I'm sorry, this just was the easiest way to get there without you being spotted."

His eyes moved down to the tattoo on my shoulder. Thankfully, I finally had on some actual clothes rather than the pajama shirt I'd been stuck wearing for the last week.

"Do all humans look like you?"

"Well, kind of. My brother and I are Caelun, so we differ a little. But the bulk of it, yes. We look like everyone else." I took in the young Hiem before me, wondering about his past. "So, Xander. You seem to know a lot about me and my brother. It's only right you tell me a little about yourself."

"I am but a humble representative. There is nothing special about me." He looked back out the plane window.

"I think being special is a matter of perspective. Are you married?"

The first hint of what could be interpreted as a smile formed on his face. "No, but I will be in two years. It is customary for the," he hesitated and then continued, " . . . men to marry on their twenty-fifth birthday."

"Okay, that's something." I raised my eyebrows in interest, trying to encourage him to talk more. "Tell me about your family."

"I live with my siblings and my parents in Pruina, our largest city. Being the eldest son, I am to inherit my family's mantle."

"And what mantle might that be?"

Marek interrupted and sat down next to me. "Hopefully a family business, something like heaters, because Iskrem is freaking cold."

"Master Marek, legends say you are the most skilled fighter in all of Caelum. Is this transport safe enough for you to teach me?"

"Have I told you how much I like this kid?" Marek elbowed me. "Sure Xander, we can scrap on a plane. Here, stand up, and I'll show you some things."

The mother in me groaned, grown men fighting on a plane. Over the next hour, Marek taught his eager new pupil.

THE FEELS.

Gabby

"Rosie!" I cried, tears already stinging my eyes.

"Gabby!" Her arms wrapped around me, the hug engulfing me completely.

I pulled back, looking at the woman who had been my Italian Grandma for so long, never fully understanding why until now. Her deeply wrinkled, soft brown eyes puddled with tears. I hadn't had time to explain everything that had happened over the last week to her, but she knew enough to feel the weight of what was ahead. She understood I knew the truth, and that was enough to practically send us both over the edge.

"Mi dispiace amore mio." She cupped my face in her hands.

"Don't be sorry Rosie, it's going to be okay. Mom is okay."

"No, my darling. I'm sorry for lying to you all this time." Her face filled with regret.

"I understand why you had to. I've seen enough in the last forty-eight hours to know how complicated it is. Do I wish everyone had told me sooner? Maybe." I shrugged. "But this is all kinda unreal."

"Si, it most definitely is. But I'm so glad you are here and so happy we get to talk about it. Let's get you settled at the house before your mother arrives." Her eyes searched the floor around me. "Where is my sweet little JJ?"

"He's coming behind with Charlie. He wanted to watch some planes land."

After picking up our luggage and a brief fight with JJ, not wanting to leave the "hugest flying planes," we made our way to Rosalina's villa in Sorrento. My mind flashed back to the first time I'd come here with my mom for the wedding. Everything looked mostly the same—not much changed on the Amalfi coast. Which at the moment I was grateful for. So much else had changed over the last week. Familiar felt good; it felt safe. I couldn't wait to see Mom and Dad and hug them for real, in this world. Part of me was frustrated at how this all went down, but not even Mom, with her gifts, could have seen this coming. I couldn't be mad at them. At this point I just wanted to be with them.

After getting JJ settled in our room with his computer and tablet, Charlie, Rosalina, and I sat around her kitchen table, catching up over some cappuccino. We laughed at memories, and I asked questions. It was great to be able to hear about my Grandmother straight from a friend of hers, not just Mom's account of it. She told me some stories about Ava that weren't in Mom's journal, which made we wish I'd had the chance to meet her. I couldn't imagine how Mom felt. I thought about how much I'd have missed out on not knowing my own mom. It made my heart ache for her. As if sensing my sadness, Rosalina spoke up.

"You know Gabby, I feel like I'm finally seeing Ava's wishes realized." She put her hand on mine. "Eden would have existed and grown up even if she had stayed in Caelum. But you . . . you wouldn't have. Ava left and sacrificed herself for you as much as your mother. You were what gave her the strength to do what she needed to, knowing you would result from it. She knew you were worth it all."

My heart swelled with emotions—emotions I hadn't really allowed myself to feel up until this point. So much had happened I hadn't really allowed myself to sort through any of it. The weight, the grief, the joy, the terror, the fear, or even the relief. Charlie's arms wrapped around me, solid and strong. He had been with me from the moment this all started, and somehow he knew I needed to wait until now to release it all. So I did. I gave myself permission to feel it all.

The sadness over never being able to talk to my best friend about everything I had learned and already experienced. The realization that prom and high school felt completely ridiculous next to the weight of the truth. The future I thought lay before me was no longer really an option. The people closest to me had been lying to me for years.

Both Charlie and Rosalina sat in silence while I cried, grieved, laughed occasionally through the tears, and formed incoherent sentences. Finally Charlie spoke up.

"James and Eden love you so much. I know you already know this, but I just want you to hear it from me. They have done everything they could to give you the life you deserve—one full of joy and free of unnecessary complications. They wanted you to be able to make your own choices—knowing who you are outside of your Door Keeper lineage. I'm really proud of how they raised you. Trust me, this is coming from someone who struggles to separate myself from my job as a Door Keeper." His voice dropped.

My mind went to the argument about Prom I had just had with my parents before Mom was kidnapped. Dad had said I would have many choices to make on my own and that they were just trying to prepare me. I had no idea how right he was, and that whole conversation took on a different meaning now that I knew the truth.

"Thanks, Bruncle." I smiled up at the man who had been a large part of my family for almost half my life. "I'm sure this wasn't easy on you."

"Are you kidding?" Charlie's mood lightened. "Your mom marrying my brother was the best thing that could have ever happened. You and JJ are the best niece and nephew sibling combo anyone could ask for."

Without warning, a sob escaped me, realizing that I hadn't even understood or acknowledged that Charlie's Dad had been missing most of his life.

"Charlie, I'm so sorry about Grandpa. I can't believe that whole time you thought he was dead. How awful."

A tear formed in the corner of his eye. "I can't regret any of that, Gabbs. It allowed James and me to grow up and become who we did, together. I missed him, but getting you and your mom in our lives was worth it. Even my dad thinks so."

I leaned over and rubbed my snotty, tear stained face on his shoulder. He fake gagged, and Rosalina chuckled just as my dad burst through the door. Seeing my face, all red and blotchy, he looked worried.

"Gabbs?"

"Dad!" I ran over, and he wrapped me in my favorite bear hug.

JJ ran in the room and squeezed his little arms around us both. Dad picked him up. "Daddy! I missed you! It's so great to see you!"

"JJ, I missed you too buddy. How was the big plane?"

"I flew in the air!" My little brother beamed. Mimicking his hand as an airplane he added, "No crashing. No crash the plane."

I started laughing. "Yeah, I only had to reassure him about a hundred and fifty times."

Dad gave me a knowing look. "Well, your mom and Uncle Marek are going to be landing soon. Let me put my stuff up, and we can head over to St. Frances to wait on them."

THE COUNSEL.

Gabby

Gio was just as my mother described—big, burly, hairy, with ruddy cheeks and a voice that boomed like a trombone. Tonight however, he didn't look like the gardener I pictured when reading about him in Mom's book, *The Door Keeper*. He looked more like he did officiating Mom and Dad's wedding. Of course, even in slacks and a nice dress shirt, the top button was undone revealing his black, bushy chest hair. He welcomed us into the courtyard of the old Church. It was quiet, and the moonlight highlighted the stone archways and porticos, giving the whole garden a beautiful, magical vibe. Christmas lights hung from the giant oak tree in the center of the courtyard for nighttime events at the church. Although, tonight's event wasn't open to the public. Rosalina sat on a bench in the corner of the courtyard with JJ, so he could see Mom before bed.

When she entered through the door on the far side of the courtyard, I couldn't contain myself, running and flinging my arms around her neck.

"Hey, baby."

"Mom, I'm so glad you're here, like *actually* here."

She wore a simple white v-neck T-shirt and jeans, but I'd never seen her look more beautiful. Something about her felt different—she looked different. Taller maybe? Were her eyes brighter? Regal somehow. Perhaps after learning the truth I'm seeing her true self for the first time. We exchanged hugs and kisses and gratitude that everyone was together and safe. It wasn't until my mom had moved on toward the rest of the family that I noticed the hooded man standing against the wall. His face was covered in shadow, but as he slowly raised his head, a glint of silver flashed in his eyes. His dark, coal black eyes, against white skin. The scream escaped me before I knew why.

"*Mom*! He's here!" I yelled and ran towards her. "Run!"

Everyone froze and looked at each other.

"Gabby?" Marek reached out as I flew past him.

"No, honey, it's okay." Mom grabbed my shoulders and looked calm. "That's not Aslak. He's a friend."

"What?" I attempted to calm down, feeling confused and stupid. "Well, why is he here?" I stammered.

"He is representing the Hiems, his people. It's alright—come on. I'll introduce you."

Feeling mortified and embarrassed, I followed her reluctantly, mumbling apologies to everyone for freaking out. But they hadn't seen what I did—how terrible Aslak was. How was I supposed to know there were more of them? The man still stood with his back against the wall. His skin looked like a thick hide, white and stretched over his muscular chest under the cloak he wore. An involuntary shiver went up my spine. I dreaded looking into those dead black eyes—at someone who reminded me so much of my mother's kidnapper. He reached his hands up and lowered his hood revealing his crazy, long, dreaded white hair.

"Xander, this is my daughter, Gabrielle. We call her Gabby." Mom smiled.

"I'm sorry I freaked out on you." I made myself look into his face. His black eyes were highlighted in silver, making him look less terrifying than Aslak. He gave no hint of emotion and nodded slightly.

"You need not apologize, Gabrielle. I am full of remorse for what your mother went through. I am only here to help." Xander's eyes never left mine, making me feel uncomfortable.

"You can just call me Gabby."

"A woman of your lineage deserves the birth name you were given."

"Um, okay, whatever." I turned quickly to escape this dude's creepy vibes. I made eye contact with Uncle Marek, and he seemed like he was stifling a laugh.

Xander remained against the wall while the rest of us caught up for a bit. When my mother finally spoke up to start the oncoming discussion, Rosalina left with JJ to put him to bed. After watching my little brother leave, Xander walked over and joined the rest of us. I was surprised when the men encircled my mom, making it immediately obvious that she would be the one running the meeting. Most everyone sat in chairs, except for Xander, who remained standing. I plopped down on a bench next to Charlie, who eyed Xander with open curiosity.

"He is amazing," he whispered.

"Are you serious? He's downright creepy."

"Gabbs, he's a Hiem. They are rarely sighted, even in their own world. I've never even seen a picture of one and only heard pieces of stories."

"You *would* find him fascinating." I rolled my eyes.

My mom raised her voice to get our attention.

"Before we get started, I'd like to welcome Xander officially. He has offered his services to help us and will be representing the Hiems and the Stags of Iskrem." I noticed Gio and Xander subtly exchange nods. Mom continued, "Now, down to business. Charlie, you went to Terra Arborum to see Strix. Did he have a message or any insight for us?"

Charlie stood. "Yes, he had a request. He wanted you to come see him in Terra Arborum through Caelum's door. He knows Caelum will be our home base through this and wanted to make it easier. He said he had some questions for you specifically before he tells us what he thinks. In the meantime, he will be blockading the doors into other worlds the best he can, especially Palus and Iskrem."

"Okay." Mom sighed. "I was hoping for more, but I'm sure he has his reasons."

"Eden, would you mind telling us exactly what happened and what Aslak said?" Gio spoke up.

"Of course, I'm sorry. I should have started there."

Mom recounted the past week from her abduction, Taran's murder, and her *almost* execution. My dad interrupted her after she explained how she was taken.

"My biggest question is how did the Paluns open the door, and how did they knock out our surveillance while they were there?"

My mom answered him. "The Paluns got a copy of a key from Aslak, and as for their ability to block the cameras, I'm not sure." She continued on with her story. Every eye around the circle turned to me when she explained how she escaped Aslak.

"Impressive," Gio murmured.

"Just like her Mom." Marek smiled.

Xander nodded towards me solemnly.

Feeling flattered, yet slightly uncomfortable with the attention, I steered everyone back towards Mom.

"One thing I don't get . . . " I started. "You said Taran told you that Aslak only had access to three of the thirteen doors, but in your book, you wrote that there are only twelve worlds."

Everyone turned their attention to Gio. He cleared his throat and slowly stood.

"We all know about the twelve worlds. Granted, we know more about some than others. Eden, do you remember when I met you for the first time and told you about the world that most of us no longer have access to? The world with the metal we make the keys and doors from?"

Mom looked down and played with her wedding band.

"I do," she answered simply. My dad smiled at her as she said it.

"That is the thirteenth world, one that has been lost for over five hundred years. There was a war that began between worlds over harvesting it's metal. Certain worlds turned to using the metal for profit, and in order to protect the precious material, the Door Keepers of that world destroyed all evidence of the door locations and went underground. Their lineages have died off, and the secrets died with their ancestors. If Aslak found the portal to that world, it would change everything. His armies would be indestructible."

"What makes you think he wants to?" Dad asked.

"I had word sent to me shortly after Eden escaped that Aslak broke into Iskrem's Door Maker's shop and stole the remaining metal he had. It would seem that he might be after more. The metal from the Lost World is the strongest we've found in any world. It's why we use it for the doors and locks. It provides the strongest protection."

We all sat in silence for a moment, contemplating what Gio's words. Dad was the first to speak.

"What if we found it first? Could we use the metal to seal the doors permanently around Palus and Iskrem? If we could trap them, it would at least allow us to determine when and where the fight would happen."

"Do you think that is what it will come to?" Charlie asked.

"Yes. I'm sure it will." Eyebrows knitted together and lips pursed in frustration, Mom turned to my dad. "You said it yourself. Our crossing worlds should have instigated a war, and now it seems it has. This is our fault. If we'd never gone to Palus, Aslak would have never have known about the Paluns wanting access to Doors."

"Eden, we did the best we could with what we knew at the time. We had no idea this would happen." Dad approached Mom and put his arm around her.

She didn't seem appeased or convinced.

"Aslak would have found another way. This is not your fault," Xander said just loud enough for us to hear. He walked into the middle of the circle. "He feels denied. He has been looking for an ally for years. When we first learned of his intent of betrayal, we exiled him and appointed a new Door Keeper."

"Why exactly does he feel denied? Denied what?" Charlie questioned.

"Caelum." Xander looked at Mom.

Realization flooded her face. "Of course, the land Hiems are originally from—it's Caelum."

"Wait . . . so you are Caelun?" Dad looked at Xander with confusion.

"Originally, yes. But as you can see, we have changed ever so slightly." It was the first hint of a joke from the Hiem, and none of us laughed. Xander didn't skip a beat. "Three thousand years ago, your ancestors explored the different worlds, attempting to gain a better understanding of them. When the Caeluns found the Tree of Light in Iskrem, there were no inhabitants other than the Stags, and they were indifferent to the importance of the tree and the impact it could have on the other lands. So your people negotiated with them to allow some of their people to stay in Iskrem to protect the Tree of Light. The Caelun Door Keeper at the time charged her brother as Iskrem's Door Keeper. He took his family as well as his whole village to live and inhabit the world. What you see before you is the evolution of us living in Iskrem's conditions for three thousand years."

"No wonder Aslak was mad," Charlie mumbled under his breath. I elbowed him.

"The Hiems understand the importance of the Tree of Light. We would never consider it a burden to protect it." Xander turned his dark eyes on Charlie. "Aslak acts alone. He is selfish and does not represent our people. I do." Xander's voice rose just enough to unnerve me.

"Sorry man—um, Hiem, I mean," Charlie stumbled.

"I apologize if I was harsh. This has been very upsetting for our people."

"We understand, Xander. Thank you for filling us in. This makes a lot of sense." Mom said, although talking more to herself than the group. "He told me he was tied to the world he was condemned to, so it is safe to assume he wants to escape Iskrem. Caelum is too obvious, so the problem is, we have no idea what world he wants."

Dad followed her train of thought. "We know he's working with General Sapp because he had Paluns with him. That's bad news because Sapp wants all the worlds, not just to escape Palus. These two could be seriously dangerous together."

Mom continued, "So, until we know where he is going, we need to close the doors to every world," she said with a heavy realization, looking around at everyone.

"But 'Ass-lick' already has access to three doors." Charlie threw his hands in the air. Dad and Marek stifled laughs.

"It's pronounced 'Az-lak,'" Xander corrected.

"I know, but this guy is starting to piss me off, so I'm gonna call him 'Ass-lick' if that's okay with you." Charlie stood. "Do you guys understand how difficult it will be to try to close all the doors? There are twelve different worlds, all with doors leading to each other. Thats . . . " He counted his fingers.

"132 doors, not including the lost ones to the thirteenth world." Marek groaned.

"But we don't need to close them all," Gio interrupted. "Remember what James said, we just need to confine Aslak to Palus and Iskrem."

"Okay, so even with only ten worlds to protect and two doors to lock per world, that's still twenty doors. We're gonna need a lot of cooperation from Door Keepers." Marek crossed his arms.

"Leave that to me," Gio said. "I'll contact the ten Door Makers. They will inform the Door Keepers to be on high alert and ready for your arrival."

"Our arrival?" I looked around. "Why do we need to go? Why don't we just contact the Door Keepers to close the doors themselves?"

"Gabbs, we need to secure the door and check surrounding areas before we close the portal permanently. Plus, if there has been a breach, we can't expect a single Door Keeper to handle that alone," Dad explained.

"We need to divide and conquer. There are too many doors for us to stay together," Marek added.

Everyone looked around nervously. We had just been reunited. None of us liked the thought of splitting up again. Everyone looked to Mom.

She took a deep breath and spoke slowly, "Marek, you and Charlie take Gabby. Xander can come with me and James." Her eyes met mine, full of despair.

"Mom, I wanna be with you." My eyes stung. She walked over to me and knelt down, grabbing my hands. "I know sweetie, you have no idea how much I don't want to leave you again. But we are the only two who can communicate with the other group immediately if something bad happens. Our separation is our best shot at keeping everyone safe. Plus, you've already proven that you and Charlie make a good team. None of us would be here without the quick thinking from you both. Between your gifts and your Uncle's strength, you guys will be unstoppable." She kissed me on the forehead and stood, continuing the conversation to the whole group.

"But before we split up, I think it's time we get the whole story about what happened in Palus with Ava all those years ago.

Whatever happened resulted in Sapp's intent on crossing worlds. We need to go to Caelum and see my father and Aunt Mae."

Marek looked over at me and smiled. "It's time for us to go home."

THE ITALIAN FAREWELL.

Eden

Once my family had settled in at Rosalina's villa, I changed into my tennis shoes and grabbed the two bags sitting on the floor. Walking to the door of the guest bedroom, I glanced back at James, propped up reading in bed. He raised his chin and gave me a knowing look, saying the only thing I needed him to.

"You're doing the right thing."

"You know it wigs me out when you read my mind."

"I'd think you'd be used to it by now."

"Thank you."

"Prego." He grinned, saying *you're welcome* in Italian. Which of course, made me love him more, if that were possible.

Rosalina stood out on her veranda, the lights shining along the Gulf of Naples coastline. I'd always said she had the best view in all of Sorrento. I didn't want to disturb her, knowing how difficult this moment must be.

"Rosalina, are you ready for our walk?"

With her back to me, she wiped tears from her eyes. She turned slowly and faced me with a determined smile.

"Yes, I believe so."

As we passed through the kitchen, I stopped to refill my water bottle and Rosalina gingerly placed her fingertips on her kitchen table. She traced the plastic yellow sunflower painted on the cloth. Laughing gently, she looked back up at me.

"You know how many times I went to the store to buy a new tablecloth? Probably a dozen times. Some things just witness too many memories and are impossible to replace."

"Don't I know it. Ask me how many times I've thought about buying a new couch, but even the different stains have come to mean something to me."

"I'm sorry I'm feeling so nostalgic."

"Don't apologize for that, Rosalina. We've been through so much the past few years."

"Let's go. I'm ready." Her eyes hardened just ever so slightly.

We walked down a quiet Corso Italia, arm in arm. All of the shops had closed and only a few restaurants were still open. I let the stillness hang in the air, unwilling to fill the void with mindless chatter. I took my cues from Rosalina, when she wanted to talk we did. When she needed space, I obliged. Although, as we made our way to the coastline, she surprised me with an interesting question.

"Eden, do you have any regrets?"

I sighed. "Huh, that's a tough question." I thought about Eric, my late husband who died almost fifteen years ago, seemingly in another life. I thought about my mother, Ava, and not being able to have ever met her. I considered James and his father's absence in his life because of my father. JJ's face filled my mind and his difficult childhood, and of course I thought about Gabby and all she had been through the past week. Finally, I was ready to answer.

"You know, regret is a tricky thing. So many things we experience and go through mold us and make us who we are. Without those difficulties and trials, we wouldn't become who we are supposed to become. It's hard to regret things that teach us important lessons. But that being said, I regret the way Gabby found out the truth about us, about herself." I didn't attempt to hide my sadness.

"Why?" Rosalina asked simply.

"Because, I'm not sure her finding out without me served any purpose. Over the past seven years, I imagined taking her away on a trip, giving her the book, and being able to spend a couple days laughing, crying, and answering her millions of questions. Selfishly, I'm upset we didn't get to experience it together."

Rosalina reached over and grabbed my hand. We had just reached a cliff with stairs climbing down to the coast, to a rock beach nestled on the water's edge. She motioned to the outstretched sea sprawled before us.

"This is a big world, and it's only one of them. In *this* world, you have been the only constant in Gabby's life. Gabby will soon have to learn how to manage in all of the other worlds without you. It only seems fitting that she learned how to do that here, in this one, first."

Rosalina's words weighed heavy on me. The realization of the truth hit me unexpectedly. She was right, of course. Just as Ava couldn't be there to guide and direct me, I wouldn't always be there for Gabby. Eventually, she would have to learn to do this all without me. Maybe learning the truth the way she did would prepare her and serve a purpose after all.

Rosalina continued, "Do you think you would let her go on this adventure without you if she hadn't already experienced what she has?"

"No. I wouldn't let her out of my sight in another world if the past seventy-two hours hadn't happened." I surprised myself with this particular truth.

"Then it sounds like it should no longer be a regret."

"Yes, m'am." My heart filled with love and adoration for the wise Italian woman next to me.

We made our way down the steps that lead to Leonelli's beach, finally reaching the T-shaped pier that lead to the rock beach at the end. The bright moon's reflection glistened as we stood in silence.

"Do you have any regrets, Rosalina?"

"No," she answered quickly. "I've thought about it much over the past few weeks. I've never regretted meeting Ava or keeping her secret. It's been one of the greatest adventures of my life outside of having my own family. I miss my husband dearly, but nothing about him or my marriage do I regret. I'm sad my daughter and her family live so far away, but that is out of my control, and I got to spend two weeks with them last month, so that makes this easier."

"Do they know? About the cancer?" I asked gently.

"My daughter and her husband know, but my grandchildren do not. Knowing it would be one of our last visits, we decided not to tell them so we could just enjoy our time together." Wiping a tear, Rosalina changed the subject. "You know, my husband and I used to come here often when we were dating. He was obsessed with Mount Vesuvius, and this is one of the best views of it on the coast." She smiled, reminiscing.

"Were you ever tempted to tell him—about my mom?"

"A couple of times. We would drink wine at night and talk about our lives before each other, and I would almost bring it up. But I knew he would just think I was crazy." She laughed, then her eyes turned mischievous. "But I must confess, I did tell my daughter bedtime stories about Ava when she was little. She thought Ava was a fairy queen from a made up land I imagined. And this last visit, I told stories about you and Gabby to my grandchildren every night. Of course, I over exaggerated them enough to make them sound made up. But it felt good to talk about you to my family, even if they think you are just a bedtime story. My daughter overheard me one night and teased me that I needed new material."

My laughter floated over the waves. "I should send her a copy of *Lolli's World*. I bet your grandkids would love it."

"Oh, you should. Celia's address is in my apartment—for when you need it." Her smile faded slightly. "Should we move on?"

"If you're ready, I'm ready."

We ascended the stairs and took a left onto Via S Francesco, passing the church and opera house, as well as some of Rosalina's favorite restaurants. She told me stories of different friends met and meals eaten at each one. We passed Corso Italia, our turn that would have taken Rosalina home, and instead turned onto Via Fourimura, the road that led us to mine.

I followed the now familiar routine that led to Caelum, only slower and more intentional with my older traveling partner. As I held her hand, leading her carefully, her pulse quickened with each step closer.

Finally, we landed in the dark stone room, the lantern casting shadows over the high arched ceilings. The gray wooden door was perched on the wall in front of us, it's stone steps beckoning me home.

Rosalina let out a long held breath. "So this is it? This whole time, it's been here, right under my feet?"

"Yes."

"I can't imagine. On the other side of that door is Caelum? How can it be?"

"I know. It's difficult to understand."

We both stood in the still silence of the cold room, staring at the arched door that changed both of our lives.

"You are sure you want to do this?"

"Eden, I've never been more sure about anything." Her smile lines deepened as the shadows from the lantern danced across her face.

We inched towards the steps, and I pulled out my key.

"It'll be dark, without the suns, so it'll make traveling to the island easier for you. Father is waiting with horses to take you the rest of the way. I'll come with everyone else in the morning. I'd take your shoes off. You're about to get your feet wet."

"I'd say." She laughed at my pun. I handed her the packed bag with her personal items she had wanted to take with her, and as I reached to open the door that would take her to another world, she grabbed my arm.

"Thank you, Eden for giving me this. I know what it means, and I hope you know how much I appreciate it."

"Rosalina, I wouldn't even know any of this existed without you. I owe you the life I'm currently living. The least I can do is make the rest of yours the most spectacular yet." I hugged my friend and gently led her through the door into another world.

As the warm waters of Caelum spilled over her feet, her face was all the thanks I needed.

THE ROAD HOME.

Eden

At first I thought I'd made a mistake. JJ had been yelling, extremely frustrated for the better part of an hour.

"No more feet wet!"

"My eyes burning!"

"Go home, *now*!"

"How many more minutes, please?"

At this point James was carrying JJ on his back, and I felt terrible for him every time our child screamed in his ear. Gabby and I walked on either side of them attempting to calm him down and reassure him it would get better. Not quite sure if we were reassuring JJ or James. Both seemed equally grumpy at our group's current state. Thankfully, Cocoa, Marek's horse showed up not to long after we entered Caelum, apparently sensing our struggle. Even with Xander's skin fully covered with his cloak, he was suffering due to the heat, his body being so unaccustomed to it. Thankfully, he rode on the horse to exert the least amount of energy possible. The only bright spot in our trip home so far was Charlie's sudden bursts of observation and awestruck wonder. He would make us smile every couple of minutes with his hysterics.

"Holy bananas, is that seriously a banana tree?"

"Ah! That's a giant turquoise bird!"

"Oooooo, that tree is ginormous!"

"Gabbs, James, do you see all of this?!"

Within minutes of walking through Caelum's door, my skin turned its familiar shade of coffee. Every single fiber of my insides breathed a deep sigh of relief as the suns penetrated my skin. Apparently there were still a few cold spots from being in Iskrem so long. I even noticed Gabby's skin was less red and more brown since her first visit. We had JJ mostly covered, so he could acclimate more slowly than the rest of us, with the exception of Xander, who might need the better part of a decade.

Gradually, JJ complained less and less as we trekked along, allowing the walk to be much more peaceful. My dad, the reigning King of Caelum, waited for us on the outskirts of the island, on the tiny, barely existent beach.

"Hi Poppy!" JJ squealed and wiggled off of James' back.

"JJ, I've missed you little one!" My father bent down and scooped him up. It was a bit surreal to see my father and son embrace in our own world, not having to worry about covers or lies to mask the truth.

Gabby put her hand in mine and whispered, "So this is it, your real home. And that is Poppy how he really is."

We looked at the tall, large, bare chested man wearing a long, light gray skirt that matched his long grayish white mane flowing onto his shoulders. He laughed and tickled JJ, who begged him to stop, quite unconvincingly.

I raised my eyebrows at the sight.

"Yup. In all his Caelun glory." We both giggled. She dropped my hand and walked towards them. "Poppy." He shifted JJ and looked at his granddaughter.

"Oh, Gabby. I can't even tell you how happy it makes me to see you here." He sat JJ down and approached her, wrapping his large arms around her. "I can't wait to show you around the land. This will all be yours!" he bellowed.

"Okay, Dad, let's let her breath for a second before we bestow her the kingdom," I teased, and he just responded with laughter.

"Come here, daughter. I've missed you. It's been too long since you visited," he scolded. We embraced as James walked up with Charlie.

"King Samuel, you remember my brother Charlie from the wedding."

"You have grown into a fine young man." Father shook his hand. Charlie half curtseyed and half bowed making everyone chuckle.

"Poppy, tickle me again!" JJ pulled on Samuel's skirt.

He lifted him up as Xander slid off of Cocoa and made his way towards them. He slipped off his hood and knelt.

"King Samuel, it is an honor and privilege." He spoke in Caelum, much to our surprise.

"Yikes! Scary man!" JJ's face wore an over exaggerated expression. We had kept him away from Xander for this very reason. Although, in our defense, we weren't expecting Xander to reveal himself under the Caelun suns.

James jumped in before I could. "JJ, that's not very nice. We don't say things like that . . . " But Xander raised his hand to stop James before he could finish.

"It's okay," Xander said softly. He turned towards my son. "JJ, may I hold your hand?"

"That's okay. I'm fine!" he responded in a loud voice.

"Please?" I was surprised by Xander's persistence.

"Okay." JJ relented and held out his still slightly chubby hand. Xander took it gently, and JJ eyed his white leathery skin. A smile crept on JJ's face, and he looked into Xander's and beamed.

"You are a nice man. All done now." No one else seemed to think anything of it, but James and I looked at each other. What had just happened? Does Xander have a gift, and did he just use it on our son?

"Thank you for coming and helping our efforts. You are welcome here anytime, Xander of Iskrem." My father reached out towards the Hiem, and they grasped each other's forearms. "Now, let's get you out of the suns before you turn crispy and get you cleaned up for dinner tonight. The rest of the family will arrive soon to join us for the celebration! I've had Wynn prepare your baths. Eden and Gabby, Rosalina is waiting for you in the bath house."

"Oh man, I'm excited. Of everything I've heard about, this is one of the things I'm most pumped about trying." Gabby's eyes widened.

Within the hour, I'd been reunited with Wynn and my friend Shay, and relaxing deep into my favorite Caelun bath—peaches and honey. On either side of me, Rosalina and Gabby's immediate ooo'ing and ahh'ing had quieted to the occasional sigh of relaxation. I couldn't quite contain my elation at being sandwiched between two of the most important ladies in my life, experiencing one of Caelum's oldest traditions. Rosalina would ask random questions every now and then, but it always took a minute for her to form them coherently.

"Eden . . ." Pause followed by a sigh. "Why . . . I want . . . sorry, so relaxed."

I finally figured out she was asking why we couldn't take these types of baths at home, back on Earth. I listened as Shay explained to her the plant that the bath milk was harvested from only grew in Caelum.

After a while, the milk cooled and conversations turned to our travels here.

"Mom, what do you think Xander did to JJ?" Gabby asked seemingly from nowhere.

"Honey, I don't know. I wondered the same thing."

"I don't trust him. I just can't get past his face and creepy eyes."

I responded with my "Mom disapproval" face. "Gabbs, you know you can't judge people on their appearance. Come on, I raised you better than that."

"It'd be different if he didn't look so much like 'Ass-lick.'" She looked straight ahead, but her dimple deepened, signaling a smirk forming.

"Oh, come on! Not you too. Charlie's a bad influence on you."

"Seriously, do you really trust him? Is that why you are taking him with you and Dad?"

"I think I do. I'm not absolutely sure why, but I feel like there is more to his story than he's letting on, and I want to get to the bottom of it."

"Well, I don't. But, I'm not too worried. You'll be with Dad, and he would crush him if he betrayed you."

"He wouldn't be the only one," Rosalina piped up.

"Oh my gosh, I'd pay to see you beat someone up, Rosie." Gabby laughed easily.

I joined her. "Alright ladies, I think it's time we let the boys have a turn. Let's go get dressed." Suddenly I was anxious to see the new dressmaker.

That night at dinner, everyone glowed and looked radiant after a day in the Caelum suns and moisturizing baths. All of the non-Caeluns had been soaked in a cactus sap to help protect their skin and keep it from burning. The most noticeable transformation was Xander. His skin was no longer painfully white, but had a tint of a pinkish hue, and the leather creases of his skin seemed slightly smoother. The silver around his eyes had increased just enough to make his black eyes less menacing. His white dreads were piled up high on his head wrapped in a large bun.

I noticed Gabby give him a quick once over in his light purple with darker purple trimmed Caelum garb.

She looked amazing in a one-shouldered light blue silk dress that was striking against her already darkened skin. The hair around her face had been braided and pulled back, laying softly at the nape of her neck. Shay had painted around her eyes with gold to highlight them even more.

Earlier that evening, Mae, her husband, and their daughter had arrived to visit from the village of Ramus, my mother's childhood village. Ramus was the town where the treehouse was located and where we normally stayed when visiting. Magnus, Mae's husband was the prison guard who had watched over her for so many years. Within weeks of our family confrontation years ago, they were married and shortly there after had a baby girl, Lilia. She and JJ ran around the table chasing each other, giggling and causing quite a commotion.

Vera had come with them along with her new husband, and they sat quietly at the end of the table just taking in the scene. Vera and I hadn't spoken much since everything happened years ago, but I knew she still frequently suffered from the nightmares of my mother dying. I went and visited her a few years ago after her wedding and made peace with her on a personal level, although a slight tension remained within the family. However, it was nothing that could dampen the spirits of us being together after so long.

Every now and again, I'd catch Rosalina's eye and see the wonder and excitement that filled her. I was so grateful she could experience all of this.

After much laughter and story telling, and once the adult beverages started flowing, we knew it was time to get down to business. Rosalina offered to take the children down to the shallow sea and fruit orchard to play while we talked about our plan to protect the remaining ten worlds.

Mae spoke up from the far end of the table.

"Alright everyone, quiet down. Especially you, Xander. You've just been insufferable with your incessant talking." Everyone dissolved into laughter considering he hadn't said a word all night. My aunt Mae was always funnier after Serenbe tea. "Seriously though, as much as we want tonight to be a celebratory reunion, we know why we're really here. You need to know the truth about Ava and the Paluns and why General Sapp has aligned himself with Aslak. I could tell you the story, or you can just watch it unfold."

As she said the last couple of words, a haze filled my eyesight, darkness encroached, the stone beneath my feet transformed into mud. I shuddered, recognizing the Palus jungle immediately—the droopy leaves, vines intertwined, and the yellowish green sky barely visible through the dense brush surrounding me. Even knowing it was just a dream, I slipped my hand into James' next to me, who felt equally as tense. As if sensing my dread, Mae whispered in my subconscious that Gabby was safe. She did not allow her body to follow her mind. She also told me that as long as Gabby is not the one controlling her dreams, her physical body would not follow. Even though I knew we were all seeing the same thing, I felt utterly alone, and the feeling left me uncomfortable.

We were in a part of Palus I don't remember seeing before. The land was deeply sloped, and the rise and fall of hills surrounded me in every direction. A sound off to my left startled me, so I walked over towards it. Traversing Palus in the dream world was much easier, without sinking in the mud or being obstructed at every turn with vines and tree branches.

The noise came from a a large circular hobbit door, built into the hillside. As it creaked open, a beautiful woman crouched through to enter the dreary jungle. Her long, wavy, lavender hair covered her face, but I didn't need to see it to know who she was. As she straightened, regal in her mint green, two piece dress, Gabby inhaled sharply beside me. She had never seen Ava other than the one picture I had of her. I could never throw her a dream of her without giving away the truth.

Ava closed the door behind her and turned facing the jungle, standing still for a few moments, getting her bearings. Walking closer to her, I watched her eyes dilate into light purple disks. Her chest was wrapped tightly in light green cotton, and she reached down and pulled up her skirt, tying it with a belt fashioned from the same material. She wrapped her long thick hair up and tied it back into a ponytail. Then, with a look of determination in her eyes, she trudged through the mud. I followed about ten yards behind her watching her pass effortlessly through the trees and obstacles. I remembered how difficult it was for James and me to navigate.

Then I saw him. The giant, hairy, disgusting ground sloth sitting on his hindquarters, completely still so as not to draw attention to himself. His nose followed her as she went by. He was camouflaged enough with mud and leaves for her not to see him. Suddenly, Ava started singing softly under her breath, a sweet lullaby in Caelun. I wanted to yell at her, "*Stop it! He's right here!*" Tension radiated through everyone sitting around the table.

Mae flashed us forward to Ava sitting by the river, cleaning her hands and feet, with Sapp just down river, following her every movement.

Next she flashed us to a shed, very much like Squash's hideout by the Brazilian door, with Ava leaving a round, smooth circular device on the cot and heading back to her door. Horror rippled through us all as Sapp entered the shack and picked up the device and pushed the single button on top. Ava's recorded message played softly.

"I'm sorry to have missed you, my friend. I won't be able to visit for several more months, as I am pregnant with my firstborn. I just wanted to thank you in person for telling me about your world, your customs, and the Paluns. I have enjoyed our visits and cannot wait until we meet again. Being a Door Keeper with you has been one of my highest honors. May your world's peace continue."

As only powerless spectators, we watched as Sapp took the recorder and followed Ava back to the door. He hid behind a huge tree as she opened the door, and with a cursory glance back into the jungle, she disappeared back to Caelum.

Sapp approached the now locked door, and tried everything he could to open it. He tried picking the lock with his talons, smashing it with boulders, and even throwing his entire body up against it. Mae preceded to show us a thirty second montage of General Sapp coming back to the door, again and again, year after year, trying different methods to open it. Until he decided to turn his focus to finding his own world's Door Keeper.

Then, everything melted away, and we sat around the table, stunned into silence.

I glanced over at my father and saw the sadness in his eyes. It must be difficult for him to see her again, alive, if even in only a dream. I reached over Gabby and grabbed his hand. His eyes betrayed his smile as he cleared his throat.

"Okay, so it's clear that Ava caused General Sapp's obsession, and that obsession was obviously passed down to his son, Sapp Jr. But General Sapp's son is only half the problem. What do we do now that he has Aslak as an ally? Aslak was a Door Keeper, which means he knows about at least three of the other worlds, so it's reasonable to believe Sapp now knows about even more doors."

I shook off the mental image of Paluns in our world and had an idea. "Aslak has the knowledge, and Sapp Jr has the army. One without the other is much less threatening. Is there anyway we can turn them against each other?"

"Not a bad thought, but it is doubtful." Xander spoke for the first time. "It is safe to assume, with everything we have seen, that Aslak and Sapp have reached a mutual agreement. I know my uncle, and he will not merely want to escape Iskrem, but conquer another world, or at least part of one. But he is just one Hiem, and needs Sapp and his army. Sapp most likely wants any or everything else and requires Aslak's knowledge to succeed. The problem is that they are the perfect allies, both get what they want."

"It sounds like the best way to stop both of them is to find and stop Aslak." James looked grim. "Perhaps the Paluns would retreat if they lost their brains behind the operation."

"That only works if he hasn't already given them everything they need," Marek pointed out.

Feeling frustrated and overwhelmed with information, I rose out of my chair. "I think we need to secure Caelum first and foremost. If Caelum falls, every other world will fall faster, considering it's the easiest to travel from door to door." I looked down at Gabby, whose eyebrows seemed knitted together in worry. "Gabbs, you haven't said much tonight. What do you think?"

She met my eyes with trepidation. "I think we need to follow the plan we made in Italy. We need to split up and reinforce all of the doors we can leading to Palus and Iskrem. Dad was right. Once we trap them in those worlds, we can then figure out what to do next."

"I agree with Gabrielle. We should stick to our original plan." Xander nodded at Gabby. She returned a one sided smile.

Marek pushed away from the table. "It'll take me a day or two to get the supplies we will need for our journeys and Gio enough time to coordinate with the Door Keepers. Let's get some good sleep and take some time to be together tomorrow before we separate again."

"That sounds perfect. I've missed my family." Samuel beamed looking around the table.

I sat back down and wrapped my arm around Gabby, my heart filling with anticipation, "I know just the place I wanna go."

THE DAY OFF.

Eden

  I paid closer attention to my dreams that night, knowing being in Caelum always brought out my gift more than in any other world.

  JJ and I walked hand in hand along the shallow seas. He couldn't stop talking about how much he loved the beach. He let go of my hand and ran off ahead of me, and I called out to him to slow down and let me catch up. Suddenly, my toes stubbed up against something hard. I looked down to see a huge submarine-looking hatch door in the sand floor below me. It was a brass oval about six feet at it's longest. I knelt down to get a closer look, but something pulled my attention behind me.

  There she was, standing on the cliff, tears streaming down her face. Why was she so sad? I glanced back and couldn't see JJ anywhere, but remembered this was a dream, relieved he was actually sleeping in his bed. I willed myself next to my daughter, and within a millisecond, stood next to her. She read the piece of paper in her grasp, a hand painted flower stationary. The letter looked to be several pages long. The handwriting was blurry, but vaguely familiar. Her eyes and cheeks were blotchy from crying. She sniffled and looked out onto the horizon and after a few seconds, closed her eyes.

  She drew the letter to her chest.

  "Why?" she asked simply.

I jolted awake, sitting up, sweating, I welcomed the wind that blew through the open window off the sea below. What was that letter? What was she reading? Every time I tried to get back to that part of the dream, it grew fuzzier and fuzzier. I wasn't supposed to see it, and something was keeping me from it. Whatever it was, I knew it was the future, and I absolutely hated that something was bringing Gabby so much pain.

I looked over at James, sleeping peacefully in the bed that I stayed in the very first time I came here. Above us hung the Elisium flower painting my mother created, complete with the rip from Marek's and my fight. We decided to mend it and leave it, to remind us that some things were worth salvaging.

I closed my eyes and attempted to check on Gabby's dreams, but she wasn't in one. Whether it was dreamless sleep or she was still awake, I didn't know. Realizing I wouldn't receive any answers tonight, I laid back down, closed my eyes, and drifted off into another dream-filled sleep.

The next morning, between us, we had over a dozen horses that hauled our entire family, plus one Hiem, to our special place. We spent the day swimming and diving off cliffs. Even JJ got in on the action, jumping off one of the smaller ridges. We laid out under the suns, the guys catching fish for us to cook for dinner. We lounged around telling stories and took a hike to catch the view from one of the smaller mountains.

Every moment that passed being in Caelum and being outside, JJ steadily relaxed and self regulated. We didn't have to correct his sentences quite as much, or prompt him to answer people when they spoke to him. At one point, he even asked a proper question without prompting. JJ never asked questions. He only told us what he wanted in statement form. Normally, he would simply say, "I want dinner." But instead he asked, "When is dinner?" James and I almost fell over in excitement. Of course, we wanted to oblige him immediately, positive reinforcement and all. So, Rosalina and my father set up a large picnic area on the flat side of the lake, while the kids ran around, climbing trees and playing hide and seek. Marek built a fire with Charlie and James to cook the fish, while Mae, Vera, and their husbands collected firewood. Xander had wandered off to find a secluded spot in the shade, which just left Gabby and me standing on a small, rocky beach overlooking the mountain's reflection off the lake.

"Mom, this is beautiful."

"Yes it is," I sighed, fully content.

"It's just like you described in your journals—wait, are those the boulders from your and Ava's dream?" She pointed to two, large, pastel rocks protruding from the water.

"Yup, that's them." I looked at her, already knowing what she was gonna say next.

"Shall we?" Her eyes beamed.

"I thought you'd never ask."

We walked down to the water's edge, picking out some smaller, flat rocks. We made our way carefully to the two large boulders, colors equally faded. After scrambling up on them, we relaxed there for a moment, allowing ourselves to feel the weight of the moment. Even she, in her youth, understood that this was a fulfillment of sorts. That this moment represented what Ava gave up so that we could experience it.

Finally, I broke the silence and commenced with the trash talking that instigated quite a competition. We were teasing each other and neck and neck with our amount of skips, when Mae called out my name.

"Eden!"

I turned around and saw my two Aunts, arm in arm, watching us with tears in their eyes.

This was it, the very moment in the dream. I realized my hair was still tinted lavender to match my dress from the night before. Behind Gabby, the dark orange sky and two suns setting behind the sharp mountain, shone their final rays over the smooth, glassy water. The wind had picked up and as Gabby stared back at me with wild and bright eyes, a couple strands of her hair flitting across her face. Her hand was poised behind her back holding the last stone, anxious to prove her skills.

I looked back at my aunts, thankful that we could experience one more beautiful moment of Ava's hopes and dreams fulfilled.

THE CONFESSION.

Gabby

My great aunts looked at us teary-eyed. I remembered from Mom's journal that they knew about the dream Ava had, the one we were currently living out. I couldn't imagine how painful it must have been for my grandmother, to see something and know she wouldn't be able to see it come to fruition. What a heartbreaking, yet beautiful gift.

A gift I now knew I did not have.

My mom had it, she could pull memories from past and see events in the future, but every time I've tried to conjure this particular dream or the one where I became Queen of Caelum, my subconscious did not follow. The only stream I seemed to be able to pull from was the present. I'd been testing myself, to see how far my gifts stretched. I could command myself to go practically anywhere, sleep whenever I needed to, and connect with anyone living, wherever they may be. But anytime I tried to pull one of my Mom's stories or attempted to see the future, it was just blank. Nothingness.

I glanced around at my family laughing, eating, and spending time together—my family in the environment we were created for. A combination of joy and sorrow warred within me. I was elated that we were all together and I finally knew the truth, but also sad because up until this point, everyone had just been waiting on me to grow up. Until now, my life hadn't really been real. It had been a temporary fake life of school, friends, parties, and dates with boys who were boring. I didn't want to be mad with my mom. I understood she had done what she thought was best, and I trusted her, but I couldn't help feeling frustrated at this whole situation. There was no easing into this insanity. I was simply thrown in without my consent. But as I looked at my mom and remembered her journal, I guess she was too. She went from zero to sixty in a matter of weeks.

But at least it was her choice.

I knew I was being childish. Of course everything I'd done up until this point was my choice. Every dream was of my own free will. It was unfair for me to pretend otherwise. I was the one that went after Mom in Iskrem. If I asked her not to make me go on this mission, she wouldn't. If I told her the truth, she would understand. If I explained how scared and completely unprepared I felt, she wouldn't be upset or angry. But I didn't want to tell her the truth. I needed her to be proud of me. I needed to prove my family right and to be as brave as her and my grandmother.

I turned, ready to skip my last rock when I caught him looking at us. Xander was perched on the ledge, shaded under a giant pine tree. He leaned on one knee, eyeing us carefully. He had been there, watching us the whole time.

Feeling awkward making eye contact with him, I raised my eyebrows and my hand, waving slightly. Maybe if I acknowledged he was staring, he'd back off and leave us alone. Instead, Xander bowed his head, as he had every other time we'd greeted. That dude was so weird.

Shaking my head, I turned back to my mom, who observed our little interaction with her own eyebrows raised.

"What was that?"

"You tell me. You brought him here." I shrugged.

"You still don't trust him?" she asked.

"He barely talks, treats us like royalty, and he's apparently fond of stalking." I flared my nostrils and made my eyes wide. "No. Not really."

Her hair brushed her tattooed shoulder as she chuckled. "He barely talks because he chooses his words wisely, unlike the people in *this* family. And I hate to tell you this, but he treats you like royalty because you *are* royalty. The stalking thing, I will admit is a little weird."

I changed the subject.

"So, I've been trying to throw myself dreams from your journals, and it's not working. Why can't I see them?"

"What do you mean?" She sat down on the huge rock underneath us and I followed suit.

"I can't seem to conjure the same type of dreams you can. You can see things that happened before and things in the future. I don't think I can."

"Huh. I wonder if it has something to do with your physical body being tied to your mind." She looked past me thoughtfully. "Mae told me that when you aren't the dream thrower, your body doesn't go with you. It's much safer for me or her to throw you dreams than for you to dream yourself."

"Really? So it would be safe if you threw me into the past or future?"

"I guess so." She didn't say anything more, and I guessed she realized what was coming.

"Can I see what you saw, when I became Queen?"

She scrunched her eyes and cocked her head to the side. "What is it exactly you want to see?"

"I don't know. Wouldn't you want to see your future?"

"Sweetie, I do. Sometimes I don't like it." A twinge of pain crossed her face. Then she seemed to snap out of it and smiled. "Maybe once the fate of the worlds have been settled, I'll throw you a little peek. I just don't want you to feel unnecessary pressure to fill some pre-determined destiny. This is still your choice."

"Yeah, okay." While slightly disappointed, I was grateful she acknowledged my decision. I took comfort in her not pushing me into anything. I glanced over towards Xander's hideout, but he wasn't there anymore.

"But how about I show you some of my favorite moments of your grandmother?" Mom's gray eyes sparkled.

"Yeah, I'd like that." I returned her smile.

We laid back on the rocks, looking up at the increasingly dark pink and orange sky. I closed my eyes and relaxed as Mom threw me into dream after dream of Ava's life in Caelum. She showed me Ava teaching Marek how to sword fight, Ava painting in the garden, even her leaving Caelum for Earth when she was pregnant with my mom.

It was simply incredible. Tears formed and hovered in the corners of my eyes.

"Thank's Mom. I wish I had that gift."

"Honey, you have one of the most amazing abilities I've ever seen. No one, not even Gio, has heard of someone being able to be physically present in his or her dreams. I think that is enough of a responsibility in of itself." Then her face became serious. "If you need me, at any point in what is to come . . . " She trailed off.

"Mom." I reached over and grabbed her hand.

"I'm serious. We have no idea what we are walking into. What we can do, Gabby is be there for each other. Please never hesitate to reach out to me. And if something happens, and you can't reach me, go to Aunt Mae, and she'll help you."

"Why are you saying this? Have you seen something?" Worry took hold of my mind.

"No, you know me. I just like to be prepared for all scenarios," she reassured me and put her other hand on mine.

"Oh I remember. Prepare for the worst, but always hope for the best." I quoted her from the zillion times I'd heard it growing up. You'd never meet someone who was more optimistic, yet prepared for trouble, than my mom.

My gut told me this was our goodbye before the trip. Things would be chaotic when we got back to my grandfather's house, and I sensed Mom knew that too. She took her hand and put it on my cheek.

"I love you, Gabbs and am so incredibly proud of you. You have handled all of this with a crazy amount of grace."

Her words forced the tears that still sat in the corners of my eyes to fall. Truth spilled from my mouth before I could stop it.

"Mom, I'm so scared. What if I can't do what I think? What if something bad happens, and I can't do anything to stop it?" I cried.

"Oh honey, if I've made you think that any of this rests on you, I've done a terrible job as your mother and your Door Keeper for that matter." She hugged me. "This is not your battle to fight or your war to win. You are not queen of this realm yet, and you should not be feeling that burden. This is not your weight to carry—it's ours. Anything that happens from here on out, it rests on us. And we promise not to hand anything over to you until we have righted our mistakes. I promise you, Gabby. I will not allow Samuel to hand you the crown or key to this kingdom until there is peace across all of the worlds."

"Okay," I sniffed. "But you know that's easier said than done, right?"

"Yes, and I'm sorry." She pulled back and looked at me. "It's okay to be scared, as long as you don't sit in it very long. Feel it, and then let it go. If it starts to drive you or your decisions, then you are in dangerous territory. It sounds silly, but I like to talk to it like it's a person. If I can personify it, then it's outside of me, and I can control it easier. You know, tell it what it can do and where it can go." She winked at me.

Laughter erupted in between my tears, causing hiccups. I imagined my Mom cussing fear out loud, and it just struck me as the funniest thing ever. I would definitely be trying that.

Her stormy eyes pierced into mine. "And just remember, whenever you are scared or afraid, or just need some encouragement, I'm only a dream away."

THE UNKNOWN GOOD-BYE.

Gabby

As the guys gathered our weapons and horses for our journey, Mom met with Aunt Mae, talking about Mae staying in Caelum, and attempting to find information about the lost door to the thirteenth world. I was in the bathhouse, Shay and Wynn loading me up with healing herbs and oils to use if anyone got injured. They gave me a crash course on some medicinal herbs and different techniques to fix things in a pinch, all sorts of creams and concoctions. I loved learning about the homeopathic methods, and I couldn't wait to incorporate some of these herbs back home and show Emmie some of these beauty tricks. My stomach dropped a bit when I realized I wasn't sure how long that would be. As far as my best friend was concerned, I was traveling in Europe with my family, while she was stuck at home, grounded. My life with her and my friends seemed a million miles away. Technically, I guess it was.

The large bag the ladies gave was surprisingly light considering it's size. I was anxious to get back to the room, to divide little bags and jars of herb and salves up between the two teams. But when I returned, Rosalina was still curled up under the covers, her face a little pale.

"Rosie, you're still in bed? Are you feeling okay?"

She lifted her head slightly. "I'm okay, Amore. I think all of this excitement has just made me tired." She sat up more, exposing her pretty, rose, silk nightgown. The beautiful, deep color made her skin look even whiter.

"Do you want me to go get Mom?"

"No, I'm fine. We talked last night and already said our goodbyes." Her half smile faltered.

"I feel bad that we're leaving you behind. I know you came so we could be together." I joined her on the bed. "Are you going back home after we leave?"

"No, your mom and grandfather are generous enough to let me stay a bit longer, as sort of a vacation."

"Well, I couldn't imagine a better place to va-cay." I perked up, looking out the window that overlooked rows of peach trees growing out from the bright turquoise water.

"Indeed." She took my hand into her soft, weathered one. "You have grown into one of the most beautiful, talented, and sweetest young women I have ever met." Her warm brown eyes looked milkier than I remembered. "I love you Gabby. I love you like you were my own grandchild."

"I love you too, Rosie." My eyebrows scrunched together. "But we will be back in a few weeks to check in and de-brief. We don't have to say goodbye."

"I know, but I never want to waste a moment to tell you how proud of you I am."

I wondered what I ever did to deserve such strong, wonderful women in my life that supported me and loved me. So many of the kids at school didn't have people in their lives that believed in them or fought for them, and I had an army behind me. It fueled my courage, made me feel strong, and ready to take on all the worlds. I hugged Rosie gently, her body feeling frail under my touch. After kissing her forehead, I got up, and picked up my bags.

In the doorway, I stopped and with my free hand, blew her a kiss. Smiling, she blew one back.

"Sogno bene il mio amore," she whispered. *Dream well my love.*

"Fino a quando ci incontreremo di nuovo, amica," I answered. *Until we meet again, friend.*

THE JOURNEY BEGINS.

Gabby

The six of us divided up supplies and talked strategy when my Grandfather, Aunt Mae, and JJ approached. JJ hollered and tore over to our Mom, embracing her waist. She bent down and none of us missed the tears forming in her eyes.

"Don't be sad, Momma. It's okay." JJ never liked seeing anyone unhappy.

"I know, baby. I'm just going to miss you." She wrapped her arms around him and squeezed him tight.

"I miss you too." He placed his hands on her cheeks. "Don't be sad. I'm happy! I ride horses and fight swords with Poppy."

"Yes, I know you will have a lot of fun with the family while we're gone." Then Mom's face went blank for a couple seconds, and she turned to my Dad eyes wide with wonder.

My brother continued, "What day home, Momma?"

She faced JJ again and slightly shook her head. "Um, two weeks, sweetie."

"Fourteen days? Okay, I love you." He hugged her and then ran to Dad. "See you in fourteen days, Daddy. I love you!"

Dad picked him up and practically engulfed him.

"Dad," JJ laughed. "That's too hard. You hurting me!"

"Sorry, buddy. I'll miss you. Have fun, okay?"

"Yes sir!" he yelled. "You have fun too!"

Man, I loved my brother. I teared up, knowing I was next. He didn't make it easy on me with his sweet smile and chubby cheeks. I knelt down anticipating the oncoming attack hug. But he surprised me, approaching and hugging me slowly.

He whispered in my ear, like he always wanted me to do to him. "Don't be scared Gabby. You are strong. You are brave, like Momma." Suddenly, my mind raced, flying through Caelum in hyper-speed, it landed with a vision of myself, wielding Ava's hook sword against one of the largest sloths I've ever seen. The giant swung his large blade at me, and I blocked it with the handle of my weapon, ducking and slicing him up the middle. He fell back, and I stood over his body, wearing goldish bronze chain mail, face covered in gold tattoos, and hair flying wildly behind me. I looked like a freaking warrior.

Snapping back in the present, I stared down at my baby brother. His giant chocolate eyes bore into mine. He giggled and ran over to Charlie to continue his good-byes. I glanced over at Mom, dumbfounded. She smiled knowingly, like she understood what had happened. She must have seen something herself.

"Did JJ just show you something?" I whispered as I approached her.

"Somehow he knew how sad I was to leave him, so he showed me the fun things he was going to do with Sam, Mae, and Vera." She still looked shocked. "What did he show you?"

"He told me not to be scared, that I was brave, like you. Then he showed me fighting and killing a sloth. It was crazy."

Dad came up behind us. "Interesting. It seems like he has both of our gifts, melded into one. My ability to know what you are thinking and feeling, and yours to be able to show you in your subconscious what you need to feel better."

"But he's only seven!" Mom looked as freaked out as I felt.

"We always knew he was special . . . " My Dad smiled. "Looks like being here has helped unlock something after all."

"I'd say. Now, let's just hope it unlocks something in me."

"I do not doubt that it will," Xander said from behind us, making me jump.

"Dude, don't do that!" I yelped.

"My apologizes, Gabrielle."

"It's Gabby . . . " I practically growled.

"Alright, break it up you two," Marek chimed in. "It's time we get going, so we can get where we need to before nightfall."

Charlie walked up in a daze.

"Um, why did my nephew just enter my mind and show me almost getting trampled to death by a giant elephant being ridden by a crazy looking leaf wearing woman?"

We all looked at each other before bursting out laughing.

"Sounds like a personal problem to me." My dad smacked Charlie on the back.

Mom turned to me with a more serious expression and pulled out her weapon from her back. It was my grandmother's hook sword, the one JJ had just shown me defeating the sloth with.

"This is traditionally the weapon of Caelum's Queen. While it's not technically yours yet, I think it's only right you get accustomed to using it. I've enjoyed taking care of it for you all these years." She handed me the intense sword, that was much lighter than it looked. She continued, "Have Marek teach you how to use it. He's a good teacher."

My mind flashed back to the vision JJ had shown me. I found some confidence hidden somewhere deep, knowing I would learn how to fight with this massive death trap in my hands.

"Thanks, Mom." I hugged her one last time before we split up.

"Looks like I'm gonna have my hands full." Marek hugged Mom, and I over heard him telling her to be careful.

Dad made me blush while giving my two uncles the traditional Dad speech, *you take care of my daughter, or I'll hurt you both*. The weight of Xander's gaze rested on me as everyone talked and said goodbye.

He didn't look quite as jarring as he did the first time we met, now that his skin had a shade or two of color, and I'd gotten used to his crinkly leather covered muscles exposed all the time, even beginning to find them rather intriguing. His long white dreads were piled on the top of his head, and his eyes were now almost half iris half pupil, which softened his appearance a great deal. Xander would win the most exotic and mysterious award if one existed, I'd give him that. He knelt down in front of me, grabbing my hand. Feeling super awkward, everyone stopped talking as he mumbled something in his native tongue, then rose looking me in the eyes.

"Peace and health to you, Gabrielle. Until we meet again." His face contorted into what I assumed was the closest thing he's ever done to smiling.

"Uh, sure. Thanks, Xander." Feeling so weird about the whole interaction, I slightly curtsied and felt like a complete moron. I quickly turned and walked towards my horse, trying to turn the focus away from me. Glancing over my shoulder, despite myself, I watched him mount his oversized gray mare.

"Looks like I'm not the only one who finds him fascinating now," Charlie teased.

"Whatever. I still think he's nuts."

Let Charlie think what he wanted.

"Deny all you want little Neester, but your blushing tells a different story."

"Oh, you're just jealous, Charlie, because you've never been pursued by a Hiem warrior before," Marek teased, climbing his horse next to us.

"Ha, ha, ha guys, get it out of your system now. Because this is the last I'm gonna hear of it . . . " I rolled my eyes, completely annoyed.

"Or what—you're gonna—*oof*!" My foot kicking him off his horse interrupted his attempt at mockery.

"Gonna beat your ass? Yes, Charlie, that is exactly what will happen if you don't shut up." I glared down at my uncle covered in sand and salt water.

He shook the sand out of his short cropped hair and stared up at me with a wicked looking grin. "Yaas, Queen."

He was going to pay for that.

THE WISE OLD OWL.

Eden

I sighed, as my daughter chased Charlie around the orchard on horseback. He tripped and fell every twenty yards or so, taking refuge behind the twisted trunk of a peach tree. The visual gave me a momentary flashback to when Charlie used to chase Gabby around the house as a little girl, threatening to tickle her until she cried. It was becoming difficult for me to accept she wasn't that sweet ten year old anymore.

Maybe this wasn't such a good idea. I looked over to James, who just shook his head. "Poor Marek," he mumbled.

"You think they can handle this? Because I'm having second thoughts . . . " I said only half joking.

"They're about to grow up faster than we can imagine. Let them have their fun." James grinned at me. Something about his smile calmed my nerves. The three of us watched from horseback as they finally settled and rode off toward the next island a few hundred miles away. I purposefully didn't say goodbye to Gabby, knowing we would be checking in with each other later tonight. Saying goodbye to her wasn't an option. I wouldn't let it be.

Glancing at Xander, I wondered what was going on in his mind. I tried to use my gifts with respect for other's privacy, but was rethinking it, desperately wanting to know what his story was. I was just going to have to be patient. We needed to get to Terra Arborum's door before nightfall, knowing we would need to be there for a couple of days before we could move on to the next world. Plus, Strix was expecting us tonight.

We rode hard all day, only stopping every couple of hours to allow our horses to rest and eat. I had yet to travel Caelum to Terra Arborum's door because we had such easy access to the Land of Trees from our Earth home. The journey was long, but I appreciated the opportunity to see other parts of Caelum I hadn't explored yet.

The islands were large and flatter than the mountainous island back where my family lived, with more vegetable farms and less fruit orchards. We passed green, grassy islands sprawling on for miles and miles, each covered with thousands of grazing sheep. It was an incredible sight, watching them move in sync with each other, and then scatter in every direction as we rode past.

We reached the island housing the Terra Arborum door just as the first sun touched the horizon. It was densely forested, with trees every color of the rainbow. The immense beauty sparked the first words from Xander since we left the others.

"I have never seen so much color." He gazed up at the foliage ranging from deep fuchsias to bright pinks, golden yellows to glowing greens, even with the occasional blue and silver. Walking through the forest, a steady rain of leaves fell around us, like a permanent autumn, the floor brightly colored below our feet. We stopped under one of the largest trees I'd ever seen, in any world. Following Marek's instructions, we walked around it until we found the strategically hidden pegs that would allow us to climb the gargantuan trunk. All three of us hiked up our Caelun skirts and tied them to allow for easier climbing. I went first, slowly and steadily until reaching a large branch, big enough to stand on comfortably in front of the door. I waited for James and Xander to join me before pulling out the key.

The door was practically invisible to the naked eye. Only the change in the bark's grain indicated anything out of the ordinary. The trunk's bark wrapped around the tree swirling towards the left, but the door's bark seemed to be running straight up and down. I reached out, touching the wood, wondering how this was even created. The only man-made looking thing on this tree was the lock and knob in the goldish bronze metal from the lost thirteenth world.

"Incredible," James exhaled.

Anxious to see my old friend Strix, who I hadn't seen in months, as well as get some answers, I unlocked the door stepping into the now familiar world of Terra Arborum.

Prepared for the dusty flatland and dense air, I was pleasantly surprised to walk directly into the trees above the moisture/mist cover. The clean, fresh scent of nature and flowers filled my nose making me feel nostalgic. The temperature was at least thirty degrees cooler, and Xander visibly relaxed. As I closed and locked the door behind us, the familiar whooshing sound of Strix's wings approached. I turned and grinned as my friend landed in front of us and then completely engulfed James and I in his feathery embrace. He stepped one talon back and bowed.

"Xander of the Hiems, it is an honor to finally meet you. I have heard wonderful things about your people and the important work they do." His deep yellow eyes bore into our guest's.

"Likewise, Strix, Peace Keeper of Terra Arborum. I hope our visit will not be an inconvenience to you." He returned the bow.

"Never!" Strix's deep voice bellowed. "Come, let's pour some Serenbe tea and get you settled for the evening. We have much to discuss."

We followed the giant, brown, horn-rimmed owl through a short maze of flowering bushes that looked like exotic azaleas. We came upon a canopy made out of honeysuckle vines, complete with a table and chairs, and three cots arranged comfortably. Lolli and Vi waited for us with Serenbe tea brewing.

"Lolli!" I exclaimed as she flittered up to me with her bubble wings and landed at my feet. "I've missed you, friend."

"Oh, Eden, Strix told us the extraordinary tales of your adventures. Please, sit, and I'll pour you some tea." Her voice rang like bells.

"Thank you, that would be wonderful."

"How is my sweet JJ?" she asked, handing me a cup of tea with her multicolored stained hand. "I miss his hugs."

"He misses you too, Lolli. He talks about you all the time." James answered as he sat next to Vi, Lolli's mother, her skin covered in different shades of purple.

"Oh, that fills me with such glee! Would your friend like some tea?" She nodded toward Xander.

"I would, thank you." Xander nodded in return. The two of them couldn't have looked more hysterical interacting—Xander with his rough, intimidating appearance and Lolli looking like a walking piece of fragile candy with her transparent, colorful bubble wings.

As James and I caught up with the butterflairies, Xander remained mostly silent, watching the oversized fireflies light the space over head. Finally Strix cut into our conversation and brought Xander into it.

"I'm grateful that you decided to come along with Eden and James, Xander. There is much at stake for the Tree of Light, much more than I'm afraid you know. Eden, can you tell me specifically what Aslak said to you during your capture?"

I settled in, ready to discuss the matter at hand.

"He called me the bridge builder." I looked down at the tattoo of my mother's words on my arm. "And said that he wanted to burn them to the ground."

Strix's feathers ruffled. "That's what I was afraid of." He turned and spoke to Xander only. "I know why you followed Eden here. You know who she is."

"Yes. She carries the mark our legends refer to."

"Um, what? What legends? What mark?" My eyes darted between Strix and Xander. I thought back to what Taran had said to Aslak before he had been killed. He had mentioned a legend. Xander's dark eyes turned to me and looked at my shoulder.

"You will re-unite Iskrem and Caelum, to become one people again. You carry the mark of the Tree of Light."

I followed his gaze down to the tattoo on my arm beneath my shoulder.

"Eden, the branch of your tattoo, with the light purple flowers, those are the flowers of the Tree of light. Although, it hasn't actually bloomed in hundreds of years," Strix explained.

"What?" James and I asked in unison.

Xander leaned forward. "A legend has been told for generations of the one that would bring the blooms back to the Tree of Light. The tree only blooms when the door between Caelum and Iskrem remains open. The power of the two suns gives the tree what it needs to continue to thrive. But the door has been closed between the two worlds for centuries, since our Civil War. No one alive has ever seen its flowers.

When the Stags told me that Aslak had you, I came as fast as I could. When I met you, I knew you were the one, and that I had to do everything within my power to help you succeed."

"Wait, so Ava saying I was a bridge builder wasn't just about Caelum and Earth, or even everything with Palus . . . " I attempted to work this out in my head.

Strix interjected. "No. It's way bigger than you could have imagined. Aslak thought if he killed you, then the legend died with you. If he can destroy the bridges between worlds, than the Tree of Light is all his to misuse. You already have experienced its unique powers. It is imperative that he not succeed."

"Teik told me that the Tree had been planted from the light of another world's sun, so why does it need Caelum's suns' power?"

"The Tree has been in existence for thousands of years. In order for it not to eventually lose its energy, it must have access to another source."

"Like renewable energy?" James asked.

"Yes, your world would consider it that. Although the power of the Tree is far more deep and mystic."

I gazed down at my upper arm, where the branch of the seven tiny light purple orchid flowers curved up and around the Elisium flower. This whole time, a prophecy was tattooed on me, given to me by myself. I tried to remember the dream that sparked this flower in my imagination that day I created the painting that hung back in my gallery in Woodstock.

Woodstock. Georgia. Earth.

It all felt so far removed from this moment, this life. I wondered how it could fit in the same lifetime.

"I need some air." I sighed and walked outside the canopy tent.

Walking back past the door to Caelum, I came upon a huge field of Serenbe flowers. I knelt on the edge of the field of flowers that started this all. The Serenbe brought me to James, the Elisium brought me home, and now the—I had forgotten to ask what this flower was even called. Whatever it was, it was a prophesy leading me to unite two worlds. Even after all of these years, and everything we'd seen, this was a little much.

"It's called the Lumen." James sat down next to me and picked a Serenbe. "But the Serenbe will always hold a special place in my heart." His eyes sparkled as he handed it to me.

"There you go again, showing off your impressive skills."

"What can I say? I'm a natural." His smile faded. "Eden, everything is going to be okay. I know it's a lot to take in, but we'll handle it the way we do everything else, together."

"I know. I don't even want to think about this fourth stupid flower." I grimaced and looked down at the upside down, dark pink, pointy, lily that seemed to glow yellowish white in the middle.

"Let's just take one flower at a time."

"Deal," I sighed. "I guess I just never expected this. I thought just being Ava's daughter, and a Door Keeper, was all there was. Honestly, that was enough."

"Aw, girl, I knew there was more than that. Why do you think I stalked you until you went out with me?"

"Um, my good looks and charming personality?" I put my head on his shoulder.

"No way. I'm all about climbing the multi-world social ladder. You were my ticket to the big times." He chuckled underneath me and slid his arm around my back.

"I'm glad you're having fun with this." I looked up into his soft chocolate eyes.

"I always have fun with you." He kissed me softly, then pulled back. "I know you want some space, but if you need me, I'll be in the tent. I love you." He got up and left me to ponder what we had gotten ourselves into.

I decided to check in on Gabby, so I closed my eyes and threw myself into her consciousness. They were camping out on an island not too far from Iskrem's door, sitting around a fire and eating dinner. She told me they'd had an easy trip so far with no surprises. I knew this wasn't the time or place to tell her about the prophesy or Tree of Light, so I filled in the gaps with news of Lolli and Vi, hoping she wouldn't ask about what Strix had to say. We talked about plans for the next day, when a sound rustled behind me.

"Forgive me for startling you, Eden." Xander took a step back.

"It's okay, Xander, just let me say goodbye to Gabbs."

Gabby seemed curious as we "disconnected," but I quickly turned my attention to the Hiem kneeling beside me.

"Please, just have a seat. No need to be so formal." I patted the ground.

"Well, that is what I wanted to talk to you about, Eden. Now that you know the truth about yourself, and your relationship to the Tree of Light, it is only fair you know the truth about me."

"Okay, and what would that be?"

"I am not just a Hiem representative. I am *the* representative. I took over Iskrem's Door Keeper responsibilities from my Uncle when we exiled him, and in two years time, I will become Iskrem's King."

"King?" I had not expected this.

"Yes. Aslak is my Uncle. The first-born son in our family takes the crown, and the second son takes the key. My father is the current king of Iskrem. I took over being Door Keeper until my younger brother comes of age. He will take over as Door Keeper when I take the crown."

"So that's your *family's mantle*." I raised an eyebrow.

"I wasn't ready to reveal who I was to you. I am sorry that I misled you."

"No, Xander, I understand. If everyone knew you were going to be King, it might have changed our conversations and the way we approached this, but I think we made the right decisions. I appreciate you coming to me with this though. Now we can move forward with all of the information."

"There's something else you should know. When we banished my Uncle, we took his key. He obviously had a copy made before we found out the truth. So the three worlds we need to focus on are the three that Taran referred to, the doors leading to Earth, Palus, and Asylum."

"Asylum, I've never heard of that world."

"It's now one of my doors to guard, but it's different than the usual Door Keeper charge."

"Why? How is it different?"

Startled, we both turned when a noise interrupted us in the brush a couple yards away. I turned back to the Hiem, Door Keeper, Prince sitting beside me.

"We should cross that bridge when we get there." His choice of words was not lost on me.

"Ok, let's head back and get some rest tonight. Tomorrow, we can talk to Strix and figure out the best use of our time moving forward. But it makes sense we should secure the three doors Aslak knows about first."

THE UNFORESEEN.

Eden

James and I held on tightly to Strix's back as he soared up and over the peach colored cumulous clouds. Xander gripped the back of a smaller owl flying next to us, one of Strix's younger friends. Apparently, he was only two hundred years old or so. Xander was obviously uncomfortable flying above the clouds, especially under the unobstructed sun, but in order to get to both of the doors within a couple of days, we needed speed on our side.

James had been just as shocked as I was with the news about Xander. We hadn't had a chance to really talk about what this meant moving forward. His interest in Gabby made me nervous, and I couldn't help but remember the conversation we'd had on the plane—the one where Xander told me he was to be married in two years. I suddenly hoped that the Hiems' royal marriages were arranged.

We flew for hours, the quiet stillness hanging in the Terra Arborum sky. This was one of the quietest worlds, with no noise pollution of any kind. I used to tease Lolli that I could hear the trees growing, the land was so silent. As we finally made our descent below the clouds, the trees below were much greener than they were before. In fact, I couldn't see any bark on any branch in any direction, only green. Once we landed, my feet sank into the spongy, soft moss that coated every square inch of everything.

Strix turned his head about 240 degrees, looking behind him. "This way."

James, Xander, and I pulled our weapons just in case there had been a breach. The weapon I now carried was Taran's tree antler smoothed down and straightened with a spearhead attached by our Caelun blacksmith. As we approached a large tree trunk covered in more moss, slight indentations in the spongy material alluded to a door hidden underneath. It seemed as though the moss would've been disturbed if anyone had opened the door, but just to be sure, we searched a wide perimeter and talked to some of the birds in the area to make sure there hadn't been a disturbance.

Once we were satisfied the door hadn't been used, I pulled out the metal stopper that Gio had made for us before we left Italy. It fit perfectly in the keyhole and would block the locking mechanisms from being able to move, rendering the entire lock useless. It would at least buy us some time to find a more permanent solution.

We hopped back onto Strix and his friend's back, taking off for Iskrem's door. It would take us about fifteen hours to get there, and while flying on a giant owl's back is fun, it's looses it's allure after an hour or so. None of us were looking forward to the long flight ahead.

About twenty hours later, after a couple hour breaks for water and rest during the night, we touched down close to Iskrem's door. We were a little on edge, more so than Palus' door, considering what was happening there. We hiked towards the door when I pulled out my spear. Immediately a vision of Aslak's smug face flashed in my mind when he killed Taran. James, noticing my reaction, was next to me in seconds.

"Eden, what's wrong?"

"It's nothing, I saw a weird vision of Aslak's face . . . "

"When? Just now?" Xander questioned.

"Yes, when I drew my spear."

"It's Taran—the energy in his antler—it's warning you." Xander swung his axe from his back and sprinted towards the door.

"Wait, Xander!" James ran after him, his own sword drawn. I followed behind, still not grasping what was happening. Strix flew above us as we ran through the trees. James and I both almost fell over when we rounded a large oak to see the chaos that exploded before us.

Xander fought for his life against five Paluns—jumping, diving, rolling, and swinging his weapon with all his might. Strix flew down, grabbing one sloth with his talons and forcing him to the ground, ripping him open as fur flew everywhere. Seeing my peacekeeping friend become a fighter snapped me into action. James and I leapt into the madness, yelling warnings, taking down as many enemies as we could.

I forgot how much I hated sloth's claws.

Pain shot up my spine as a Palun got a swipe in while my back was turned. Although, running my spear through his midsection suppressed the pain enough to move on to the sloth towering over James, stuck underneath him. I jumped on the Palun's back, with Taran's antler pressed against his throat. I squeezed with every ounce of energy I had in my body until he fell limp. The spear handle vibrated under my grip, Aslak's face flashing before me once again.

He was close—somehow I knew it. Taran knew it.

I looked around and saw two remaining sloths, but no one else. Aslak was either running, or just on the other side of the door. Both James and Xander were finishing off the last two Paluns, and I bolted towards the door, noticing it was cracked open. I would end this once and for all. As I reached out with my arm to open the door and confront Aslak, a heavy weight crashed into me and knocked me to the ground. Xander had tackled me and slammed the door closed with his foot.

"Xander!" I growled. "He's right there, I know it!"

"So do I. Quick, give me the stopper."

"No, we have to end this!"

"Eden! Give it to me now!" His voice carried an authority and tone that surprised me, so I obeyed. He grabbed it, jumped up, and locked the door.

James killed the last sloth and ran to my side.

"What just happened?"

"Ask him!" I pointed to Xander angrily.

"Eden, you do not understand. I just saved your life. It was a trap, I am sure of it. He was waiting for us on the other side with an army."

"But, how could he know we were coming?" James turned on Xander, getting in his face. "You! Did you betray us?"

Xander put one hand on my husband's chest, pushing him away. "I swear on the Tree of Light, I would never."

"Why should we believe you? You're his family!" James yelled, understandably shaken.

"You aren't thinking clearly James. If I were on Aslak's side, you would be dead," he said softly.

Strix landed between the two men. "Xander is right. We underestimated our enemy. If this plan is to infiltrate so soon, then we must adjust our course of action."

We stared at each other in a panic.

Xander whispered what we each just realized. "Gabrielle. She's in danger."

"Warn her. You have to stop them. They may not have gotten there yet. They had several days to travel." James grabbed my arm.

I closed my eyes and screamed within my own head to get her attention.

Gabby, stop! Don't go to the door! We must change the plan, they are waiting on us!

No response.

Gabby, please answer me! Don't go to the door!

Nothing.

God, no. Please help me.

"She's not answering." Panic rose in my chest making it difficult to breath. I tried again, this time to my brother.

Marek! Stop! Don't go to the door. Aslak knew we were coming, and we just got attacked.

Nothing. This can't be happening.

Marek, please!

Charlie?

No response from anyone.

My blood turned ice cold. I was separated from my family and had no way of knowing if they were okay.

"I don't hear or see any of them. Something is wrong. They're not dreaming or answering when I try to contact their subconscious." Fear and dread took root in my gut.

"What do we do?" James' frustration had turned to alarm.

"Go to them. Do what you have to. I must go home," Xander answered. "Go back through Caelum, and I'll head that way through Iskrem. I can travel much faster there, and we can flank them from both sides."

I couldn't bring myself to say anything, completely frozen in terror. James spoke up for me.

"How are you going to get through if Aslak is on the other side of the door?" The argument from just moments ago already forgotten.

"I'll wait here until nightfall. If my uncle thinks we permanently closed the door, he'll move on to his next course of action."

"Okay. Strix can you get us back to the door to Caelum?"

"Of course James. We will fly through the night if we must."

I pulled myself up, despite the paralyzing anxiety and nausea creeping through me. "Xander, thank you. Thank you for everything."

"We will see each other again very soon, Eden. I am sure of it." He clasped my hand in his. "Now go and save your daughter."

THE HAPPENING.

Gabby

My uncles were driving me crazy.

We currently sat around the fire eating dinner after a long day of riding. Marek informed us we only had another day and a half before arriving at Iskrem's door, but at this rate, I didn't think I was going to make it. Charlie taught Uncle Marek the game two truths and a lie, and they were going back and forth trying to outdo one another's lies and truths.

Thankfully, my mom pressed in on my subconscious, and I welcomed the distraction from the ridiculousness happening in front of me. She filled me in on their travels to Terra Arborum and updates on Lolli and Vi, neither of which I had even met yet. I was about to interrupt her and ask about her conversation with Strix when she startled.

Xander's voice interrupted us, sounding muffled, like hearing someone on the other end of the telephone.

"Forgive me for startling you, Eden."

Mom seemed anxious to end our conversation, so I let her go. But I had a nagging suspicion she wasn't telling me something, so I did what any good teenage girl would. I eavesdropped. I laid down, pretending to doze off, but instead threw myself to my Mom's and Xander's conversation.

When I opened my eyes, I was covered in an azalea bush, and they were talking a few yards away. Quietly as possible, I turned myself to hear them easier. Xander sat next to Mom, wearing his oversized fur lined cape that he'd worn the first time I'd met him.

"Well, that is what I wanted to talk to you about, Eden. Now that you know the truth about yourself, and your relationship to the Tree of Light, it is only fair you know the truth about me," he said simply.

Truth about Mom? What truth? What was he talking about?

"I am not just a Hiem representative. I am *the* representative. I took over Iskrem's Door Keeper responsibilities from my Uncle and in two years time, I will become Iskrem's king."

Um, what in the world? King? Did I hear him right?

He explained to Mom about his family, but I couldn't stay focused. This whole time, he lied about who he was, and Mom didn't even look upset. I was furious.

"So that's your *family's mantle*." Mom's voice snapped me back to the present.

"I wasn't ready to reveal who I was to you. I am sorry that I misled you."

"No, Xander, I understand." She kept talking, but I was too angry to listen anymore. How could she be so understanding? I guess maybe she understood, having lied to me for so long. Maybe it came easier for her . . .

But why would he lie about who he really was? It didn't make sense. I'd want everyone to know I was in charge if it was the case. No wonder he never talked. It's so much easier not to spill the truth if your mouth's shut.

And what was the truth Xander referred to about Mom? Her relationship with the Tree of Light? I knew whatever it was, whatever Strix had revealed to her, was what Mom hid from our conversation earlier. More secrets, more half-truths. I was getting sick of this. I had a good mind to just pop out of the bushes and demand to know everything, when something crawled across my bare foot. Glancing down, a centipede climbed over the top of my foot, and I kicked it off, causing me to fall on my butt. I woke up immediately to keep from being discovered.

I found myself back at camp, with a whole heap of new knowledge.

Charlie looked over at me. "You okay, Gabbs?"

"Yeah, just tired. Think I'm going to sleep for tonight." I needed a minute to process this myself, but tomorrow, I would tell both of them the truth. I'm not going to be the one to keep lies.

After a dreamless sleep, I woke up to my Uncles having already packed up. For a couple of hours, we rode nonstop which helped calm my overwhelming emotions. I wasn't so much angry or mad anymore, just frustrated. Why did people think shielding me from the truth was what was best? We stopped under a giant Banyan tree that had multiple low hanging branches, allowing us to string up some hammocks and rest above the shallow sea.

"Hey, I got one for you guys," I spoke up, while pulling out a snack.

"One what?" Marek looked up eating his fruit.

"Two truths and a lie."

"Okay, shoot."

"My birth father is still alive, my mom is still lying to me, and Xander is in line to be King of the Hiems."

Both of them sat up in their hammocks and turned to face me.

"Gabbs, the game is *two truths* and a lie, not *three lies*," Marek said slowly.

"Well, what if I told you I found out two of those truths last night. And I know for sure that my real dad is dead," I said dryly.

"Damn, that's harsh." Charlie raised his eyebrows.

"I'm sorry. I'm just insanely frustrated." I jumped out of the hammock and paced, splashing water everywhere. "I overheard Mom and Xander last night, and he told her the truth about himself. She wasn't even upset." My voice raised more than I'd meant it to.

Marek digested the new information, his eyes darting around the water below. His eyes finally landed back on me. "So why are *you* so upset?"

"What do you mean? He lied to us."

"But why do you care? You think he's weird and don't really like him," Charlie countered.

"I know but . . . "

Why were my uncles making this so difficult? More importantly, why *did* I care so much?

"Why do you think Eden is lying to you?" Marek changed the subject.

"Because she is. Xander said something about 'now that she knows the truth about herself.'"

"And?" Marek looked at me to finish.

"And she didn't tell me anything last night."

"Gabbs, she probably just didn't want to tell you over your insane telepathic thing you do. It's most likely more complicated than just a one-time conversation. Pretty much like every new piece of information that we *ever* learn," Charlie reassured. "Don't assume the worst. I'm sure she's planning on telling us as soon as she can. You don't have a reason not to trust her."

"Oh, you mean like the seven years she lied to me about all of this?" I waved my hands around pointing in every direction.

"That's not fair, Gabbs. That was a family decision. We all decided that was for the best, for you. So be mad at everyone, not just your mom," Marek said firmly.

Sighing, I plopped down in the warm water.

"I'm not mad. Not at anyone, really. I'm just so over secrets. I'm over not knowing what my future looks like, and having the one I used to imagine, simply ripped away. A month ago, I just wanted to turn eighteen and get more social media followers, and now—here we are. Everything I used to think about and dream about just seems so trivial and stupid."

Charlie studied me, walking over and sitting down, putt his arm around me.

"I don't know what you're complaining about. You have like three times the amount of followers I do."

I threw his arm off me as he chuckled. Leave it to Charlie to try to make me laugh when I'm grumpy. Marek joined us in the water, sitting in front of us, with a very serious look.

"Gabby, no one faults you for being frustrated. We get it. And just so you know, we have all had to face hard truths that made our previous lives feel false. But your mom showed me that trying to hold onto fake truths so that we don't have to face reality is wrong, and dangerous. I almost punished you and Eden because I was unwilling to accept a very difficult truth. I promise, we will be patient while you accept yours."

I allowed myself to fill with emotion as I looked at my Uncles. "Thanks guys. I'm glad I'm here with you both, even if you do sometimes drive me crazy."

"I just can't believe that I have met the future King of Iskrem, protector of the Tree of Light!" Charlie exclaimed from nowhere.

Marek looked at me and rolled his eyes. "And don't be mad at Xander. That is exactly why he hasn't told us the truth. He's just a private guy and is probably trying to avoid the groupies."

THE INCIDENT.

Gabby

I processed everything Marek said later that night, lying under the bright Caelum stars. The three full moons cast an eerie glow on the shallow sea as it ebbed and flowed in all directions. He was right of course. Every member in my family had lived under a false pretense, only to have it removed and the truth be told to them, dissolving the life they thought there were living. My mom, learning the truth of where she was really from. My dad and Charlie finding out their father was alive. Poppy and my grandmother's death. All of them had to accept a new normal and realize that they couldn't return to their old lives.

I guess it was my time to do the same.

But then I tried to think about the things that I had expected for my life that were no longer possible, and I couldn't think of one. I could still do and be the things I wanted to be, it just might be a little more complicated. I would still fall in love, get married, have children and a job that I loved doing and was good at. It might be ruling a nation versus being an art teacher, but a job's a job. I could still travel and have friends, and create things and make a difference in the world. Or worlds. Hopefully, none of that had changed.

So I might have to live a double life until I graduated, or eventually say good bye to my high school friends. That would inevitably happen anyway once everyone went to college. College.

Do Queens need a college degree? Mom said I had a choice in the timing. Maybe I could go to college first.

I dozed off imagining myself walking a college campus while wearing a tiara and Caelun dress.

When my mind wandered into the space between wake and sleep, I found myself soaring under the stars in the black of night. Nothing was below me but clouds whirling past, my shadow being cast under the large singular moon. This wasn't Caelum. I was somewhere else, and I was totally flying. I glanced to my right and almost fell into the clouds when the largest owl I'd ever seen flew with my mother and father on it's back. Dad laid between the owl's shoulder blades up along it's neck, peacefully asleep, and Mom's arms wrapped around Dad's waist, also asleep. The huge owl, that I could only assume was Strix, had massive wings that created a methodic, swooshing noise that was hypnotizing. To my left, Xander sat motionless on a smaller owl, awake and unaware of my presence. The moon's glow washed his skin a ghostly white, reminding me again of when we first met, before the effect of Caelum's suns. His cape and long dreads flew out behind him, whipping in the wind.

He actually resembled a future king flying on the back of that owl.

"You need not worry about your parents. I swear to keep them safe," Xander said as if to no one. He didn't look towards me, or seem to know where I was. Yet he spoke directly to me.

"How do you know I'm here?"

"I sense you close. I always feel when you are close."

"Not always." I tried to fly closer to him, but had no control over my flight plan.

"I felt you earlier when I told Eden the truth about who I was."

"Why didn't you say anything?"

"I wanted you to work through it on your own. I imagine you were angry." He looked down into the back of the owl below him.

"Why would you assume that?" I countered.

"Were you not?" He finally turned his dark eyes toward me, the perimeter of silver gleaming in the moonlight, making a shiver run down my spine.

"Yes, I was. But that doesn't mean you know me."

"I have watched you and Eden. You both have the same impulsive and stubborn emotions. She has just learned to sift and navigate hers better."

"Is that so?" I huffed.

"Yes."

"You know, I don't like you very much." I glared.

"I understand." He nodded slightly. "But I will earn your trust, perhaps even your friendship. I swear to that as well."

I sighed in exhaustion. "Yeah, sure Xander, whatever you say. Sorry to intrude on your flight."

"Seeing you is always a pleasure, Gabrielle."

Even after waking up, and knowing it was a dream, my imaginary conversation with Xander sat in the pit of my stomach like a heavy brick. It nagged at my subconscious the entire ride to Iskrem's door. Almost as though, the closer we got to his homeland, the more Xander weighed on my mind and the more it annoyed me.

It was mid afternoon the next day when we finally got to the island where the door was located. There was a singular mountain on the island, rocky and taller than most I'd seen in Caelum. Charlie, Marek, and I found an easier path up the steep mountainside and for the better part of two hours, climbed until our legs hurt. We came upon a large flat area on the side of the cliff face where we knew the door to be. There was a stone archway made of stacked boulders that housed the dark wooden door. A beautiful ornate tree, molded out of a metal that matched the key material, hung on the door like a work of art. The Tree of Light.

Uncle Marek pulled out his key to make sure it was locked before inserting the key stopper, when a deep guttural panic rose within me. My heart beat almost out of my chest, but I saw no reason to feel nervous.

Until my eyes landed on the door, barely cracked open.

"How?" Charlie's face crumpled in pain.

"Charlie!" Marek screamed and sprang into action.

Horror coursed through me as a spear stuck out through the center of Charlie's gut.

"*No!*" I ran towards my best friend as he fell to his knees. Metal scraped and rang against metal behind me, but the only thing I could focus on was the blood pouring from Charlie's midsection.

"Gabby!" Marek screamed my name, but I was frozen.

"*Gabby!*"

Then claws wrapped around my feet and pull me backward. Every fiber of my being was on fire with rage as I flipped onto my back and stared up at the giant sloth towering over me, his arm coming down towards me in slow motion. I kicked upwards, knocking the creature's knees out and ran towards my pack with my weapon.

I grabbed my grandmother's hook sword as I raced towards Marek fighting against two Paluns. As I reached him, I noticed a gargantuan sloth wearing a ton of military gear watching everything unfold from his perch on the hill. My attention shot back to the huge Palun behind Marek, and I brought my sword up, slicing him up the middle. A monstrous sound left the sloth's disgusting mouth as he turned, hitting my head with his claw. I fell over, seeing Charlie had completely crumpled to the ground, and allowed the sight to fuel my adrenaline. I rolled over and out the beast's reach and pulled myself up, my blood boiling with a mixture of anger and fear.

Marek and I fought one on one with the creatures and made no headway. For every blow I dealt, I received one in return. I was exhausted and losing steam quickly. I tried to summon the memory JJ had shown me for strength, but my mind was as weak as my body. Marek finally killed the one he fought, but by that time, the larger sloth on the hill slowly made his way down to us. One of his eyes was missing and a large protruding scar was left where it should have been. General Sapp's son. He had one of his claws on the ground navigating his way down the hill and the other raised with something in it.

An enormous rock.

I screamed Marek's name as it flew through the air towards his head. As Marek's body fell to the ground, lifeless, I dropped my weapon and fell to my knees, sobbing uncontrollably. The Palun General's shadow engulfed me.

"You son of a bitch," I gasped.

Everything went black.

THE BURNING QUESTIONS.

Eden

I was perched on Strix's back basically unconscious, James sitting behind me with his arms holding me upright. I dedicated every moment trying to find out what happened, trying to locate my brother, Charlie, Gabby, or any of their dreams. I tried to throw myself into any situation that might give me information on what happened, but nothing came. I reached out to Mae to let her and Dad know what happened and to remain on the lookout. My father immediately sent a rescue team to Iskrem's door, but it would take days to get there.

The tension in my body tightened as every minute of uncertainty passed, wreaking havoc on the few injures I'd sustained during our brief encounter with the Paluns. Every inch of my body hurt, as I poured so much effort into concentrating within my own subconscious.

Finally I sensed Marek, and quickly threw myself into his mind.

Oh God, Eden are you there?
"I'm here. Marek, don't go to the door."
It's too late, we were attacked . . . Charlie . . . Oh God.
"What happened to Charlie?"
Eden, they took her. Gabby's gone.
My body went limp.
"Who took her? How?"

The Paluns. They ambushed us.

"Are you and Charlie okay?"

No, Charlie's badly hurt. I'm trying to help him with the supplies Gabby brought, but he's lost so much blood. I don't know how long I was out before I came to.

"Dad sent help. They're on their way and should be there tomorrow. Do you have enough supplies to hold out?"

Forget it, I have Charlie on a horse heading back home. Meet us there.

There was a long pause on his end.

I'm so sorry, Eden. I was supposed to protect her. I can't believe this happened.

"We had no way of knowing. We were ambushed too. Just get Charlie back home."

Somehow knowing Gabby was taken gave me new resolve. They wouldn't kill her without trying to use her to get to me. Even this slight hope fueled my adrenaline. I shook my head and came to hearing James in my ear over the wind.

"I heard your end of the conversation. What happened to Charlie?" His words were heavy with concern.

"I don't know, but he was hurt, badly. Marek is taking him home, so that's where we're going."

"Charlie will be fine. And we'll find Gabby," he said somewhat unconvincingly.

"Yes. Yes, we will. Now hold onto me again. I need to tell Xander what happened. If they have Gabby in Iskrem, the Stags will know about it."

It was easier to get a hold of Xander's mind than I thought he would be. I think after spending so much time with us and our gifts, he learned a way to open himself to our communication. He agreed to find and talk to the Stags and get information back to me about where Gabby was being held as soon as possible.

That night, we reached the Caelum door. Strix went through the door with us to get us home faster. Within hours of passing through the door we were back home at Caelum. Strix dropped us off, and went after Charlie and Marek to bring them home faster. I couldn't ignore the exhaustion in his huge yellow eyes, but he was determined to help anyway he could.

James, Dad, Mae, and I paced the courtyard floor. Finally my father spoke up.

"Why doesn't one of you use your gift to find Aslak or Sapp? Can't you throw yourself in their minds to find out where they are?"

"I can only enter the dream state. So, I'm afraid I can't locate or infiltrate someone's mind when they are awake." Mae said, still pacing.

"I can do it for people I've seen and met in person. The closer I am to them, the better. I haven't spent much time with either of them, but I tried anyway. I can't find either of them. It's like they have fallen off the face of the worlds." My head throbbed after straining my mind for so long.

We sat in silence for about an hour before we heard Strix approach from the North. He landed with Charlie spread across his back, unconscious while Marek sat behind him, holding him on. Marek didn't look too good himself, dried blood stained his face and head a dark reddish brown. Shay and Wynn were ready to take Charlie to the bathhouse where the doctor waited. They had turned the large herbal remedy room into a hospital of sorts, since Caelum had no need for such things on most occasions. Most medicinal work was done within people's own homes.

James and Dad gently lowered Charlie off of Strix's back, and a groan escaped James' lips. Charlie's face was pale, and the skin around his eyes had turned yellowish. His entire stomach area was caked with blood. They rushed him off, and I turned to help my brother. He sat at the table in the middle of the courtyard, bloodied head in his hands.

Strix needed to get back before the two suns rose, so after we said our goodbyes and well wishes, he left to return Terra

Arborum. I joined Marek, having no words to say to make him feel better. Alone in the courtyard, scared and defeated, we simply sat in silence.

I tried to imagine what our mother would say if she were here right now. Would she offer advice, solace, or simply sit here with us in our grief? Would she chastise us for sitting here, frozen in our fear? Or would she understand because she's been here? I thought about Gabby—whether she was scared, alone, or hurt.

Two years ago, she and I had traveled to Thailand for a week and had gotten lost on the outskirts of the city after dark. I was afraid and frustrated, and she was scared out of her mind. We both knew we were in a bad situation, and I remembered something I'd told her that night. So I turned to Marek, put on the bravest "mom" face I could muster, and laid out the plan.

"Okay, here it is. This was completely worst-case scenario. We were blind-sided, and we are all freaked out. This is on us, we underestimated Aslak and whatever his plan is. So we are both going to take five minutes and cry, yell, and get angry, but then we've got to move on and figure out how to get us out of this mess."

"You're gonna try to pull the old Thailand mind trick on me right now?" His eyes were swollen.

"Yes."

He sighed, and then the tears fell. His tears quickly turned to anger.

"This is all my fault. I'm the leader, the warrior. I'm the one with the experience, I was the one in charge of keeping them safe. They followed me to that door and now look where we are? How could I be so careless?" His voice rose. "How the hell did this happen? We have no idea where Gabby is and that disgusting monster has her!"

He stood as his rage boiled. "And Charlie is laying somewhere dying, and there is nothing I can do. I can't fix it. Those damn Paluns! Why would our mom even go there? Did she not think through the ramifications of her presence in that stupid swamp? They wouldn't even know we existed if she hadn't left that damn note for Squash. None of this is even our fault!" He threw his hands in the air and paused when he realized what he'd said. It was the one thing none of us wanted to say since learning the truth. There was a deep-seated sense of frustration rising in both of us with the realization that this didn't start with us. We inherited this shit storm.

Knowing it was now my turn, I picked up where my brother left off.

"You're right. It's not our fault and now Gabby is paying the price. We don't even know if she's alive." My voice fell to a whisper not even wanted to say it. But this was the point, to feel everything I was afraid to. To cry and get it all out of our system so we could move forward. The tears fell fast.

"And I'm just sitting here, with no idea what to do next. Completely helpless. How could I not think Aslak was capable of something like this? He broke into our beach house and freaking kidnapped me! Is this what we get for not assuming that the worlds are selfish, greedy, hateful, and just plain awful? It's not bad enough that humans can't even manage to be decent, but now we have Paluns and Hiems and other worldly races to deal with. I freaking hate General Sapp. He killed Squash, he tried to kill James, and me, and now he has taken my daughter. I will gut that ass hole."

I began to pace, allowing myself to fall down the rabbit hole.

"Do you know what really makes me angry?" I shouted to no-one particular. "I should have seen this coming! This is karma. I lied to my daughter for years and years and this is what I get for it. At least if I'd told her the truth we could have trained and she would have been ready. She might have been prepared. Instead I led my sweet little lamb to the slaughter with no more than a stupid pep talk and a sword she had never used before!"

This wasn't Marek's or Ava's fault—it was all mine.

I never should have separated from Gabby.

I should have killed Aslak when I had the chance.

It was a mistake I would not make again.

I sat back down next to my brother, emptied. No more tears to fall or expletives to yell. No more anger or hate. Just an empty shell of a mother. I looked over at my brother.

"You feel better?"

"Slightly."

"Good enough. Let's get to work."

THE MILLISECOND.

Eden

As we walked towards to the bathhouse to find the others, even after our five minutes of raging, everything crept back into my head again. Where should we go? What's our next step? My head ached and was so jumbled I couldn't have picked Gabby's subconscious out of a line up if it were right in front of me.

In order to find Gabby, I needed to clear my head and relax. My gift was always more powerful the more rested I was, and right now, my body was drained beyond comprehension. Not knowing what else to do, besides sleeping for three days straight, which was *not* an option, I told my brother where I was going.

We separated in the main hall. He joined the others to wait for word on Charlie, and I walked up to my father's private quarters. Opening the large double stained glass doors, I passed through his bedroom towards what I needed. Through another set of double doors, I found what I was looking for, his private bath—an oversized stone hole in the middle of the floor. I ran the water immediately and added the milky powder. Finding his herbal cabinet, I pulled down the two fragrances I craved at the moment. Orchid and lavender. I looked down at the tattoo of the Lumens above my elbow, deciding to tap into however I was connected to the Tree of Light. Maybe if I embraced my newly discovered connection to the Tree, it's energy would help me find Gabby.

Throwing the crushed dried petals and leaves in the bath, the aroma quickly filled the room. It was quiet here. Everyone else waited on the other side of the building. It would be the perfect place to decompress and try to clear my head. This was my only chance to find Gabby. Not even bothering to remove my dirty Caelun garb, I eased into the bath, and a sigh escaped my lips. The creamy milk substance absorbed into the scratches on my back, and the slight pain was welcomed, knowing the medicinal properties of the flowers would help heal them. I sunk low, submerging everything except my head in the steamy hot bath.

Now, to clear my head and straighten out my thoughts. I could do this. Focus on one thing at a time. What did I know for sure?

Gabby is missing.

Charlie is hurt.

Aslak has a key to open the doors and has already breached two worlds.

Which means he'll do it again.

But Gabby comes first.

How do I find her? She was taken at the door to Iskrem, so if Aslak has her there, then chances are the Stags or Hiems will know about it. If we have to, we will eliminate one world at a time until we find her, starting with Iskrem. At least this was something I could do and action I could take to get me one step closer. I reached out my mind to Xander to let him know we would be coming and where to meet us. One step down and an unknown amount to go.

My head swam, overwhelmed at the thought.

I regulated my breathing, closed my eyes, and lowered my ears under the water. My heartbeat pulsed loudly through the milky bath while my head was submerged. It finally slowed down.

Gabby. Sweetie, where are you?

Nothing.

So I pictured her face, her laying on the couch back at home, reading one of her books, feet kicked up behind her.

Nothing.

Sitting back up, I reached my arms out of the bath in frustration, running my hands through my hair and resting them on top of my head. Why couldn't I find her? I wouldn't even let myself consider the possibilities.

My eyes became mesmerized with the huge waves of steam rolling off my skin, dissipating into the air above me. Feeling sightly dazed, I was unable to focus on anything other than the white air rising above me.

One of the doors slowly opened into the bathroom, and a mop of brown curly hair poked in.

"Momma?"

"Oh hey, sweetie. You can come in. It's okay."

"Momma, you're home early!" He smiled, then looked at my face. "Are you sad?"

"A little, but I promise I'll be okay." My reassurance sounded hollow.

"Where is Gabby?"

I fought to keep my composure.

"I'm not sure, buddy," I said quietly.

"Is she lost?" His eyes grew in concern.

My heart sank.

"Just for a minute, but I'll find her very soon."

He carefully considered my words and sat by the edge of the bath, perched like the bird he imitated back home. Even in his light blue traditional Caelun skirt and his skin a couple shades darker, he looked just like he always did. Long gangly limbs with every rib exposed along his back and chest. His presence relaxed me. At least everything hadn't changed in the past couple of weeks.

"Gabby is afraid." JJ frowned neither a statement nor a question.

I reached up and and grabbed his hand. "I know buddy, but it's okay."

"I don't like it," he said simply. "I want my family to be happy, like when Gabby has a crown." Within a second, my head soared through the house into the courtyard to the very scene I had shown my father so many years ago. Gabby entered, wearing her golden crown and gorgeous pink dress. Everyone in the scene was smiling and laughing, including Gabby. Looking at her glowing face, something clicked within my mind. Her subconscious connected with mine for a millisecond then it was gone—then for another second, then it was gone again. As though it bounced around, unable to stay focused. Almost like I'd felt when I was drugged before . . .

She was alive.

My eyes shot open. JJ was perched above me with an expectant look on his face. He had done it. He had not only shown me that Gabby was alive, but he had helped boost my signal in some way to reach her, if only for a second.

"You did it, sugar bean!" I reached up and grabbed him, pulling him in the bath with me. "I love you, you crazy little man!"

"Momma!" He laughed uncontrollably. Milky water splashed everywhere as he tried and failed to get out of the tub. "You're a sugar bean!" he repeated what I'd call him but yelled it, like he was trying to insult me. "Momma, you're making a mess!"

"JJ, thank you. I feel so much better. Thank you for making me happy."

"You're welcome." He beamed. "All done with the bath now?"

I laughed. "Yes, let's dry off."

Before we could get out, the doors burst open, and James barreled through. Looking down at us his face went from determined to confused within seconds.

"What happened?"

"Momma's a silly sugar bean!"

"Everything's okay." I answered pulling him from the in ground bathtub. "JJ helped me feel Gabby's subconscious, just for a moment. I think she's being drugged like I was before, so she can't use her gifts."

"I knew it. Oh my God, what a relief." He closed his eyes and smiled, and then it grew larger. "I have good news, too. Charlie is awake, and he's going to be okay."

THE ARGUMENT.

Eden

As soon as JJ and I had changed into new, fresh clothes, the three of us made our way to Charlie's room, where he had been moved since getting cleaned up. Thanks to Marek stopping and maintaining blood loss during their trip back, Charlie was going to be okay. When we entered, Shay and Wynn as well as the other caretakers left, giving us space and allowing him to tell us his side of what happened.

He got really quiet after recounting the story. Finally, he looked up at us with tears in his eyes.

"Marek was too busy fighting to see who it was, but I recognized him from your description. It was Sapp. He was the one that hit Marek and knocked out Gabby. I couldn't do anything to stop him as he dragged her through the door. I'm so sorry." He choked out the last part.

I knelt in front beside Charlie's bed and grabbed his hand.

"Nope, don't you do that. This is not your fault. The responsibility lay with us. We should have assumed Aslak would be more aggressive. We won't make that mistake again." I turned my attention towards the rest of the group. "Gabby is alive. JJ helped me sense her for just a moment, long enough to think she is being drugged as I was, which means it's up to us to find her. Marek and I will go to Iskrem and meet up with Xander to gather information. If she's anywhere in Iskrem, the Stags will know about it, and if she's not, then we move onto the next world. James, you stay with Charlie."

My husband interrupted me before I continued.

"We are not splitting up, Eden," he said simply. "Marek can stay with Charlie. We will go to Iskrem."

I looked at James, knowing this wasn't going to be pretty.

"Guys, give us a minute?" I grabbed James and led him out to the courtyard.

"No way, Eden. You don't get to pull rank and make decisions without me." The frustration built in James' voice.

"That's not what I'm doing."

"Yes it is! It's what you always do. Gabby is my daughter too. I want to find her— no, I *need* to find her as much as you do."

"I know that."

"After everything we just went through. You want to split up again?!"

"No!" My voice raised an octave. "I want us to be smart. I don't want anything else happening to anyone I love."

"Ok, fine. Let's hear it. Why do you really want Marek to go?"

"He feels responsible!" I threw my hands in the air. "He knows he was the one in charge, and this happened on his watch. I want to give him a chance to do something. If he stays behind with Charlie, he'll go crazy."

"So you are willing to tie my hands and keep me on the side lines to pacify your brother?" he argued.

"That's not fair. Don't make this a choice between you and him."

"But it is! You know how I feel about staying behind when my daughter's life is at stake, and you are choosing his bruised ego over me."

"James! Charlie is your brother. He's going to get better within a few weeks, probably enough to join us. You can meet up with us then. But you know him better than anyone, and you'll know when he's ready to come back. I don't trust Marek to make the same call."

"Then I guess you have it all figured out, just like always," he said bitterly and turned away from me. I put my hand on his shoulder.

"Please don't push me away. We are both going through this." My eyes welled up.

"I'm not the one pushing you away, Eden. I'm not the one leaving you behind." His voice turned cold.

I had been with James long enough to know when a conversation was over and when to give it space. So I turned and left to give him time to process. This was not what I wanted. I needed him to trust me and not see this as more than it was. It wasn't a choice between him and Marek. I wished both of them could go with me. Actually, if I had to choose I'd rather it be James. He made me stronger. But I knew Marek's abilities and his knowledge of Iskrem would be more important. Someone had to stay with Charlie, someone we trusted to know when he was ready to rejoin us. Or, was that just the excuse I was telling myself?

As I walked through the kitchen, toward my room to gather my things, Aunt Mae and Vera stopped me. They were chopping a mound of vegetables and fruits, and Vera hesitantly pulled out a chair for me to join them.

"What's wrong?" Aunt Mae's eyes never left the table.

"It's nothing—just my daughter missing, and my brother-in-law being almost speared to death. You know, the usual."

"No darling, it's more than that. I can see you are torn." Mae's light purple eyes rose from chopping and forced mine to look into hers.

"James is upset with me because I'm asking him to stay behind."

"Do you want him to stay here?" Vera asked.

"No, I don't. I think we should be together, but I'm scared."

"Of?" Vera raised her eyebrows.

"What do you mean? Look around us, Vera. Our family is falling apart. I have to keep James and JJ safe."

"I once thought making someone stay here was keeping them safe. I once thought I could control what happened to the people I loved. We both know what happened because of it," Vera said softly.

"You say it's about keeping James and JJ safe, but the truth is this is about you," Mae said as she looked to the painting hanging on the wall beside us. It was a picture my mother had painted of the two suns setting on the shallow sea horizon. "Do you remember the message Ava left you behind this one?"

I sighed. "Trust yourself."

Mae put her hand on my arm. "Don't just trust yourself but also the people around you. Trust your instincts. If you don't want to split up, then don't. You know better than to let fear drive your decisions. We've all learned that lesson the hard way. You heard Vera. I'll stay with Charlie, and I'll reach out to you when he is ready and not a moment before." She smiled. "Now go to your husband and say you were wrong."

A chuckle bubbled up in my throat. "This family and our pep talks, good heavens." I hugged both of my Aunts, knowing they were right and turned to find James.

"And Eden." I looked back to Mae. "No more doubting yourself. You will need each other to face what is to come."

I knew better than to ask what she had seen. I've seen enough to know that knowing the future isn't always easiest or best, so I simply nodded and turned to find my other half, who I needed now more than ever.

THE RENDEZVOUS.

Eden

I vaguely remembered Wanda warning me next time she wouldn't be so nice, but I had little patience for her this go around. James, Marek, and I stood in the cemetery of the Urnes Staves Church, the setting sun casting deep and dark shadows across the tombstones. The fjord below us glistened, tempting us towards it, and away from the tiny viking of a women yelling at us at the moment.

"You are telling me after centuries of peace, you three have managed to start a war within the worlds?" Her thick Norwegian accent harshened her words.

"Wanda." Marek attempted to charm her. "We didn't start it. Iskrem's Door Keeper did. You of all people know how dangerous the Dökkálfar are . . . "

"This coming from a *Caelun* who is friends with one." She huffed and crossed her arms.

"You listen here, woman. We don't have time for your asinine racist issues. Now are you going to let us through or what?" I towered over her, trying to restrain myself.

"Niflheim, no! I don't trust you. You'll just keep screwing everything up and making everything worse."

"Wanda, I don't think you understand. We are going through that door." James looked like a giant bear next to the petite Norwegian.

"Over my dead, cold, frozen body."

I narrowed my eyes and mumbled, "Don't tempt me."

"Ladies." Marek stepped between us and put his hands out. "I think I have an arrangement we can all agree on. Eden, may I have a word?"

"That's right, you back off, *Jentunge*," Wanda said smugly. "This is one world you *don't* rule."

"Oh. My. Gosh. I'm going to hit her. And what in the heck is a *Jentunge*?" My eyes cut to her as Marek dragged me outside. James grimaced, following behind us.

"It's slang and means 'little girl." Kinda funny all things considered. But seriously, why are you letting her get to you? I've never seen you like this."

"I don't know. She just drives me crazy." I tried to shake the frustration off me.

"Well, then you aren't going to like my idea." Marek scrunched his face.

"What?"

"We take her with us."

"Are you insane? That is the worst idea you've ever had."

"Look, she's not going to let us go through the door, and we can't hurt another Door Keeper. She has to willingly let us pass. She says she doesn't trust us, so I say we ask her to come. I think it's the only way she'll agree to let us through."

I looked to James to back me up, but I didn't like what I saw there. His eyes betrayed whose side he was on.

"Guys, I can't even have a conversation with her. How can I trust her with what's at stake? Plus, she's racist towards Hiems and apparently us."

"I'm not too worried about it. I'm human." James shrugged.

I sighed and cut my eyes at my husband.

Marek ignored us both.

"She's smart and strong as an ox, granted a tiny ox. She can handle the cold and snow. Plus, Gio has seen her fight, and apparently she's good with a blade. I think she could be helpful."

I blew out a long and steady stream of air, knowing this was the fastest way to the Tree of Light, and we couldn't afford to go back through Caelum at this point. Marek and James knew I was resigning and both moved towards the church's main door.

"Just let me handle the talking, okay? It's best you keep your 'little girl' mouth shut." Marek didn't even attempt to curb his amusement, and I punched him hard in the arm.

"Alright Wanda, we've discussed it, and we think you're right. We will just botch this up, which is why we need a seasoned Door Keeper who knows what she's doing. Would you be willing to help us?"

"Help you?" Wanda considered. "Go into that frozen tundra and help those leathery monsters?" She scrunched her face.

I rolled my eyes and took a deep breath.

"Mrs. Von Stron, there is more at stake than just my daughter's life. The Tree of Light is in danger, and I know you have to value that as Iskrem's Door Keeper," James spoke up.

"Of course I know about the Tree," she snapped. "It's fall would devastate all of the worlds, not just Iskrem." She looked towards the backside of the North Portal and continued, "I suppose I could have my brother lock the door behind us with that little contraption you have from Gio. If we go through the door to do this, we can't come back through. I won't risk the door's exposure to this war. It's my job to protect it."

"Of course, we understand and completely accept those terms," Marek said quickly.

"Okay," Wanda uncrossed her arms. "I'll go with you. But not to help you or your daughter, but to protect the Tree of Light. I've never trusted the Hiems."

This was going to be a long journey. By the time Wanda had packed her things and arranged for her brother to come take her place and lock the door permanently behind us, we entered Iskrem in the dark. The North Portal creaked and echoed through the halls of the cave as it shut behind us.

The four of us walked slowly in the frigid temperature for hours. At least this time, I was dressed and prepared for the weather. Fleece lined layers, wool socks with boots, and a weather resistant outer layer to protect from any moisture.

The snow fell down hard in sheets as we trudged north. Talking used too much energy in this weather, so we walked in silence. The warmth and energy of the Tree of Light tingled my skin before we could see it. Taran's antler vibrated with energy in my hand, the spearhead covered with a leather pouch.

James whispered behind me, *"I can feel it."*

Finally, the glow and flickering of the light became visible ahead, dancing on the snow. Illuminating the night with warmth, the Tree of Light shone bright in the dark of night. Wanda audibly gasped once it was within sight. We walked up, staring up at the thousands of flickering candlelights springing up from every branch. I moved toward four smaller trees around the larger in the distance, recognizing them. The Stags slowly rose, the snow falling off of their branches.

Xander emerged from the snow, camouflaged with his fur cloak. I made my way towards my friend, seeing the sorrow in his eyes. I realized he worried for Gabby as much as we did. All sense of propriety was gone as reached out his arms and embraced me. No bows, no formal greetings. For the first time since our first encounter, the stoic Hiem I'd met, melted away into a Caelun who stood before me. His eyes still held the silver that had increased around his pupils, his skin still held the tint of color he'd received from our two suns.

"We will find Gabby."

"I know." I smiled trying to ease his worry. "I know." I said again, this time trying to ease my own.

THE EXTINCT.

Eden

Teik was not with Xander and was quite literally on the other side of the world, scouting for news of Aslak. I missed my no nonsense friend and hoped to see him again. We sat under the Tree, soaking in its healing energy, which was welcomed after traipsing through the snow all night. After updating Xander on the details of Gabby's abduction, he regrettably told us he had heard nothing about Aslak having her. Gabby's presence in Iskrem would have definitely spread if he had her here.

"Well, we know she was here at some point. Charlie saw her go through the door," I said frustrated.

"I'm not sure what to say, Eden. There hasn't been a whisper of her here. If Aslak did pass her through Iskrem into another world, he would have done it quietly enough not to tip anyone off."

James stood, his arms crossed, looking as unsure as I felt. "It would make no sense for him to be quiet here. He has no idea you are working with us." He motioned to Xander. "And this is where he's making his stand. Iskrem is his domain, and he knows it. Why would he even feel the need to hide her?"

Marek spoke up, "Not to mention, his having her would just be leverage to get to you. So why hasn't he reached out to us?"

"Because he doesn't have her . . . " It dawned on me as the words left my mouth. "You haven't heard that Aslak has her because he doesn't, and we haven't heard of her being here, because she isn't."

"Who else would want her?"

"General Sapp. I don't know why, but for some reason he wants her to himself and doesn't want Aslak to know." It was the only thing I could figure based on what Charlie told us.

"He wants her for the same reason Aslak would, leverage." Wanda spoke for the first time since arriving at the tree. "If this Aslak character is half as sketchy as you make him out to be, then I would want some insurance he wouldn't double cross me. If the sloth doesn't trust him, having Gabby in his pocket is the perfect thing to use in case Aslak tries to betray him."

"In some weird way, it makes sense," Marek said.

I hated to admit it, but Wanda's theory felt plausible.

"Okay, let's play out this scenario. If Sapp has Gabby, and Aslak has no idea, and she definitely isn't here, then where is she?"

"Asylum." Xander said and looked up at us.

"Asylum isn't real, dökkálfar." Wanda glared at the future king of the Hiems.

"Wanda, my name is Xander, and yes, I assure you it is very real."

Marek whistled low. "Asylum is a dangerous place. Are you sure?"

"I know it's where Sapp would hide her because Aslak would never dare set foot there again."

"Why?" Marek asked.

"When my uncle was much younger and new to being a Door Keeper, he once crossed into the world, despite the rules and almost lost his life trying to return," Xander replied.

"What is Asylum, and why is it dangerous?" My heart drummed in my chest, not sure if I wanted to know the answer.

James looked at me and raised an eyebrow. "Name something that you think is extinct."

"That I *think* is extinct? Um, dinosaurs."

"Nope, they just migrated—to Asylum."

I looked around the circle unbelieving. "Are you guys serious?"

"Deadly." Xander eyed me. "Anything that you think is extinct, is not. Your world's Door Keeper just wanted you to think it was. Asylum is full of animals and plants that no longer could survive in their home worlds for whatever reason. Sometimes it was just endangered, sometimes it was just no longer compatible living conditions. Sometimes the animals themselves chose to migrate.

But that's not the hard part. Once you enter Asylum, you can never leave. That's the deal. The doors only unlock one way, allowing the world to remain secret." He glanced to Wanda as if her unawareness of the world confirmed what he was saying.

"So how do we leave once we find Gabby?" James looked to Xander.

"Well, Aslak made it back. Also, years ago when I was a just boy, Taran told me a story of once seeing a unicorn in Iskrem, so it must be possible to escape. We just need to make allies in Asylum who can point us in the right direction."

"A unicorn? Let me guess, they live in Asylum."

Xander nodded once as though we were talking about a completely regular animal.

Marek stood. "Okay, so which way should we enter Asylum? We've got a couple options—Earth, Caelum, Terra Arborum, or here."

"Hold on there, cowboy, we aren't going back to Earth, at least not through Iskrem's door. Off limits." Wanda grunted.

Xander intervened before we could argue.

"I think we should pass through this world. Our presence here will disrupt whatever Aslak is currently working on and when we pass through into Asylum, it should distract him enough to buy us some time. I assume it will also send Sapp into a fury knowing we are going for Gabby. It might drive a wedge between them which would work to our advantage."

"Okay, it's settled." I turned to the pouting Viking still sitting with her arms crossed. "Wanda, I know entering another world you assumed was mythical isn't what you signed up for, so if you want to go back, we will understand."

"No way, little lassie. You're not getting rid of me that easy."

"Wanda, is there any particular reason your using weird southern dialect when you insult us?"

Her mouth twitched, out of humor or annoyance, I couldn't tell. "I like watching American westerns. I watched them growing up with my brothers."

Marek laughed. "A viking cowboy, now that's a western I would actually watch."

"What is a cowboy?" Xander asked.

"Um, it's a man in America that herds cattle and drives them where they need to go. They usually ride horses and wear big hats." I tried to gesture the hat and suddenly felt ridiculous trying to explain this in another world to an otherworldly prince.

"So we will be like cowboys, except we will be moving Stags." He half smiled as dozens of huge, snow laden, Stags emerged slowly from the woods, apparently waiting there the entire time for Xander's signal.

"Yippee ki-yay," James whispered under his breath, so only I could hear.

"We will leave at first morning's light. Tonight, we sleep under the Tree's energy to fully recharge for our journey. The Stags will remain with us, so we can rest without worry," Xander said solemnly.

We all gathered, huddling at the tree's base, using its trunk to lean against. Even though snow covered every square inch, the tree's warmth counteracted the cold emanating from under us. As everyone began to doze off, a thought crept into my mind I couldn't shake.

"Xander," I whispered. "If Aslak knows about the door to Earth, why hasn't he attempted to breach it?"

Xander answered without opening his eyes. "It's too close to the Tree of Light. Aslak underestimated the Stags and their investment in the Tree. When he killed Taran, most of the Stags migrated here, ready to protect it. Aslak will not come here until he absolutely has to, but strategy and planning is his Door Keeper gifting. So, I assure you, he has a plan. I just hope we can stop him before he can implement it."

My mind rolled over Xander's words for the next hour. Planning and strategy was Aslak's gift. It made sense to me that he would attempt to win a war before it began by trying to kill me, it would have been the easiest way. I just wondered and worried what he would do once the war actually started. What were his plans now that his attempt on me failed?

Unlike my first night sleeping under the tree, tonight was full of dreams. It was almost as though it waited for me to learn the truth before it revealed itself to me in the way that it did. Intense didn't even begin to describe it.

As I dozed off, I found myself flying through a montage of pictures, flashing before me, fast and unfocused. Gabby curled up on a stone floor, covered in a blanket made of green moss. Xander clashing swords with Aslak. JJ laughing by the ocean. Me clutching Rosalina's hand and crying. Swimming underwater towards a red glowing light. Gabby staring back at me, tears streaming down her face.

I found myself standing at the bottom of a metal spiral staircase. It was dark wherever I was, and a few rays of light shone through small paneled windows. The glass seemed bubbled, so it distorted the outside, giving me no clue as to where I was. I slowly climbed each stair, sending an odd echoing noise through the tight space. Something in me knew I was looking for JJ. I called out his name but received no response. Slow dread rose in my gut, and I called for him again. His giggle rang out from the top of the staircase. Relief spread through me, interrupted by the frightened voice calling out behind me.

"Mom?"

As I opened my eyes, the glow of the illuminating tree above me eased all tensions remaining from the dream. Through the dancing flames and dark limbs, the sky turned a light gray, signaling dawn. Knowing we needed to get an early start, I woke everyone up to pack and get moving.

With the Stags protection, we easily made our way to a remote part of Iskrem, one that even Xander had only been to a handful of times. Even with hiding ourselves within the moving forest, our passage still made quite a stir among the world. Nothing like thirty moving trees to disrupt the day-to-day lives of the animals and inhabitants of Iskrem. We traveled nonstop for days, not wanting to waste any more time than necessary, and Stags switched out for each other to keep our protection strong and intact.

We finally made it to the frozen ocean, where glaciers melted and refroze, creating a slick and difficult passage to Asylum's door. Only five Stags accompanied us across the ocean, one for each of us. The others returned to their scouting duties. We moved slow and methodical, never staying in one place too long. Not knowing how thick the ice was beneath us, we didn't want to put ourselves in unnecessary danger. Once we got back onto solid land, we picked up speed and reached the isolated door within two hours.

I wasn't prepared for the door that towered before us.

THE ENTRANCE.

Eden

The colossal double gate arched almost twenty feet above us, constructed of thick glass and silver. Its maker made no attempt to hide or camouflage it within it's surroundings. Freestanding, attached to nothing, it stood on the edge of a cliff. If a traveler had happened by, it simply looked like it opened up into nothing, with the icy seas raging below. I guess the Door Maker thought it enough of a deterrent. Even knowing the truth, it frightened me enough to think twice.

I walked towards the door, running my fingers along the glass. It almost resembled ice chiseled with beautiful intricate engravings, but it was too warm to be ice. The glass had been etched with giant swirl patterns, each ending in a silver star about twelve inches in size. Even the three-dimensional stars were patterned with the same swirl cut outs. Every door I'd seen up until this point was breath taking in it's own way, but this was a masterful piece of art.

I noticed the odd-shaped keyhole, which was practically the size of my head. There was no way my key would open these doors. The lock would just swallow it. I startled when Xander swung his axe.

"I'm pretty sure that's not how it works, Hiem." Wanda's face scrunched in the wind.

"For a Door Keeper of thirty years, you sure do not know much about the worlds." Xander didn't even look back at her, focused on his task at hand.

James eyed his axe, and a smile lit up his face. "What a minute—is *that* the key?"

I followed his eye line and inspected the large double-sided axe, each blade curving outward back towards each other. The keyhole in the doors was almost the same size. This whole time, he'd been carrying the key to Asylum right under our noses. He slid the axe in vertically, and after hearing a click, he turned it clockwise, a series of creaks and noisy gears turning followed.

Xander slung the axe back over his shoulder and looked over at me, placing his hands on both the doors. "Are you ready to see what only a handful of humans have ever seen?"

"Have you ever seen it?" I asked hesitantly.

"No. But I am ready if you are."

"I'm ready." James grinned like a kid in a candy shop.

"I'm not." Wanda looked frightened for the first time since I'd met her.

"Well, I sure as hell am!" Marek set himself in a ready position.

"Alright, let's go."

Xander pushed with all of his might and the hinges screamed. The doors opened out over the frigid churning waters below, but everyone stood still, unwilling to move.

Bright blue sky with deep lush landscape sprawled in every direction. At least fifty miles from us a volcano spewed angrily in the distance. The wind blew in through the opening, the air hot and richly fragrant. Xander and Marek walked through first together, followed by Wanda.

James walked over, grabbed my hand and whispered, "In every world."

"In every world."

"Let's go get our daughter."

We walked through, the humidity hitting us like a wet blanket. After closing the door and hearing the locking mechanisms reengage, we instantly stripped off all our Iskrem attire, only stopping at the bare minimum. Sweat covered our skin before we had even stripped down. Around us, a tropical jungle landscape flourished with flat African looking plains that sat at the base of the volcano.

"I feel like we're in 'the land before time.'"

"Well, if legends are true . . . people groups of any world aren't allowed here. So it is the land before our time." He looked over and caught Wanda staring at his tattoos. Her cheeks instantly flushed pink.

"Don't you get any ideas, cowboy, I was just looking. I may be old, but I'm not dead."

"Shoot, Wanda." Marek grinned. "You've got less than a decade on me."

"Pokker," she swore in Norwegian. "Caeluns age well."

Chuckling under my breath, I faced the angry volcano. Ash filled the sky, and Mount Vesuvius floated into my mind. The familiar dread I'd felt that day visiting the entombed city so many years ago, crept back into my gut.

"Where do we even begin?" I was desperate for a plan.

Xander glanced up at me, folding his fur cape into his pack, already looking tired in the dense heat. The silver in his eyes shone bright against his black dilated pupils, and his face carried more stress than usual. "We start searching here, fanning out in all directions. I do not believe Sapp would attempt to enter this world, so he most likely has an ally here. Whoever that is, is most likely hiding her. We should try to gain the trust of this world's inhabitants to learn what we can."

"Why wouldn't he 'attempt to enter this world' exactly?" Wanda asked, mimicking Xander's formal accent.

"Well, besides the not being able to leave part, he knows what happens to outsiders." Xander eyed her.

"Dare I ask?" James looked to the Hiem.

"Probably best that you not." Marek answered, putting his hand on James' shoulder.

I breathed in the heavily humid air and threw my pack over my shoulder. "Let's go. I feel eyes on us, and I don't love the idea of being watched."

"I would get used to it." Xander walked next to me. "I doubt we will be alone from here on out."

THE FOREVER DREAM.

Gabby

It was as if all of the dreams I'd ever had were stuck on a loop. I couldn't see or experience anything other than things I already had, and it was incredibly frustrating. I attempted to think of something new, anything new. A new thought, a new experience, a new idea. Nothing. Nothing other than what I'd seen a hundred times already. It was as though my brain had disconnected from my mind, unable to be controlled by my own thoughts and instead held captive by someone else.

Mom being dragged behind that Palun in the snow. The panic on her face when she saw me. The picture shifting to the look in her eye, just a couple days ago, when she told me this wasn't goodbye.

The relief on Dad's face when I found him in the Palun jungle and told him Mom was alive and okay. The concern on his face when we parted ways in Caelum.

Uncle Marek's surprise when I appeared in front of him in Caelum. His crumpled body hitting the ground unconscious. My body shuddered in anger and fear.

Charlie laughing with his arm around me, making me feel safe and secure. Kicking him off his horse after he made fun of me. His face draining of color while bleeding out sprawled just a few feet from me.

An involuntary scream escaped from deep within me.

A cold, damp rag was placed on my head with a quiet singsong voice murmuring something unintelligible. My swollen eyes opened long enough to see a pile of messy, fire-red hair hanging over me with striking, green, oval eyes against a pink complexion.

I wanted to demand to know who she was, where I was, and how long I'd been here. But I lost my train of thought even before putting words to it. Before I even remembered how to speak, my mind had reverted back into the dreams.

JJ perched on the counter back home in our kitchen. It was always one of his favorite places to sit while Mom made his dinner. She pulled his handmade pizza out of the oven, and he thanked her. Always so polite and sweet.

"Thank you, Momma. You are the best ever!" He beamed.

Her shoulder length silver hair brushed her shoulders, and she laughed easily while slicing up the pieces. "How many pieces you want, buddy?"

"Three!"

"That's a lot of pizza." Mom smiled.

"This is fantastic! So delicious." JJ said with pizza sauce smeared all over his face.

I always loved how little it took to bring him joy. As if sensing my thoughts he added, "I'm so happy!"

Then his eyes darted to me and added, "I'm so happy like Gabby is Queen!"

My thoughts cleared for a millisecond, and I saw what he wanted me to see. The dream my mother had described in *The Door Keeper*. I stood before my family in a beautiful pink dress that hung off my shoulders, my hair falling long down my back. Wearing a rose gold crown of leaves, my face was bright and flushed. Mom had tears in her eyes looking at me, and JJ giggled, hanging on Charlie's back.

Something new. For the first time, I saw something new.

This vision, this dream—I'd never seen it before, but something told me I had wanted to so badly. Confused and unsure, I knew JJ had gotten through to me. My family knew I was alive and were coming to find me. If that scene was the future, then Charlie was alive. Everything was going to be okay. Before I could do, say, or even think anything else, I drifted back into the cycle.

Mom being dragged in the snow behind the giant sloths…

THE HEARTBREAK.

Eden

Finding an ally in this world proved difficult. The jungle was packed full of animals, the constant noises attested to that. However, none revealed themselves to us. Apparently their fear trumped their curiosity. Every time we heard a new animal, we would follow the sound to an open, empty clearing. We even tried talking into a few burrows we noticed, but no one wanted to help us. In all honesty, we weren't even sure animals could talk in this land. My hunch was no.

"If we don't have help, this is going to be harder than we thought," I spoke up.

Marek hollered over his shoulder, "I don't know. I thought it was going to be pretty hard."

"Look on the bright side, I'd rather be ignored than attacked." James pointed out from the back of the group.

Wanda stopped walking in front of me and dropped her bag. "We have been walking for hours. My knees need a break."

We found an open ledge that over looked the valley below and decided to stop to eat. We didn't want to risk a fire, so we simply ate some snacks from our packs. The menacing roar of prehistoric animals wasn't too far in the distance. There was something incredibly creepy about knowing you are the only humans anywhere in a world.

Other than our missing daughter.

I sat on the ledge looking out, getting lost in the lava flowing out of the volcano looming in front of me. I tried not to think about Gabby, but it was difficult. Attempting to focus on the landscape and scouting a plan for our next trek worked for a few minutes, until her face popped back into my head. James joined me.

"Do you still feel like we're being watched?" he asked.

"Definitely." I looked around. "What ever it is hasn't left us since we arrived."

He looked out over the horizon and said somewhat absentmindedly, "Thanks for changing your mind and letting me come with you."

"Who was I kidding? I need you by my side. I was stupid to think that I didn't."

"I don't think it was stupid. I just think you were scared. You know Eden, it's okay that you are. No one is above being afraid." He put his hand on my leg.

"I know," I said simply.

But at his touch, the realization that had been creeping in my mind for days, that I had been trying to suppress, surfaced unexpectedly, and I began to sob.

"What is it?"

"It's her birthday. Today is Gabby's eighteenth birthday," I cried. James wrapped his long arms around me and held me while my body shook violently.

"I'm sorry. I know. I wasn't going to say anything."

"I just can't believe *this* is where we are," I choked out. "That this will forever be her eighteenth birthday. You know what it meant to her. What it was supposed to mean to me, to us. And she's completely alone."

Thankfully, James just let me cry and express the complete range of emotion coursing through me, allowing me to say everything I needed to. "This was not the way it should have been. We were supposed to have her favorite chocolate chip pancakes for breakfast, take her shopping, and then go to the cabin. I should be giving her the book and answering her questions. We were supposed to make memories we would talk about for the rest of our lives. It was supposed to be a montage of laughter, tears, baking, and swimming in the lake. Instead we're getting kidnapped, wounded, and fighting for our freaking lives," I practically yelled.

"Nothing about the past month has played out like we hoped it would," James said.

"Yeah, and it sucks!" I sobbed. "We're her parents, we're supposed to protect her, keep her safe until she became an adult."

"Eden, she became an adult the second she learned the truth." He tucked my hair behind my ear. "And she has been one ever since."

"It happened too fast." I wiped the snot off my face with my tank top.

"Yes, it did," he sighed.

My brother sat down on the other side of me.

"Who knows, maybe we will find her and bust her out today. At least that would make her eighteenth birthday pretty epic." I couldn't see his face, but I knew he was grinning. My sob hiccuped into a laugh that was muffled by James' chest.

"I promise you Eden, we will celebrate Gabrielle's birth when we take her back to your homeland," Xander said standing behind us.

Wanda must have been standing next to him because she scoffed, "My eighteenth birthday was one of the worst days of my life, and I turned out okay."

"Um, Wanda, you're definitely not helping," Marek retorted.

Without warning, ear-piercing shrieks rang above us. Startled, I looked up just in time to see two giant pterodactyls swoop down towards us. Time seemed to move in slow motion as Xander pulled his axe from his back and tried to push Wanda out of the way with his other hand. But it was too late. We watched in horror as their talons grabbed Xander and Wanda. As they flew off the ledge, almost knocking us off, all we could see was their flailing arms and legs in the dinosaur's grasp. The Hiem's axe fell from his hand and dropped into the valley below.

Paralyzed and unable to comprehend what had just transpired, we stared at the two giant birds fading into the sky above.

"Damn," Marek moaned. "Just when that old viking was beginning to grow on me."

THE FLYING RESCUE.

Eden

My mind raced with ways to save our friends, all of them required flying, obviously one skill I'd yet to master. "What are we supposed to do?" I panicked.

A long loud whistle, followed by three short staccato bursts echoed through the trees and bounced off the hill above us. We looked around, unable to see the culprit or where it originated. Wanda and Xander were barely in view anymore, the dinosaurs only specks flying in the clouds. The sound reserved for when Strix approached, the steady swooshing of wind, filled my ears. My eyes grew twice their normal size when witnessing the animal that made the sounds. Marek followed my gaze, his own surprise mirroring mine.

"Whoa."

Three horses, with wingspans of at least twenty feet swooped down and landed next to us on the ledge, folding their wings and bowing their heads. All three were probably white at one time but their wings and lower halves were stained brown with mud. Without waiting for a formal invitation, we grabbed our weapons and jumped on their backs. They galloped and jumped off the cliff one at a time, swooping straight down then bolted up into the clouds.

The wind felt incredible after the hours of intense humidity, and I said a silent thanks to Strix for helping me feel so comfortable flying on the back of a large animal. Although, with the Pegusus' wingspan, it flew immensely faster than Strix. I held onto to its mane tightly with one hand and readied my spear in the other. Marek and James flanked me on either side. Marek yelled over the wind, "Eden, get in front and distract those blasted things. James, go for Xander. I'll get Wanda!"

Like I knew how to control a flying horse.

Feeling stupid, but not knowing what else to do, I told the Pegasus that we needed to fly in front of the pterodactyls. The horse seemed to ignore me, but then we shot up even higher in the cloud and picked up speed. Within a few minutes, I looked down and spotted the two flying dinosaurs soaring below us. I rubbed the horse's neck, *good job Peggy*. I pointed down at my friends, and we descended.

Behind us James and Marek approached the pterodactyls from below. The flying dinosaurs finally sensed our presence and squawked. It's horrible screeching almost busted my eardrum. I cut down in front of them, sending one of the birds spiraling out of control. It was the pterodactyl carrying Xander, and he took the opportunity to stab the giant dinosaurs leg with a knife he had strapped around his ankle. The bird opened his grip, dropping Xander into the clouds beneath him. My stomach filled with dread as he disappeared out of sight. I screamed his name as James raced down after him, but I couldn't see anything through the dense cumulous coverage.

Not paying attention to what was happening around me, the impact of a pterodactyl's wing snapped me back to my own perilous situation. Peggy neighed, as she turned vertical, kicking the giant bird in the face, while I hung on for dear life. Wanda's body hung lifeless, tight in its grip, just a few feet away from me. I prayed she had simply passed out. Peggy recovered from the bird's attack, and we righted ourselves. The bird flew off again. Marek got my attention and mimed throwing the spear then catching something.

At that very moment, James re-emerged from the cloud with Xander sitting behind him on his horse's back. Relief flooded me as we chased after the other dinosaur. I knew I had to be close to hit the flying target, and not my friend dangling underneath. The pterodactyl took a hard nosedive, and I almost fell off my horse as she followed suit, but thankfully her giant wing kept me from plunging to my death.

Coming out from under the cloud, the prehistoric bird was nowhere in sight. We sat, flying idly for half a minute when a paralyzing scream ripped through the sky. It grew closer and closer as her body fell down straight past me toward the ground. Peggy didn't wait for me to react as she folded up her wings and hurled us toward the ground right above Wanda. Her face was filled with pure terror, and she stretched a hand towards me as I reached out my own to grab her. Not quite close enough, we were running out of time.

Taran's face flashed in my mind and the safety his antler trees had provided while in Iskrem. Even now, Taran could help me. I extended the spear, and it was just long enough for Wanda to grab. I yanked her to me, and Peggy whipped out her wings, slamming both Wanda and me into her back. Peggy swooped up, barely missing the tree line. Both of us gasped and struggled to catch our breaths.

"Søren, Eden." She gulped. "Cutting it a little close there."

I attempted to catch my breath, "You just called me Eden. No insult?"

"I'm sorry. My life flashed before my eyes. I'm a little off my game." She turned her face up to mine. "I know I can be a bitch sometimes."

"I'm just glad you and Xander are okay," I said.

"Thank you. I've been a Door Keeper for a long time, but I've never almost died."

"Wanda, hang around with us for much longer, and you'll get used to it."

THE NEXT INCIDENT.

Eden

"Geez, that was too close." Marek hopped off his horse back on the ledge. As soon as we were all safe and back on the ground, the horses flew off. We didn't even have the time to thank them.

"Where did they come from?" James watched as they disappeared.

"Who knows? I'm really glad they showed up though." I sighed. "What happened up there? Wanda, why did you fall?"

"Cowboy over here decided it was a good time to try to ride a pterodactyl." Wanda thumbed towards my brother.

"I saw an opportunity, and I took it." He shrugged.

"You jumped on it?"

"I thought it would be my only chance to ride a pre-historic animal, and I didn't want to miss out."

"Thank you." Xander bowed his head. "That was the least pleasant thing that has happened to me, perhaps ever."

Smiling, and shaking my head, I reached down and grabbed my pack. "Let's get going. That whole episode freaked me out. I think it would be best if we found some cover."

It took us the better part of an hour before we hit the valley floor. Even with the cover it provided under the trees, I didn't feel comfortable being in the lowest point of the valley. We needed to search everywhere though, and I wanted to get this area over with as soon as possible. I felt like a sitting duck.

The ground underneath us was spongy and soft, and was unstable putting us on edge. I think after what we had already been through, we wanted our feet on solid ground. Trees towered above us in all directions, with oversized trunks wrapped in thick tangled vines, the size of my arm.

The constant onslaught of animal sounds didn't help our nerves, and combining it with the unsteady ground and limited sunlight through the tree cover, we finally gave up and decided to head back up the mountain to reevaluate. The eerie feeling of being watched stayed with me, except now it felt like everything watched as we moved.

As though even the trees had eyes—

We walked in a straight line towards the cliff face, ducking and dodging limbs, vines, and fallen logs. I couldn't help but think about the Palun Tango that James and I had perfected so many years ago.

"You know what this reminds me of?" James laughed.

"Yes, I was just thinking the same thing." I smiled.

"Of course you . . . " before he could finish, he fell flat on his face in front of me. I had never seen him fall so hard or abruptly before.

"Geez, hon. Are you okay?" I reached down to help him up.

"Yeah, that was weird." He looked down at the large vine lying across our path. "Guess I didn't see that."

Those ahead of us kept walking and out of nowhere my brother cursed, falling on the ground face up.

"What the—?" he cried. A vine had clotheslined him, knocking him off his feet.

"This isn't a coincidence!" I pulled out my knife instead of my spear.

Everyone drew his or her weapons, and all hell broke loose. Before I knew what happened, I was flat on my back staring into the tree canopy above. A vine flew across my line of vision, and Wanda was knocked on her butt. Xander yelled and then got cut off. I heard him struggling, and I tried crawling towards him. Something grabbed my leg and pulled me backwards away from the group. I called out, and James jumped next to me gripping my hand, trying to pull me back.

"It's the vines! They're alive!" He struggled to free me.

"Of course they are," I growled.

This place was the worst.

He pulled out his machete and cut the oversized vine that had grabbed my leg. We jumped up just in time to see Xander being choked, Wanda tied to a tree, and Marek hanging upside down with his legs tied together. James and I lunged toward them to help when two vines wrapped around both of my arms squeezing until I dropped my knife, pulling me upward into the trees. James hollered, then was suddenly silent. I struggled to look down and panic raced through me when my eyes found him completely covered in vines, only a part of his torso still visible.

This was it. Everyone was incapacitated, and we had no way to free ourselves. Gabby was here somewhere. I was so close and realized I was never going to see her again. We were going to die in this crazy God-forsaken world.

"Gabby, I'm sorry," I whimpered. I had lost feeling in my hands, and the numbing sensation spread up my arms. Tears stung my eyes as I whispered the poem we said every night as a family. I pictured my two children piled in my lap as I gently stroked their backs.

Then, out of nowhere, a strong breeze tore through the tree tops, and a faint whisper carried in the wind. It grew louder and then softer as the grip on my arms loosened. As I dropped slowly to the ground, the soft words left tickles in my ears. Everyone had been freed. The vines had dropped to the ground and around the trees where they had been originally.

Everyone was too stunned to say anything for a few minutes, trying to regain their breath and composure. Finally, James spoke up first.

"Did you guys hear that voice?"

We all nodded.

"Super creepy. It sounded like what ever it was was right next to my ear," Marek added.

"I think it was in the wind, but I don't know." I still felt very uneasy.

"Whatever it was bought us some time, but I don't think we should tempt fate. We need to find a safe place to stay the night. I think we should rest before we continue our search," Xander said.

"I saw a cave back on the cliff's ledge earlier. That should be a good option." I gathered our gear off the ground.

"Let's just hope some giant, prehistoric, lion-bear combo doesn't already live there." Wanda huffed.

"At this rate, nothing would surprise me," I said without an ounce of humor.

THE LAND BEFORE TIME.

Eden

We had been in Asylum for almost five full days, with no leads about where Gabby was being held but no more life or death incidents either. Having scoured every square inch around the door leading to Iskrem, we made our way outwards slowly, now finding ourselves on the other side of the massive volcano.

I'd been in constant communication with Mae back home to check in on JJ and Charlie's recovery process. He got stronger everyday. Shay and Wynn's medicinal work was apparently working miracles. He had left yesterday to join us, meeting us closer to the door leading from Terra Arborum. Strix picked him up from Caelum's door and crossed the Land of the Trees to get him to us quicker. We decided to camp out here to wait for him to arrive within the next twenty-four hours. Our constant search left us drained and tired, so we took the opportunity to eat, rest, and revive our energy. We found a large river that ran along the border of the jungle, a long stretch of desert plains on the other side. We made a base camp best we could out of what we had. Cooling off and bathing in the river for the first time since our arrival here, did wonders for our spirits. Even Wanda was more agreeable.

Cooking some fish we caught in the river, we ate only what we had to in order to survive, realizing that every animal here was endangered in some way or at least extinct in some other world. I spent time journaling everything that we had been through, determined not to forget any of it to tell Gabby. If she couldn't actually be with us, I wanted her to at least feel like she was in spirit.

Marek had brought a deck of cards, so the guys were teaching Xander different card games. Wanda mostly kept to herself, despite her occasional grumblings of being *the odd viking out*. I reclined on the riverbank and watched the giant dinosaurs roam the flatlands sprawled out before us, none of them giving us the time of day. Every one that we came across were herbivores, eating the leafy greens perched at the tops of the few trees scattered around the open plains.

Even with the warnings from Xander, I found every animal we came across as a surprise. I tried to remember all of them to write in my journal, some of which I even attempted to draw so Gabby could visualize them. A couple days ago I'd seen a black lion, his long, black mane and fur shone under the sun on the boulder he sunbathed on. His bright yellow eyes looked solemn as he eyed me carefully retreating in fear.

Thankfully, ever since the vine incident, no animals or plants had made any attempt to harm us. At one point, we passed a flock of irritable dodo birds over three feet tall. Marek made a joke that Wanda should join them, being their same size and temperament. Wanda retorted that maybe he should join them, him having the same IQ and all.

I was in the middle of sketching out the huge hammerhead salamander I'd watched skirt along the river's floor earlier that morning when a noise startled me. I followed the sound to a little creature hovering on a tree branch. It was a tiny green being, flittering and glowing, and watching me intensely.

It was completely transparent, but had a greenish glow. Its head was shaped like a teardrop, with eyes that matched. It's tiny body was delicate and thin resembling plant limbs, with rounded ears coming to a point at the top. It turned its head from side to side as if sizing me up. It's mouth opened and closed but nothing but occasional water dripping sound emerged.

Wanda arrived next to me, her surprised expressed with an audible intake of breath.

"Now, I've seen everything. It's some sort of water fairy—perhaps a sprite."

"I thought we had both learned by now, Wanda, that we are never going to get to a place where we have 'seen everything.' Not in Asylum at least.'"

At that moment, hundreds of little sprites landed on the branch and surrounding branches around us. Both Wanda and I remained completely still. Green transparent light cast an eerie but beautiful glow on every surface. It was one of the most amazing things I'd ever witnessed. They all looked expectantly at us as though we would provide them with something. As soon as it became apparent that we weren't, they flew and fell into the river below us, sounding like rain falling on the water's surface.

Wanda and I turned to each other with wide eyes and laughed.

"Now, that was something," she exclaimed and sat next to me.

"Yes it was."

The older woman had her freshly washed hair braided and wrapped around her head. Wanda's face was bright, and she looked happier than I'd ever seen her.

"Thank you for coming with us. I know we haven't always seen eye to eye."

"I can't complain. Even with what I do, or have done, over my lifetime and everything I've been through with both of my husbands, none of it has compared to this." Her voice became less harsh. "I almost feel sad about it. It feels like this was the life I was supposed to be living all along. Not just guarding the door, but being part of the worlds I was born to protect." She looked down and fiddled with her fingernails. "I know it probably sounds crazy coming from an old woman like me."

"It doesn't," I assured her. "Trust me, you're not the first Door Keeper to feel that way."

"I heard about your mother." Wanda looked up at me. "After you came through the door with the Hiem, I called Gio, and he told me your family's story. I'm sorry for everything you've been through, and I'm sorry for being so harsh to you. I think you just reminded me of the life that I did not have—the life I can no longer have.

I never got to have children. Both of my husbands chased the ocean like mistresses which left me alone most of my life. Besides the title of Door Keeper, I never really had an adventure of my own. And here you come along with a family, a husband that crosses worlds for you, all the while on a grand adventure. You just represented the things I've always wanted and never had."

She sat silently staring at her hands. I rolled her words around in my mind, seeing myself through her eyes and realized how much I'd misjudged her. I put my hand on hers. "We all have our junk—the pain and the sorrows that mold us into who we are. I think the point is to embrace them, not to fight against them or allow them to make us bitter. I'm sorry I was so quick to judge you. I should have seen past the facade of the tough old viking." Her usual frown lines smoothed, revealing the first true smile I'd seen from her.

"No apologies necessary, *Jentunge*. I deserved it. Plus, this has absolutely been the most fun I've ever had, even the almost dying twice part. Also, I've really enjoyed staring at your brother. He is just delicious." She winked at me, and we both laughed.

"Wanda, can I ask you a personal question?"

"Sure."

"What is your Door Keeper gift?"

A shadow crossed behind her eyes. She was slow to answer.

"My gift is complicated. Sometimes it's a gift, and sometimes it feels like a curse." She sighed. "My Door Keeper gift is endurance. I can endure practically anything, physical pain—or grief. It has allowed me to survive some difficult situations. And definitely comes in handy during fights."

I looked at Wanda unbelieving. "If you can endure anything, then why do you complain so much?"

"It makes me feel normal. And in truth, even though I *can* endure it all, doesn't mean I want to. I'm afraid I've allowed it to turn me a bit sour."

I contemplated what she said. "You know, I was a widow. Gabby's father died when she was three. It's tough, having a partner and then losing them. You've been widowed twice. I can't imagine that pain. Then to have grown up with six older brothers, which must have made for a crazy childhood. You've survived two attempts on your life here alone. It seems like a pretty awesome gift to me. And with a gift like that, you can have whatever life you want from here on out. If you wanted adventure of your own, here you are, right smack in the middle of one. Just don't give up hope that you can have the life you've always dreamed of. Trust me, I know. Dreaming is *my* gift."

"You really like giving pep talks, don't you?"

"I'm afraid so. It's a family thing. Besides my dream gift, I inherited my mother's desire to want to bring people joy. Is it working?"

"Well, I wouldn't go that far. I'm not sure I've felt *joyful* in decades." She smirked.

"Challenge accepted."

After everything we had been through so far in Asylum, who would have thought making nice with Wanda would have been the thing to surprise me the most.

THE BROTHER RETURNS.

Eden

That night, we built a fire so Charlie could find us easier. It was growing colder in the evenings. The stars filled the sky like glowing orbs, bright and flickering and lit our camp enough even without the fire. The stars were the one thing I counted on to fill me with peace every night and was the only comfort that existed in this world.

We sat silently around the fire, watching it dance and crackle when an odd, out of place noise rose in the distance. Stamping and huffing approached rapidly from the other side of the river. Everyone stood in anticipation, alert to attack whatever approached, when Charlie busted through the brush screaming as soon as he saw us. He kept running until he fell straight into the river, flailing in the water, attempting to reach our camp on the other side of the bank. Right after he tore through the brush, a baby raptor gracefully leapt through the hole he made in the bushes and stopped cold when it noticed us. It stared for just a second then turned and went back the way it came.

The look on Charlie's face was priceless.

James laughed and jumped in after him, accidentally crushing him with his hug.

"Whoa, bro. Watch my ribs!" Charlie was still trying to catch his breath.

"You made it!"

"Barely! Did you see that thing? It's been chasing me for almost a mile!"

I chuckled thinking about the huge pterodactyls that had threatened us when we first arrived. The baby raptor would have been eaten alive by those things. Letting Charlie have his moment, I helped pull him up to get dried off by the fire. He showed us his wounds, no one imagining it could have possibly happened over just a week ago.

"Any leads?" he asked expectantly. "When I left Mae, she told me you had nada."

"Still nothing." I sighed.

"Don't worry. I'm here now, and we all know I'm the most talented of the group." He smiled. I sure had missed Charlie's sense of humor.

"I don't know, that tiny little raptor sure had you on the ropes." James teased.

"Tiny? Did you see the teeth on that thing?"

We decided it was time to tell him our stories of peril, so over the fire, we retold our heroic tales as dramatically as possible. Which of course elicited some eye rolls and sarcastic comments from Wanda. Even though, I now knew she secretly loved every minute of it.

"So, why do you think everything stopped attacking you?" Charlie asked with a furrowed brow, looking even more like his older brother.

"We do not know," Xander said plainly. "But we are grateful."

"Yes, but it's not helping our search," Marek added. "While nothing is trying to kill us, nothing is helping either."

"Have you tried asking anyone or anything?"

"Oh, like you tried asking that raptor?" Wanda retorted.

"And who are you again?" Charlie snapped.

Realizing we never formally introduced them, I did so.

"Don't worry, she grows on you eventually," I whispered to him as Charlie and I walked off to talk alone.

"I doubt it." He looked back at her. "She's got terrible RBF."

"What?"

"Resting bitch face," he said simply.

"Charlie!" I smacked him on the arm.

"What? It's a thing! Don't be mad at me. I didn't make it up."

I sighed and sat on a log, gesturing him to sit with me. "So what's going on back in Caelum? How was JJ when you left?"

"He's doing amazing, Eden. Don't you even worry about him. Without his usual tech to fall back on, he's riding horses, playing in the orchards, and his vocabulary is expanding every day. Samuel is loving spending time with him." Charlie's enthusiasm was contagious. "Seriously, Caelum seems to suit him. It suited me. I hated to leave."

"And you are feeling okay? Your injuries are well enough for you to be here?" I pushed.

"Yes, momma bear. I got a clean bill of health. But even if I hadn't, you know I had to be here." His eyes turned harder.

"I know."

"We've got to find her. I can't imagine how scared she is." Charlie's head fell into his hands.

"I know she's okay," I whispered. "She knows we are looking for her, and trust me, that's enough to keep your spirits alive, even when you're alone."

"You would know." He looked back up to me. "What do we do now? Everyday that passes I get more worried."

"We all do. Now that we are back together, tomorrow we will push the envelope a bit. There are six of us now, and here, there is safety in numbers."

Just as the words left my mouth, a giant mammoth crossed our line of vision on the plains that stretched before us. Charlie whistled under his breath.

"Yeah, not sure any number of us would be safe against crap like that."

THE PIVOTAL MOMENT.

Gabby

My eyes throbbed and only opened slightly from the swelling. Hair was smashed against my face as I spit out pieces stuck to my cracked lips. My mouth was dry, and my entire body felt like a desert. The desire for water coursed through me. As if sensing my thoughts, her warm hand cupped my cheek, turning it upwards. Cool liquid spilled over my mouth as I greedily drank. Oh heavens, so much better.

The same hand lifted and moved behind my back attempting to move me into a sitting position. The slits of vision only allowed a blurry peek at my captor. The same messy fire red hair against the pinkish complexion. Her presence was calm and reassuring. She lowered herself onto my level, her eyes inches from mine, the deep green ovals filling my gaze.

"Everything will be okay." She whispered in my head. Her lips never moved, but she talked to me all the same. *"I do not want to hurt you. However, I have no choice but to keep you here until that dreadful thing returns."*

Her overtly sweet demeanor did nothing to ease my fear. She held me here for Sapp, and nothing she said was going to convince me I wasn't going to be harmed. Maybe not today, or by her, but I knew enough to know it was coming if she waited for him to return.

Within a few minutes, my eyes adjusted. Still swollen, I couldn't open them completely. The coolness of the cavern enveloped me, the stonewalls holding me hostage. The woman wore little to no clothes, so I assumed we weren't in Iskrem. Her hair was piled on her head and down her back with twigs and leaves sticking throughout, her chest wrapped in a thin bark. Oversized leaves wrapped her lower half and legs.

Realizing I had enough brainpower to take in my surroundings, I tried to reach out to my mom, only for a fuzz to envelope my mind. I still couldn't dream.

"Where are we?" My voice strained, having not been used in—I didn't know how long.

"You are safe for now." She answered in my head, her back to me as she fiddled with cups and pots.

"Then why are you drugging me?"

"I was instructed to. I do not wish to harm you."

"But obviously someone does," I countered.

"Yes, I am afraid someone does. But you should not worry about that right now."

"Easy for you to say, you're not tied up and being held against your will."

She turned and faced me, her eyes heavy despite their large size, her thin lips taut.

"I may not physically be bound, but understand I have no choice. We protect those we love. I know you must appreciate that, knowing where you come from."

"Let me help you. My family and I can help you if you let us."

She moved toward me, but the movement was foreign, fluid, as though she grew in front of me rather than moved. Kneeling, her long fingers removed the hair stuck to my face.

"I am afraid a deal has already been made. I am sorry I did not meet you first, Gabrielle. I feel it would have been better for everyone if we had."

I involuntarily shuddered under her words, they felt ominous and dangerous. What deal had she struck, and what would result from it? I had to find a way to get out of here. I couldn't wait for my parents and uncles to find me.

She went back to working on whatever she was doing before, allowing me a moment to myself. I examined the small space, trying to find a way to escape. I sat on a pile of soft moss in the form of a cot, nothing useful. A small circle of light shone on the floor, and I finally noticed the hole in the ceiling of the cavern where the light came from. So far, it seemed the only entrance and exit from the ominous room.

After a few minutes, I noticed a depression in one of the walls across from me. I couldn't tell if it was a hole in the wall of the cavern or just a crevasse that went nowhere.

"May I stand up and stretch my legs for a moment?"

"*Please, feel free.*" She answered without turning around. If I hadn't felt so bad, I would have laughed at the irony. I tried standing, rather slowly, my legs buckling under the weight they hadn't carried in a while. But eventually, I stood and moved around the cave. Not wanting to draw attention to what I'd noticed on the far wall, I simply walked into the light and let it shine on my face. It was enough to lift my spirits ever so slightly. Mom used to always say that if I wanted to be in a better mood, go outside and sit in the sun. Her advice worked today.

I wobbled slowly over to the apparent hole in the wall, only about a foot and a half wide and about six feet high, just big enough for me to scoot through. But why wouldn't she have blocked it? Of course it was a dead end. It seemed even silly to imagine it went anywhere. But, perhaps she just didn't think I had the guts . . .

Not knowing how long I had until this woman knocked me back out, and needing to take full advantage of the moment being awake and standing, I went for it. What was the worse that could happen, getting caught and drugged again? It was now or never.

I made a break for it.

"*NO!*" She yelled in my head. "*Stop!*"

No way, crazy leaf lady.

I ran sideways in the pitch black for about six seconds until I fell. The water surrounding every inch of me was warm. I kicked upward, hands still tied behind my back, and couldn't find the hole I'd fallen in. My lungs burned, my head swam, and fear enveloped every fiber of me. What had I done? I was about to drown.

"*Calm down and stop struggling. I cannot find you if you keep moving. Stay still.*"

She was trying to find me. She would save me, only to hand me over to Sapp. I was dead either way.

JJ's sweet face flashed in my head.

My parents hugging me when I left for my first day of high school.

Charlie and Marek riding next to me on horseback in Caelum.

They faded as my consciousness swam into nothingness, just as black as the water around me.

THE BREAK.

Eden

"So much for safety in numbers!" Charlie yelled over his shoulder as he bolted ahead of us.

"Run, you idiot!" James growled at his brother while running next to me.

"I hate this place!" Wanda called out somewhere from behind us.

We ran for our lives.

The heavy rain didn't help, nor did the zero visibility. We aimed for the tree line up ahead, praying the saber tooth tigers wouldn't reach us before we hit it. Xander and Charlie hit the trees before the rest of us and vanished out of sight. Maybe we had a chance. I didn't have time to ponder it, because as soon as James and I hit the trees, we discovered why they disappeared. The trees marked the beginning of a steep downward slope and a river of mud that took the footing out from beneath us.

Downward we slid, unable to stop or control our decent in any way. We quite literally had to go with the flow. James grunted next to me as random bushes slapped against us, attempting to slow us down but to no avail. We finally landed in a lake of mud at the base of the hillside. Both Charlie and Xander wrestled the deep sludge to reach an edge without sinking too deep. Xander reached a tree branch first and helped the rest of us to safety.

Wanda and Marek landed not long after us, one groaning and the other grinning.

"I guess the tigers had enough sense not to follow us." Marek smiled, his white teeth shining bright against the mud that caked his face.

It was hard to hear anyone or anything over the pounding rain, so we made our way to some natural shelter. Thankfully, we found a large canopy tree next to the clean river. There we stripped down in silence as we cleaned as much of our clothes and belongings as we could of the red colored mud.

Finally, it was James that broke the silence.

"This is getting really old. Constantly running for our lives and not getting any closer to finding Gabby." He said, not bothering to hide his annoyance.

"This is the exact reason humans and people groups from other worlds do not come here," Xander replied.

"Yeah, Xander, picking up on that." James retorted.

"I am sorry James, I am just explaining . . ."

"Well man, I'm just not in the mood for your obvious, matter-of-fact observations anymore."

"James." I reached my hand out.

"No, Eden. I'm starting to lose it. We're in this ridiculous world, looking for our daughter, having no idea if she is even still here."

"Don't you tell me I'm going through all of this for nothing," Wanda added unhelpfully.

"Oh, cause how dare you actually do something for someone other than yourself." Charlie rose up, visibly upset. "You stay out of this. This has nothing to do with you."

"Nothing to do with me? You dragged my ass here!" Wanda rose, a vein already popping out in her forehead.

"If it were up to me, they would have left your ass freezing in Iskrem!" Charlie yelled.

"Wanda—Charlie!" I stood up, attempting to settle them down.

"No, she's been griping and complaining since I've been here, and I've only been here a couple of days!"

"Charlie relax. She's not that bad." Marek eyed him.

"Oh easy for you to say. She's nice to *you*." James plopped down, looking defeated.

"I'm sitting right here, *Drittunge*." Wanda snorted.

"I have never wanted to hit a woman more in my life," Charlie said rubbing his temples.

"Guys." I tried to get a grasp on the situation before it was too late.

"Come on, man. Give it a rest." Marek finally stood looking at Charlie angrily.

"Guys!" I tried again.

"Are you seriously defending her?" Charlie bowed up to Marek.

"Are you seriously not gonna back down?" Marek inched closer to Charlie.

"*Guys*!"

Everyone stopped and looked at me. Finally they heard it too, trees falling in the distance. We reached for our respective packs when the ground started shaking. Suddenly about half a dozen trees exploded and fell as a giant elephant tore through the jungle heading right towards us. Charlie was in it's path, and no one could reach him in time. Before the scream even left my mouth, the elephant halted suddenly just as Charlie tripped over a log, and the giant tusked beast almost crushed him.

Everyone saw her at the same time—a crazy nymph looking woman—the very one I assumed JJ had shown Charlie in the vision before we left Caelum. She slid off the elephant's back, her bare feet not making a noise on the ground. Charlie jumped up fast and stared in amazement as she walked towards me. No one said a word, all transfixed on the first human-type person we'd seen since arriving here. However, there was something very unhuman about the way she moved.

She walked straight up to me without a word, stopping only a foot from me. Her large emerald eyes bore into mine, and her thin lips didn't move despite me hearing her words.

"I have been watching you since you arrived. I know who you are and where you are from and that you are looking for someone. But why do you believe she is here, in Asylum?"

"My daughter, Gabby. We believe she was brought here and is being kept by our enemies," I answered.

"You are the first celestials to cross into this land for centuries." Her bright red, twig-laden hair caught the wind and blew behind her.

"With all due respect—" Xander bowed towards the nymph. "You are mistaken. I know for a fact one of my kinsmen entered Asylum several years ago."

So she was speaking to everyone in their heads.

"A Hiem, here? That seems most impossible."

"More impossible than all of us standing before you?" I asked carefully.

"True. I have never witnessed different worlds cooperating in the way you are. You intrigue me. I have inhabited many different lifetimes in many different worlds, and this is the first time I've seen celestials working together."

"We are looking for my daughter. She was taken from us and brought here through the Door from Iskrem," I tried again. "Can you help us?"

"I am afraid I know nothing of this."

"Do you know someone who might?" Charlie walked up slowly, still eyeing her, enamored.

She looked down, looking unsure and adjusted the thin bark wrapped around her chest absentmindedly. *"I might know of someone who could help."*

"Thank you," James broke in, sounding upbeat for the first time in days.

"We will need to find you animals to ride. We have quite a journey." And with that she whistled, summoning the three pegasus that helped us before and two of the very saber tooth tigers that had chased us here. They bowed low to the nymph and walked toward their riders. So she had been the one to help us before.

"What is your name?" Charlie breathed.

"My name is Nanik, and you are riding with me." She pointed her long slender finger towards Charlie and walked back toward the mammoth. His knees wobbled as he followed helplessly behind her.

THE WOOD NYMPH.

Eden

For the first time since we'd been in Asylum, I dreamt of Gabby.

The dream began with us walking up a small contained spiral staircase. Feelings of expectation and nerves jumbled in my stomach. The same feelings were radiating off of Gabby behind me. We looked for something, or someone. I wondered were JJ was. Once we reached the top of the staircase, my surroundings shifted, and Gabby stood on the edge of the cliff, adorned in beautiful Caelun garb. I was behind her, the suns setting over the shallow sea horizon. Walking next to her, I recognized the same watercolor stationary with yellow flowers in her hands. They trembled as she read the letter. Still unable to read the words, I looked up at her face, stained with tears.

"Why, Mom?" She clutched the letter to her chest.

What had I done?

Suddenly, we fell into the deep dark water, able to see nothing, yet feeling her presence next to me. She was terrified. She was running from someone, fearing for her life. I couldn't help her, no matter how hard I tried. I couldn't find her. My hands grasped for her, but came up empty. Her voice rang in my head, full of desperation and sadness.

I am dead either way.

No.

I jolted awake, needing to calm myself. I've seen Gabby's future so many times, I had to remind myself that no matter how desperate she felt, she would be okay. She had to be. I'd seen too much. It did nothing to ease my now growing sense of dread. The seven of us slept at the base of a huge Acacia tree in the middle of the desert we spent the day crossing. Most of us slept around a fire while Nanik slept up in the tree. Everyone else was asleep, at least the steady sound of deep breathing relaxed me a bit. I stood slowly, careful not to wake James and walked out under the stars, staring off into the silvery shade of sand expanding in every direction. The distant sounds of animals foraging for food in the middle of the night was the only thing to take my mind off the dream.

Even knowing Gabby needed me, I didn't like the idea of Aslak having free reign while we were looking for her. This would have been a great plan for him to keep us occupied, especially knowing his gifts.

I moved my attention to my arm, the Tree of Light branch covered in the orchid type flowers. The Mark. The Mark that somehow meant I would bridge two worlds together, giving Iskrem access to the two suns that would allow the tree to bloom again.

I closed my eyes as my temple throbbed. This was too much. How did we go seven years with a normal life and now this? A dark shadow approached on the ground heading right towards me. Looking up, a gigantic bird glided silently with it's wings expanded. It passed between the huge moon and myself sending a shiver down my spine.

I was separated from my family. My son in one world, my daughter lost in this one. If I had known what lay ahead, would I have stayed home and not gone to Brazil? Could I have avoided all of this by just not going? Did one yes change the course of my life?

Yes it did. But I knew enough to know it wasn't this one. It was the yes I said eight years ago when I decided to go to Italy. That yes changed everything and looking at what I had now from it, despite being separated, kidnapped, and the occasional unknown prophecy, I don't think I would have changed a thing. I thought about my conversation with Rosalina back in Italy. No regrets.

"You seem troubled."

My heart leapt out of my chest. I turned, already knowing the only one of the group that could speak inside my head. Nanik seemingly appeared out of thin air before me.

"I am troubled. My daughter is missing."

"I meant, more troubled than before."

Not wanting to over share with someone I didn't fully trust, I decided on a half-truth. "I feel like she is in danger."

"Yes. This is not a safe place for humans."

"Why do you think our enemy brought her here of all places?" I asked aloud, not necessarily to Nanik, but more to myself.

"This is a place of escape, of hiding. This is where we come to disappear. It seems fitting to me."

"How did you come to be here, Nanik?" I asked.

"Centuries ago, we lived in a land abundantly green. The Nymphs ruled over nature and kept the balance between plant and beast. Unfortunately over time, a new species grew and decided to wage war. They were not willing to live within the ways of our Mother's Nature. We are peaceful beings, except when the land and the living are threatened. Because we did not share their same willingness for violence, we were no match for them. Slowly, our people began dying, and the rest fled in fear. Some of us took the one-way passage to Asylum while others were afraid to leave, never able to return. We abandoned our homeland and live with the grief and shame of its eventual destruction.

We are trapped here just as your daughter.

Just as you now are."

In that moment, as Nanik was in my head speaking, I experienced a flash of Gabby's subconscious, a glimpse of her fear muddled with a hazy view of wild red hair. Wild fire red hair with leaves and twigs strewn throughout. Nanik eyed me carefully when I didn't respond or answer her.

I stared back into the emerald green eyes as though I were looking at her through Gabby's eyes.

And I knew.

Gabby somehow showed me who had been holding her this entire time.

This wood nymph was not to be trusted.

THE WATER UNDER.

Gabby

I had drowned.

It was the only explanation. But how was I thinking? Why could I move? How was I surrounded by water and not dead? I slowly opened my eyes and confirmed what my body already new. I was indeed underwater. Light reflected off of the ceiling of the cavern and illuminated most of the space with a bluish glow. I didn't feel the sensation that I was floating, but sitting on the floor, my legs crossed neatly. A pressure pushed on my face, and my hands involuntarily moved up to feel a mask strapped to my head. It was a hard metal with a soft, pliable film covering my mouth. Two small projectile pieces went into my nose and I immediately understood it filtered the oxygen out of the water for my lungs. Looking down cross-eyed, I saw the metal was a dull, goldish bronze.

Noticing pressure on my shoulders and chest, my hands moved to feel a chain mail of the same material, weighing me down in the water. The vision that JJ had shown me flashed through my mind. This was the chain mail I wore defeating the sloth. I was going to be okay. This was supposed to happen all along.

It startled me as it swam past. Whatever it was that had saved me from the crazy leaf lady. Catching its tail end, I thought I must be hallucinating. Of course, I've seen enough at this point not to doubt what it was. A mermaid, or merman—it's back side to me. It was huge, it's tail alone at least five or six feet long. The most colorful translucent scales covered every square inch of the mythical creature. As it turned, her eyes were the only quality that gave away her gender. There was something oddly feminine about her eyes, devoid of color, only full of light. They glowed a golden cream, insanely haunting. Her face was adorned with the same scales that covered the rest of her body. A mohawk of larger scales looked like a fin that ran down from the top of her head down her back.

 She glided through the water in one fluid movement and floated in front of me, eyeing me carefully. Her nod asked me if I was okay, so I nodded back. She opened her mouth, a bubble forming as she spoke, inaudible to me. She raised her large scaled hand and cupped it, drawing it toward my ear. As the bubble connected to my canal, her raspy voice surprised me, "You are safe. I will keep you safe until your mother arrives."

 Every ounce of my body relaxed under the weight of the chain mail. This mermaid knew Mom was looking for me. She would let me stay here. I was going to be okay. I would never be able to thank her enough. Forgetting I was underwater and had a mask strapped to my face so I could remain alive, I tried to thank her without thinking. To my surprise, a bubble formed as the words left my mouth, and my new friend sat across from me, a look of anticipation on her face. I realized she was waiting for me to give her the bubble, so I reached up, plucking it from the material covering my lips and slowly reached it to a hole on the side of her head that I assumed was her ear. It connected, and she smiled and nodded. A shiver ran down my spine when she opened her mouth, her teeth looking less human and more like those belonging to a shark.

 She had already started on another bubble. "My name is Calyio."

 "Calyio—like Calypso?" I bubbled back.

"What is Calypso?"

"Never mind." I smiled under my mask. "Thank you for rescuing me."

"You are the first human I have ever seen. Your species is so fragile and rare. I never believed I would see one."

I couldn't stop the smirk that spread across my face. Humans, rare? If we were rare compared to mermaids, then there must be a crazy amount of mermaids in the worlds. Which sparked my next question.

"What world are we in?"

"Asylum, a refuge for those from other worlds."

"I haven't heard of it. Of course, I didn't know other worlds existed until a couple of weeks ago. Is this your home?"

"Yes." She placed the bubble next to me ear. "I usually live in total blackness, but I heard myths that your kind can not see in darkness, so I brought in some friends so you were not scared."

I looked up to the blue iridescent fish glowing, asleep along the top of the cavern.

"Thank you. The myths are right. What other myths have you heard about us?" I asked curiously.

"Oh, many different things. I knew for certain that you could not breath under water, so I am glad I had the apparatus. One of my people told me humans are warm blooded and eat their first borns."

I tried not to choke on the limited air supply moving through my mask.

"No! That's not true!" I quickly answered back.

"Well, I was not judging too harshly. Each species have their traditions." Her eyes continued to glow as she looked down at my feet. "You are smaller than I imagined humans."

"Well, I'm kinda young for a human. Plus, women tend to be smaller than men." I looked down at her giant tail fin. "You are much bigger than our myths about mermaids."

"You have myths about my kind?"

"Of course we do, but you are much different than what we imagined."

"How so?"

"We tend to picture mer-people more half human, half fish."

"You mean like with those?" She pointed to my legs and looked horrified.

I laughed. "No, like your top half." I motioned from my waist up.

"Oh, that is ridiculous. With your skin and arms, we'd be dead within days."

"Really? Dead?" I wasn't laughing anymore.

"Of course. My people collect and work shaping Valen, the metal, you are wearing. Without our own protection, we would be dead before our first harvest."

"Did you make this?" I asked dumbfounded.

"Of course. I brought it with me when I came here. I fled my home many, many years ago. I brought enough material with me to make it. It has taken me over one hundred and fifty years, but I finally finished it. It is one of my most proud accomplishments."

It took her several bubbles to tell me the story of the chain mail I now wore, and with each passing bubble my wonder grew.

"Caylio, it's beautiful."

Her expression brightened. "It is yours. I would be honored to say a human wore my work."

"I couldn't possibly—it's too important and took you too long."

"Do not pretend you do not already know that it belongs to you." She inched closer to my face with a twinkle in her already glowing eye. "For I have seen the same vision you have. Why do you think I made it so small? Although, I never thought I would have the honor to give it to you personally."

She smiled exposing her sharp, intimidating teeth and swam back towards the other side of the cavern. The water pushed from her tail whirled my hair around me.

I felt as though I was living an out of body experience. This couldn't be my life, chilling underwater with a freaking mermaid. I mean, this couldn't be real. Perhaps I was dreaming. Dreaming! I needed to reach out to my family and let them know I was okay. When I tried to concentrate, my head swam, literally and metaphorically. I assumed the amount of oxygen I was in taking wasn't enough to exert myself, even in my subconsciousness. I would just have to wait.

I missed Mom. I missed Dad. I missed JJ. I hadn't seen any of their faces in ages. I didn't even know how long I'd been gone. I didn't even know if I was seventeen or eighteen years old. I had no idea if Charlie and Marek were okay. I prayed they were both all right. I clung onto the vision JJ had shown me for the brief moment before, hoping it meant that Charlie survived the attack on us. I had to stop thinking about the unknown.

What would Mom do? She would focus on the facts. What did I know for sure? What positives could I focus on? JJ had found me before, and I couldn't help but hope he would reach out to me again. He seemed to be my only lifeline to the rest of the family. His gift was strong enough to compensate for mine when it didn't work.

Thanks to my little brother, at least my family knew I was alive. At least I knew Mom was coming.

At least I knew she would eventually catch up to that crazy, kidnapping, leaf lady.

THE TRAP.

Eden

It was difficult to get time alone with James to tell him what I'd seen the night before and my conversation with Nanik. For whatever reason, even though I knew she was not to be trusted, I felt we were on the right track. As long as we kept our guard up, she would lead us where we needed to go next.

I finally found my chance when we stopped to cool off by a small river that afternoon. Everyone spread out to clean themselves, and James and I found ourselves alone.

"I think Nanik had Gabby at some point." My words were muffled as I stripped off my shirt.

"What?" James' eyebrows shot up. "Why do you think that?"

"Last night I saw of vision of Nanik through Gabby's eyes. She was scared."

"Okay, so what do we do?" James looked over my shoulder at the others further down the river.

"I think we should continue to play along—act like everything is fine. We don't want to spook her. If we did, we know she could disappear in the wind, and then we'd never get answers."

"That feels like the right move. I should warn Charlie though. He's becoming a bit obsessed."

"I wouldn't. Not yet. I think he's a good distraction for her. As long as you and I are on the same page, we should be aware enough moving forward."

James sighed, obviously not agreeing with me. "I think we need someone else knowing this could be a trap." He looked up stream in the other direction and nodded to Xander. "I think you should at least tell Xander. I'd feel better if he or Marek knew."

Xander was currently re-knotting his long dreads on top of his head to keep them off his neck and back. I nodded at my husband, very glad I had someone whose advice I trusted.

After wringing out my shirt and slipping it back on, I made my way up the bank to Xander repacking his bag. After telling him everything I told James, he squared himself and eyed me carefully.

"You are sure we should keep going with the wood nymph?"

"Yes, well mostly. She is our first solid lead. We were wandering aimlessly before Nanik. We should follow her where ever she plans on taking us and when necessary, we can corner her and find out the truth."

Xander nodded, threw his pack over his shoulder onto his back.

"I trust your judgment."

We all reconvened, and Nanik told us we would be changing course and leaving the safety of the desert.

"The forest is alive, as you have already experienced. But with me you should be safe. We need to tread as little ground as possible, so let us remain together and attempt to stay on the path that I create."

As we entered through the line of trees that marked the beginning of the forest, I fell behind Nanik, and nodded for Xander to bring up the rear. I wanted us to be protected from the front and back, having no idea what Nanik had up her tree limbs so to speak. We walked for hours and hours without an incident, until Wanda began to complain about her knees.

"We should only have another hour left, little one. Can you make it that far?"

"Little one. Who are you calling little one?" Wanda barked from behind me.

I chuckled. "You don't like being called little, huh, Wanda? Your own medicine taste a bit bitter?"

"Well, unlike you, I'm in fact short. So yeah, it stings a bit." She snorted.

"I did not mean offense."

"Uh-huh."

"Can you make it another hour, Wanda?"

"Yes. Yes I can." It sounded like she was convincing herself. I almost reminded her of her gift, but didn't know if she wanted anyone else to know it. So, I let it go.

No one spoke over the next hour. I was too busy running scenarios through my head of what may happen next, and Wanda was too busy concentrating on not falling down. Eventually the forest opened up slightly just in time for the sun to have almost set. Shadows were long and gold glowing on the trees from the early evening sun. We had maybe thirty minutes before darkness hit, and it happened fast when you were deep in the forest.

Beyond us lay a large opening to a cave. My stomach instantly tightened, knowing this would be an easy way to trap us all, if she so desired.

Nanik looked hesitant herself as she glanced into the underground tunnel.

"The person who I believe has answers retreated here. She may know what happened to your daughter."

Charlie moved to enter the cave when James grabbed his shoulder and pulled him back.

"Bro, what are you doing?"

"You're not going in there," James answered matter of factly.

"But Nanik said that's where we need to go."

Xander repositioned himself at the cave's entrance to block it. I moved close to Nanik without seeming threatening.

"I feel your hesitation to enter. I assure you it is safe, and the answers you seek lay within."

"Nanik, I appreciate your help getting us here. In fact, I appreciate everything you did to help save us when we first arrived. But you are not telling us the truth, and I think you need to tell us why you really brought us here."

"I'm afraid I do not understand your meaning."

I had to fight the urge to grab her. I was losing patience and knowing she knew the truth wore me thin.

"You know where Gabby is. You had her. Now, where is she?"

My brother looked curiously to James.

Charlie was next.

"What? Eden, no way. What are you talking about?" Charlie moved toward me, but James grabbed him.

"I do not, nor have I ever had Gabby. You are mistaken."

Her denial set me off. Swinging my spear around from my back, I pushed Nanik up against the stonewall next to the cave and pushed the blade to her throat.

"Where. Is. She?" I gritted through my teeth.

"Eden!" Charlie yelled.

"Well, this just got interesting." Wanda crossed her arms and smirked.

Marek walked up behind me and put his hand on my shoulder. "Why do you think Nanik had her?"

"I saw her. I saw Nanik through Gabby's eyes, and she was terrified of her."

"No. It wasn't me." The nymph's eyes pleaded with me, but her sweet little Mother Nature act didn't fool me anymore.

"Stop lying!"

The words hadn't completely left my mouth when Xander jumped and swung his axe towards an unseen assailant. Instantly

Marek moved towards the cave to help him when he flew backwards. I kept my blade at Nanik's throat while Xander fought someone I couldn't see. Suddenly, tree vines wrapped themselves around Xander and pinned him to the ground.

"Helsike, not this again!" Wanda cried as she was tangled within the tree vines as well.

"Stop it! Let them go!" I yelled in Nanik's face.

"*It's not me.*" She groaned within my mind.

Within seconds everyone but me was pinned to the ground or the surrounding trees, struggling to break free.

A presence materialized behind me, and my instincts kicked in. Keeping my right hand holding the blade to Nanik's neck, I spun around to grab my attacker, using my left hand to grab for the throat.

Nanik's throat.

I looked back over my other shoulder to Nanik still under my blade. She spoke in my head.

"*Let my sister go.*"

"Damn, there are two of them," Marek barely whispered.

"*Namy, these people are no threat.*"

"It doesn't look like that, considering the placement of her weapon."

Knowing I was out of options, unable to fight both of these tree-wielding nymphs, I did the only thing I knew to do. I lowered my blade. Slowly, the vines and branches released my family and friends one by one.

Eyeing the new wood nymph, I noticed her hair and "clothes" were more worn and disheveled than her sister's. The two twins embraced.

"What in the hell is going on?" Charlie stood rubbing his wrists. He'd been face down unable to see anything. His eyes grew the size of saucers when he saw the two wood nymphs hugging. "Whaaaaa?"

James walked up behind me. "I didn't see this coming."

"As if having one of God's most beautiful creatures tagging along with us wasn't enough." Wanda grumbled. "It's enough to make a woman feel inferior."

"Awe Wanda, don't feel threatened. You've got that 'older, wiser, tough thing' working for you." Marek winked at her.

Her attempt to stop the grin spreading over her face failed.

The twins pulled away from each other, and Namy was crying.

"What have you done, Namy? Why does Eden think you had her daughter?"

"I'm sorry, Nanik. I had to. General Sapp was our only chance."

"Our only chance to what?"

"To escape this place."

THE TWINS.

Eden

"*I'm sorry. I no longer have your daughter.*" Namy continued to cry. "*She escaped, into the deep.*"

"Into the deep what?" Marek asked eyeing the new twin.

"*Into the deep underwater lake below us. I cannot go into the water, so I could not follow. I lost her.*"

Trying to keep my composure, I took a lung full of air and closed my eyes. I knew Gabby would be okay, and I held onto that belief in spite of the bad news we were receiving.

"How do we find her?" I asked.

Nanik stood gracefully and stared out into the jungle surrounding us, seemingly peering through the darkness.

"*We must ask the sprites.*"

"*No,*" Namy answered quickly in our heads. "*The sprites hate our kind. They would never help us.*"

"*They may not help us,*" the twin responded. "*But they will help her.*" Her deep green eyes found mine.

"Are you crazies talking about the water sprites we saw earlier? How can they help?" Wanda questioned.

"*Just as we can speak and control the trees and creatures of the forest, the sprites' domain is the water. They will know where Gabrielle is and who has her.*"

"The closest river is miles away. At first light, we'll attempt communication with the sprites."

"No way. We aren't going to wait until morning. We go now." I stood, unable to take another second of being separated from my daughter, when a realization hit me. "What about wherever Gabbs fell in? Why don't we communicate with the sprites there?"

"Sprites make their homes among the river beds. They prefer running water. Even then, they retreat deep into the waters depths at night. Our best time to reach out to them is early morning or late dusk," Namy answered, still sitting on a low branching limb.

Xander stood. "Eden is right. We do not wait. We should go now and simply awaken the creatures."

"These are not creatures, and it will do you well to remember such. Sprites, like us, are spiritual beings that deserve deep adoration and respect. They can control and manipulate its domain and are unwilling to be condescended." Nanik glared at Xander as she berated our minds.

"Nanik." Charlie threw his palms up. "I don't think Xander meant to offend you."

"Charlie is right. I am sorry. I meant no offense. You must understand how incredibly frustrated we all are. We need to find Gabrielle, and I do not think we should wait until morning."

I turned to the twins. "Namy, Nanik, is there no way to reach the sprites tonight?"

They looked at each other and communicated without us.

"It is a risk, but if you are willing to take it, we will take you to them now."

"Yes, whatever it is, we will do it," James immediately answered. "Let's go."

The eight of us made our way through the jungle over the next couple hours. It was slow moving, but it helped having the branches and vines move themselves out of our way as we passed—the obvious benefits of walking with two wood nymphs. We reached the wide river's edge in the dead of night. Only a few stars peaked their way through the jungle canopy. Once we stopped, only the sound of the rushing water filled the night air as we all turned, facing the nymphs, waiting for our next instructions.

"While the sprites prefer to live by running water, they sleep in the depths of the pools that run off from the main river. Our best bet is to split up and look for one. Once you find one, the only way to wake the sprites is to disturb their waters, thus disturbing their slumber," Nanik informed us.

Namy picked up where she left off. *"But beware, sprites are highly territorial and will not be pleased to be awoken."*

"Well, this should be fun." Marek sighed. "Let's go, Wanda."

Xander looked untrustingly at the twins, then back at Charlie. "Charlie, why don't you come with me?"

"But . . . " Charlie looked longingly at the twins.

"Charlie, go with Xander," James ordered.

"Geez, alright." Charlie rolled his eyes.

James and I headed down river, careful to notice any pools or small creeks that protruded from the main stream. After a short distance, we saw a seemingly shallow pool coated in fallen flower petals. The tree arched above it was covered in small white blossoms, and we watched as they slowly fell and landed on the pool's surface.

"Looks shallow." James eyed it.

I took out Taran's branch and stuck it into the water to test its depth. My weapon was five feet long and did not touch the bottom. I swirled it around to disturb the water. The flowers swirled in a beautiful pattern, but we saw no sign of the sprites. James found a large rock and threw it into the center.

Nothing.

Losing my patience, I stripped off my gear and my shoes.

"Eden, I'm not sure this is the best idea. You heard the twins."

"Yes, I did. They also seemed sure they would want to help me. Let's hope they were right." I dove into the cool water.

I swam down.

Further down.

Never hitting a bottom.

As my lungs burned, I turned to head back to the surface. Warmth hit my face, and a light illumined behind my closed eyelids. Not sure what else to do, I opened my eyes, unsure what I would see.

A green glowing orb of light hovered in front of my face. I could subtly make out the tear shaped head floating before me. Little droplets of water echoed in my ears, mimicking the same noise from before. The sprite floated up to my face and a warm current of water flowed around my cheeks, then nothing. Somehow my face became dry and I knew it was okay to breath.

Slowly, sprites began to emerge from crevasses and holes in the surrounding walls. The entire pool glowed a haunting green, and within seconds, there were hundreds of sprites floating around me.

Not wanting to take advantage of their obvious patience, I asked for their help in search of Gabby. I told them who had her and where she fell into the underground lake. My voice didn't seem to go anywhere, and I really only heard myself in my head, but I assumed they understood me when they suddenly darted off in all directions. Having done what I came to, I kicked my way to the surface and broke through the flower covering, every square inch of me coated in white blossoms.

"Eden! What the hell happened?" James was half dressed. "I was about to jump in after you." He reached down and helped pull me out.

"Well, I think I got the message across."

"Was that crazy glow the sprites?"

"Yeah, I swear, after everything we've been through and seen, I'm still surprised by some of this stuff."

James crouched down next to me. "What do we do now?"

"I guess we wait and see if the sprites come back with anything."

"Okay, you wait here, and I'll go let everyone know we made contact and to head this way." He put his hand on my shoulder. "You did it. We almost have her. We're so close now."

I allowed myself to hope for the first time in a while. "I know. You better believe I'm not letting her out of my sight for a heck of a long time."

THE WAIT.

Eden

  I sat on the water's edge, my legs hanging over into the cool pool, watching the white blossoms floating gently on the water's surface. I relished the momentary silence and solitude. It had been a long journey with the group of us, and I was relieved to be alone for the moment. I wanted to be reunited with Gabby, and while I knew I couldn't have found her alone, it felt appropriate that I take this last step of it by myself. It was after all, she that rescued me back in Iskrem. She was so brave in the face of such danger. I can't imagine what the last few weeks have felt like for her.

  Lying back on the mossy blanket that covered the ground, I listened to the loud chirping of only heavens knew what extinct species. Closing my eyes for only the briefest of seconds, I found myself drifting into the dream world.

  I stood behind Gabby on the cliffs overlooking the shallow seas. Without being able to see it, I knew she was reading the letter and crying. The fabric from her dress blew out behind her, grazing my legs. I was about to reach out to her when heat radiated behind me. Turning around, the blaze of a forest fire surrounded us. Panicking, I flew around to grab Gabby and pull her to safety, but she was gone. I faced the fire, slowly retreating away from the scorching flames. My foot slipped on the cliff behind me. Completely trapped and nowhere to go, I saw a flash of someone beyond the flames. Not just someone, people. My family screamed for me on the other side of the fire, begging me to run. I wanted to run to them, but I knew I had to protect it. Something in my gut told me I was the only one who could. The fire engulfed me, searing pain and the smell of flesh burning filled my nostrils.

I jolted up sweating, still feeling the heat from this new dream. I leaned down and splashed the cool water from the pool on my face. My eyes opened to a sprite hovering inches from my face. It's tear dropped eyes looked sad and reached out it's limb of an arm, laying it's tiny hand on my nose. It's musical dripping sounded in my ears, but I was unable to understand the spirit.

"He is saying that you will hence forth never truly be alone." One of the twins' voiced in my head. *"The sprites have pledged their allegiance to you."*

Something deep within me welled up, and I didn't try to control the flow of emotion as it poured out of me. Tears streamed down my face. As I cried, hundreds of sprites raised slowly from the water and encircled me. As each tear fell, a sprite took it, returning into the pool below. Over and over, the sprites took my tears and retreated into the pool's depth until my tears finally ran dry, and they had all disappeared except the one.

It opened its mouth and dripped as Nanik translated.

"Your daughter is safe with one of our friends. She will take her to Mount Mortuus. There, you will be reunited."

"Thank you," I whispered to the water fairy.

"Remember, Bridge Builder, although we are technically confined to this world, the power of our water transcends every world. There is no door that can block it, no body of land that can contain it. Where you find it, you will find our power."

And with that last word, the sprite fell into the water, dissipating into ripples, the white blossoms bobbing up and down.

Silence radiated through the night as I replayed the words in my mind.

"Um, I'm not sure what to address first. That freaky looking water thingy, or the fact that it told us where to find Gabby."

I looked up to see Charlie gaping at me wide-eyed. James ran up behind him.

"It told us where Gabby is?" He tried to catch his breath.

"She's at Mount Mortuus, where ever that is." I stood up, relieved for the first time in weeks. I looked to Nanik. "Can you lead the way?"

"*Yes, but it is a dangerous climb to attempt at night. We should sleep and leave first thing in the morning. The Mountain is an ancient dormant volcano that is now connected with this world's oldest known underground lake system. We should be there by nightfall tomorrow night. It's not too far away. It will just take time to climb it.*"

"Let us make camp here. This moss should make for a decent arrangement for sleeping," Xander spoke up.

Exhausted and emotionally drained, I resigned to wait till morning.

As we laid out our gear to rest, the nymphs climbed up into the large tree limb that hung over the river. James made a small fire to warm us as the night air chilled several degrees. Even though I knew I needed to sleep and couldn't remember the last time I'd really slept, I couldn't slow down my thoughts and excitement of being so close to seeing Gabby again. Holding her. Knowing for certain she was safe. Everyone was dozing off around me when I noticed James eyeing me.

"Are you alright?" he whispered.

I smiled and nodded. "I'm just tired."

"I know." He rolled over and cuddled up against me. "We are almost there."

"Even once we are reunited with Gabby, how do we get out of here?" I looked down at him. "You've heard everyone—no one leaves this place. We've unknowingly brought every single person who *could* have let us out, here, into the one world that has to be opened from the outside." I rubbed my temples.

He knew I was right. We literally had the only four Door Keepers that could open the door for us, with us.

"That's not entirely true."

We looked up to see Namy peering down intently at us.

"That grotesque creature that enlisted me to keep your daughter. He can open the door, and he would again if given the proper motivation."

"How are we supposed to trust you?"

"Please, Eden. Allow me the opportunity to gain your trust, and earn my sister's once again. The only reason I aligned with that beast is because I thought it was the only way to leave. You have brought me hope of a better way. Let me help."

"I'll tell you what, Namy, you help me get to my daughter, apologize to her for the insanity you've caused, and then we can talk about how you can make it up to us."

THE SIDEREUS.

Gabby

The most surprising part about being under water for so long was how quickly I got used to it. My body adjusted to the weightlessness of my limbs and how to move when I needed to. The chain mail was the perfect weight to keep me from floating into the roof of the cave but yet still allowed me mobility. The hardest part was the hunger. There wasn't much that mermaids ate that I could, or at least that I could stomach. Most of Calyio's meals resembled a seafood slaughter, her teeth ripping into everything she devoured. I ate some kelp we gathered together. But beyond that, I was left fairly hungry.

So, when Calyio insisted I eat some fish eggs, we came to a slight disagreement.

"You must eat before we attempt our journey," she bubbled. "The sprite said to meet your family at Mount Mortuus by nightfall."

"I'd rather starve." I glanced down at the bright red cluster of eggs.

"You haven't eaten anything but kelp in days, and we have a lot of swimming to do."

"Can't you just like, pull me along?" I grimaced.

"I'm your friend, not your sea horse." She glared with her glowing eyes.

"Okay, okay." I closed my eyes and remembered when I was little, and my mom made me eat broccoli. I always held my nose and imagined I was eating something delicious, like spaghetti. *It's just cold spaghetti*, I told myself. I ate three swallows full before I gagged and had to stop. I had to admit, even with the rank taste in my mouth, my stomach was grateful something was in there besides water logged leaves.

"Calyio, you've told me a lot about your land and people, but we haven't talked about why you are here. Why did you leave your home world?"

Calyio stared at me, blinking without answering. She sunk next to me.

"It is a long and rather arduous story, but it involves a crime I committed which resulted in my banishment."

"You were banished?" I asked surprised.

"Yes, but I did the right thing for myself and my people, so I do not regret it."

"Wow, I'm so sorry. How long ago was this?"

"Several hundred years ago."

I would never get used to how long beings from other worlds lived. Owls, butterflairies, and apparently mermaids—Emmie would think I'd lost my marbles if I ever had the opportunity to tell her any of this. A mixture of sadness and joy filled me when thinking of my best friend. All of these amazing things I'm seeing and I can never share it with her. How had my mom done it this whole time?

Not shortly after our "breakfast" Calyio wrapped her large hands around my waist and hoisted me up under her. She cradled me with one arm and used the other to keep the underwater foliage from hitting us in the face.

"What happened to the sea horse thing?" I chuckled into the bubble and lifted it up to her earhole.

"Well, I do not want your sad, little, finless feet to slow us down." She attempted a smile, but just bared her razor sharp teeth down at me, making me feel queasy before we even began swimming. "Hold on."

My eyes closed tight, the water rushed around us like we were standing under a waterfall. I couldn't begin to imagine how fast we were swimming. Suddenly I wished I had a pair of goggles, wondering what all whipped past us. Here I was flying through an underwater land and was going to completely miss it! I tried to talk into a bubble, but it flew from my mouth the second I opened it. There would be no talking on this trip.

I allowed my mind to wander, the water flowing around me was a relaxing a hot shower. Mostly I thought about the life I left behind, wondering what my friends were up to, who's house they were hanging at, what movies they watched. I imagined what Emmie would say about Xander. Or how intimidated the guys at my high school would be of him.

I lost track of how long we flew/swam, until finally we stopped. Nothing could have prepared me for what I opened my eyes to. Beams of light shone straight down into the depths around me. The rays of light came from flowers. They looked like lotus flowers floating on the surface of the water, but facing down. The lights seemed to be shining from their centers.

"What are those?"

"The Sidereus. I brought one from my home world, and my little garden has grown."

"I'd say," I breathed out in awe. "They're beautiful." I didn't want to peel my eyes away from the warm light emanating from the thousands of magenta lotus looking flowers floating above me. I finally tore them away and glanced towards my new friend and found myself surprised once again. Calyio's iridescent scales shimmered under the glow of the Sidereus. Colors bounced and danced as the water bent the light. Her scales threw tiny rainbows in most directions.

"My people used to celebrate the end of harvest under the Sidereus' light. We would swim and dance—it is what I miss most about my world." Her eyes dulled ever so slightly. Resolve settled hard on her face. "Well, past is past. Come, friend, we are almost to Mount Mortuus."

As excited as I was to be reunited with my family, sympathy filled me for Calyio. This is the longest I'd ever been away from my family, and it's almost killed me. I couldn't imagine being ripped away not only from them, but all of human kind. I suddenly wished Calyio could come with us.

We swam along, much slower than before, passing first through a long narrow tunnel and then up into a bright turquoise lake. For the first time, in I wasn't sure how long, my eyes had to adjust to the sun's rays shining through the water. Calyio took me to the center of the lake, and we sank onto the sandy floor.

"This is where I leave you, my friend." Calyio's eyes dulled. "Your family is waiting for you on shore."

"I can never thank you enough." I reached out to hug the mermaid, her scales like ice against my skin.

"You will not forget me?"

"Calyio, I couldn't forget you if I tried. You are by far the coolest mermaid I've ever met." I laughed into my bubble.

"May the Valen you wear protect you always." She placed her hand on the metal heavy on my chest.

"I will wear it with honor."

Calyio nodded low as if bowing, and before I knew it, her tail whipped around, and she was gone. The only thing left was the swirling of the water in her wake.

I took the deepest breath I could through my facemask and began to swim towards the surface.

THE REUNION.

Gabby

The water surrounding me sparkled turquoise in every direction, and I was unable to see where the lake ended or began. My only goal was to break the surface above me and see the sun for the first time since my abduction. My lungs burned and my ears popped uncontrollably, as I exerted every ounce of energy I had left, kicking and swimming toward the surface consistently hovering out of my reach.

When my head finally broke through, my first instinct was gulping the deepest breath of air I could without choking. Yanking the metal out of my nose and from around my ears, I drank the oxygen in with a smile on my face. I turned around, peering at the walls of high rock searching for my family. The sunlight was ridiculously bright, so it took my eyes a minute to adjust. I finally spotted them waving and jumping like lunatics on a cliff overlooking the lake. One of them dove off, swan style into the water below.

Mom.

I swam with every ounce of my remaining energy, which was not much. But adrenaline pumped through me as I reached one arm over the other.

"Gabbs!" Her muffled cry rippled through the water.

Her hand hit against mine, then quickly grabbed my wrist pulling me into a watery embrace. We sank immediately due to our hugging rather than swimming, and laughed as we came back up for air.

"Gabby, you're okay!"

"Mom, I'm so sorry." My salty tears mingled with the waters below.

"Don't be ridiculous, you have nothing to be sorry for. I just can't believe we found you."

"Is Uncle Marek and Charlie okay?"

"Yes, they are both on the shore waiting to see you."

Relief flooded me when I realized Charlie was still alive and here. We swam towards everyone waiting on land.

"How long have I been gone?" Not sure I wanted to know the truth.

Even though I couldn't see Mom's face, I knew she was hesitant to tell me from the short pause. "You've been missing fourteen days."

"Fourteen days?" I groaned. I had missed my birthday. Of course it was trivial with everything that had happened, but as of a few months ago, my eighteenth birthday was the single most important thing in my life. It's hard to shake off something like that, even after almost dying—twice.

As if reading my mind my mother quickly answered, "Don't you worry. We will throw a party to end all parties as soon as we are safe and together again."

Neither of us said any more as we swam to shore. Once we were close enough, my dad splashed into the water and lifted me up, wrapping his comforting arms around me.

"Wow, this is new." He grinned pulling away from me, putting his hand on the Valen chain mail covering my upper body.

"Yeah, apparently all fashionable Caeluns wear this now." I beamed up at my father. Behind him, an unlikely group of people stood on shore.

The first one I recognized as my captor, and it took me a second to understand I wasn't seeing double. Mom joined us walking toward the black sand.

"Um, I'm assuming you both know one of those crazy leaf things had me, right?" I whispered in a panic.

"Yes," Mom answered low. "It's a long story, but they are with us now."

Charlie's wide smile filled his whole face before he scooped me up in an embrace. "Neester, I'm so glad you're okay."

"You're glad *I'm* okay? I'm glad *you're* okay." I hugged him back, trying not to picture him crumbled on the ground bleeding out of his gut. He pulled back and lifted his tank top revealing a bright pink oval scar.

"Almost as good as new." He grinned, but then looked around and shrugged. "I mean, it still hurts when I breath, but it's no big deal."

"Ha, yeah Charlie, we all know you're brave." Marek pushed him out of the way and barreled into me.

"I'm so sorry," he whispered into my ear.

"You have no reason to be sorry."

"Well, if it makes you feel any better, you fought your ass off. I was seriously impressed." His eyes brightened as he kissed my forehead.

Mom eyed Xander as he slowly approached. I was taken aback when he appeared from behind my Uncle. His face flushed with color, and his skin seemed smoother. He, like the rest of my family, was filthy from being outside for weeks, but it seemed to make him appear more human. He looked down on me with apprehension, reaching out a hand to me.

"May I?" His voice was hoarse.

I half smiled and put my hand in his. He slowly pulled me into him and wrapped his arms around me carefully, as if he were afraid I would break. Or perhaps that I would try to run away. I was so surprised by the unusual contact that I allowed him to hug me, unsure of how to respond. I wasn't sure why, but I was suddenly grateful he was here. Grateful that he was with my parents and was willing to follow and protect my mom. I slowly laid my hands on his back, returning his hug. His chest inhaled sharply as though I'd surprised him, when someone coughed uncomfortably behind us.

Xander pulled back, my skin tingling where he'd touched.

"I am beyond relieved that you are safe, Gabrielle."

"Thanks Xander, me too," I whispered, a bit embarrassed after our intimate moment.

"I think we should make camp here tonight. We have a lot to plan and figure out," Dad announced. Everyone nodded and broke off to get everything set up. Mom came over and walked me to a fallen log on the black sandy beach. We rested and took a moment to ourselves. She reached over to help me pull off the chain mail, my chest instantly relaxing without it's added pressure. As she laid it over the log, her shoulder tattoo caught my eye.

"Mom, I think that's the Sidereus flower!"

"What?" She looked at me confused. "Which one?"

"That one." I pointed to the dark pink lotus flower upside down under the small branch of purply flowers right above her elbow. The inside of the flower was a light yellow, almost like light. "Calyio told me it was a flower from her land. They float upside down and shine light into the darkness, underwater."

"Really? Who is Calyio?"

I half sighed half chuckled. "I think that's a story for everyone at dinner."

Mom pulled out a dry pair of her clothes for me to borrow, and I continued to observe everyone else make camp. The two nymphs had grown a dome like structure with trees for everyone to sleep under and created vine hammocks for themselves up high in the branches above.

Marek and a tiny blond older woman worked on building a fire, while Dad, Charlie, and Xander grabbed firewood along the shore.

"Hey, who's that with Uncle Marek?" I asked as I peeled the clinging, wet clothes off my body.

Mom sighed over dramatically. "That's Wanda, and I'm not honestly sure what to say about her."

"What do you mean by that?" I pulled on a pair of pants.

"I'll tell you what, I'll give you an hour in the same camp with her. Then you can tell me what I mean." She raised her eyebrows at me expectantly.

I laughed, fully realizing how much I'd missed my mom.

"Alright, challenged accepted."

THE RETELLING.

Gabby

In less than an hour, Wanda had basically insulted me twice, complained about her aging body on three different occasions, and made an inappropriate joke about my Uncle Marek. Mom was right. It was hard to explain her without experiencing it for yourself. How she got caught up with my family was still a mystery to me but one I was sure she would complain about eventually.

I didn't have to wait long.

"Then, your mother had the audacity to speak German in my sacred sanctuary!" She threw her hands in the air. "I obviously did not trust them to take care of this situation properly. It's a good thing I came along."

"Yeah, Wanda, I'm not sure who else could have filled the complaining quota on this trip if you hadn't." Charlie rolled his eyes. Then he narrowed them on me. "Speaking of complaining, you haven't complained once about your time being kidnapped."

"Well, being drugged sucked." I cut my eyes over to Namy. "But once I was underwater with Caylio, things were pretty cool."

I told them about her, the few things she told me about her past, and about the Valen chainmail she had made. I'd forgotten how nice it was to have such easy conversation, being completely coherent or not being fuzzy from being hundreds of feet underwater. Even Wanda listened to my stories without interrupting. I kept catching Xander lifting the corners of his mouth when I got particularly excited by a certain detail. I suddenly wondered what it would look like if he actually smiled or laughed and decided it was something I was curious to see.

Once I was satisfied everyone was up to speed on my side of the story, I decided to change the subject back to the proverbial elephant in the room.

"Okay, so let me make sure I've got this straight." I glanced at the faces around the fire. "Wanda's brother locked the North Portal behind you, and we have no one else left in any of the worlds that can let us out."

"That about sums it up." Uncle Marek sighed.

"Wait, how did you get here Charlie?" I asked.

"Strix dropped me off at the door to Terra Arborum, but he had to fly to the other side of the world to continue securing and locking the other doors. It'll take him weeks to finish them all. We didn't want him to wait around and risk exposing their world to any more attacks, he's done enough for us already."

I considered that. "Okay, what about Grandpa?"

"Which one?" Charlie answered. "Caelum or Earth?"

"Either."

Mom interjected. "Well, neither Mae or my father has a key. Only Marek and I have one. I wish we'd thought about leaving one behind. Of course, we weren't expecting to get trapped behind one-way doors. What about Earth? If we could get a message to Gio, he might be able to reach out to the Door Keeper of Asylum. Do either of you know where the door to Earth is located?" She looked towards the two twins on opposite sides of the circle.

"The door to Earth is very far." One of the nymphs answered.

"It would take us weeks to travel there." The other one added.

"So what are we gonna do? We can't be here that long." I looked to the two people who have always had the answers, my parents. But it wasn't them that held the answer.

"General Sapp is going to open the door for us." Namy, the twin nymph that held me hostage answered in my head. *"I know that you do not trust me nor should you. But allow me to earn your good will. The General had a pre-set meeting with me scheduled two weeks from the day he brought Gabrielle, to check up on her.* She nodded towards me. *That meeting is supposed to be tomorrow."*

"That doesn't give us enough time to come up with a plan," Dad countered.

"No, but I could buy us some additional time. I could tell him that you and your family have entered Asylum, and I fear it is not safe to keep Gabrielle here any longer. I could suggest the best course of action is for him to take Gabrielle back and trap you all here indefinitely. It would force him to make arrangements and pick Gabrielle up within a few days. Would that suffice?"

"With all due respect Namy but what assurances do we have this was not your plan all along?" Xander's dark eyes bore into the nymph.

"With all due respect Hiem, if this were my plan all along, I would have killed you back at the cave and taken her then."

"She makes an excellent point." Charlie raised his eyebrows and nodded.

My eyes rolled involuntarily. Charlie retaliated with his own, emphasized version.

"Okay, so let's say we attempted this. What are we supposed to do? Just fight our way through the door when he opens it? It seems risky." Uncle Marek rested his elbows on his knees.

"No more risky than being trapped here for eternity." Wanda gestured around the volcano.

My mom looked over to me. "No, there is no way we could simply fight our way out. All he'd have to do is slam the door at the first sight of us, and it'd be over before it began. If we went through with this plan, we would need to use Gabbs as bait to get through the door. Sapp would have to think everything was going according to plan, it's the only way for him to let his guard down. And for obvious reasons, we are not putting Gabbs in harms way when we just got her back. There has to be another option."

"I agree." Dad put his arm around me. I looked up at him and smiled, so thankful for my parent's protection, but realizing I no longer needed it as much as I used to.

"Thanks Mom. Dad. But I think Namy is right on this one. If Sapp doesn't see me with her, we might as well announce the double cross."

"No way," Dad argued.

Marek looked from me to the nymph on the far side of the fire. "Well it's the only plan we have at the moment and we can work out the details later. But first things first, Nanik, can you meet with Sapp tomorrow to set the plan in motion? Forgive us for not trusting your sister to do it."

Everyone watched in silence as the two fire-red headed nymphs telepathically communicated. Namy closed her large emerald eyes and nodded towards her sister. She then floated towards me and knelt on the black sand.

"I promised your mother I would apologize to you, and I haven't done so yet. Gabrielle, I am so sorry that I put you through what I did. Although I was not the one who took you, I did hold you against your will, and I vow to you I will do everything I can to get you home to the rest of your family." She stood and turned toward everyone. *"I will do whatever I must to make this right.*

I only ask that once our task is completed and you are safe and back home, that you allow my sister and I passage to our native world."

"Of course." My mom nodded. "Just tell us where you want to go."

"*We want to go home—to Palus."*

THE TRAINING.

Eden

The idea that these two beautiful nymphs came from Palus felt absurd. At least, not the Palus James and I went to so many years ago. But the fact that Sapp reached out to them for help made sense. He knew he had something they wanted. A ticket home.

That night, cuddled up next to my daughter, I welcomed a dreamless sleep. Waking the next morning feeling truly rested for the first time in weeks, we took inventory of our weaponry and supplies. I was shocked when Charlie pulled two 9mm Glocks out of his pack and handed one to James.

"Charlie! Where did you get those?"

"Gio passed them to me before I left Caelum. Once we knew that you guys ended up in Asylum, he thought we'd need something more than swords. It's a good thing I brought them all things considered."

I shot an unbelieving look over to my husband. "What happened to the 'world balance' crap you gave me years ago before we went to Palus?"

"That was before they stole our daughter and war was inevitable."

He was right, of course. If we were going up against the sloths, we needed to have all the help we could get. Thankfully, everyone else that didn't have a gun had the weapons they were most comfortable with. Marek had brought Ava's hook blade and returned it to Gabby.

After breakfast, Nanik left to meet with Sapp. We wanted to send one of us with her, but it was too far, and she planned on "spiriting through the foliage" whatever that meant. Shortly after she left, the rest of us paired up and started training. I felt confident with everyone's fighting skills besides Gabby and Wanda, and after everything that happened, preparing Gabby was a top priority. We decided to partner up and switch every hour, so no one got used to any one fighting technique.

I started with Namy, Gabby with James, Xander with Charlie, and Marek and Wanda. It didn't take long for me to realize that anyone going up against Namy didn't have a chance, despite her objection to violence. Even after two blocks and three slices of vines, I hung upside down, unarmed in a tangle of brush that had grown up around me without warning. After resigning my defeat, I walked around observing the others and offered pointers where I could. James had Gabby covered, so I approached Xander and Charlie trash talking as only twenty somethings can do. I laughed hearing Charlie's slang up against Xander's formal speech. Definitely two worlds colliding in more than one way.

I also found myself chuckling at Wanda's attempts to pull Marek in to close hand to hand combat. I think she just wanted an excuse to get handsy. He had her upper body in a lock, looked my way, and shrugged, flinging her down to the ground, and they wrestled on the black sand. Despite the cuss words flying from her mouth, I was sure she loved every moment of it.

I went in for one more grapple with Namy, but it was no use. Every movement of my feet was thwarted with vines. I tripped every step I tried to take in any direction. After the hour was up everyone rotated partners so that we could get used to going up against different weapons and fighting styles.

Taking my turn sparring with Xander, I used the opportunity to voice a growing fear.

"Do you think there is any chance this could all be Aslak?" I exhaled while swinging my spear around my head.

"It could be." He ducked and swung around me, facing my back as he continued. "We have spent weeks searching for Gabrielle, and now we could possibly be stuck here. Aslak's gifting is strategy, and this feels like a good one."

I threw my leg out kicking him before he could attack. As I thought about his words, Xander caught my legs, and my back hit the ground, knocking the air from my lungs. He reached down to help me up.

"The only thing about my uncle is that he values certainty. He will not pursue action that leaves variables in play. I don't think this is him, considering there are too many unknown factors. But even if it were him, we had no choice. We had to come for Gabrielle."

I nodded, mulling over what he said. If anyone knew Aslak's playbook, it would be his family. Deciding to let it go for the moment, I observed Gabby practicing with Charlie. Since her hour long training with James, Gabby's form had improved tremendously. It was obvious that Charlie had more experience, but I bet over time they would be fairly evenly matched. I smiled noticing the determination on her face. It's the same look she had as a child attempting to master a new gymnastic skill.

Which of course gave me an idea for my hour with her.

"Gabbs, I think it's time we harness your unique abilities." I walked up to her when her hour with Charlie was over.

"You want me to just throw everyone in a dream state and knock them out?" She puffed, hands on her knees.

"Use your Door Keeper gift if and when you can, but I don't want either of us to rely on it. I meant your physical gifts."

"What do you mean?"

"You've been a gymnast almost your whole life. Why don't we use those strengths in your fighting style?"

"Huh," she breathed heavily. "Gymnastics is definitely more comfortable for me. Sounds like a good idea. What did you have in mind?"

"Well, first thing to remember is a moving target is harder to hit. So if you see me coming in for a punch or an attack, what would be the easiest way to get out of the way?" I mimicked rounding my spear towards her head like a bat. She jumped backwards into a backhand spring avoiding my weapon, but fumbling her own.

"Good!" I smiled with pride.

"I dropped my weapon." She grimaced.

"You're not going to get it on the first try." I reminded her. "Just practice the handspring while hanging onto the handle. Once you get that we'll move on."

It only took a couple tries before she had mastered it. Then we practiced the same move a few more times with me coming at different angles and attacking different ways.

"Okay, now, after your backhand spring, stay crouched low and just do what comes natural."

"Alright." She threw her weapon into her other hand and waited for my attack. I thrusted forward, barely missing her. Just when I was pulling back around to swing again her legs swept mine in a quick fluid motion, and I was on my back staring out the mouth of the volcano.

"Mom!" She hurried over to me, her face flooded with anxiety. "I'm so sorry."

"Honey, that was incredible!" The anxiety melted, and her eyes danced.

"It felt good. It was like my body knew what to do before I did." She sounded bubbly and more like herself than she had been since learning the truth.

"I know the feeling." I hopped up. "More of that, just allow yourself to go with the flow. Don't worry so much about what you look like. Just focus on incapacitating your opponent."

"Yes, m'am." She beamed.

"Speaking of opponent, may I have a turn?" Xander stood next to us.

"Wait, me or Mom?" Gabby looked over her shoulder at him.

"I would love to see what you have learned so far, Gabrielle."

"Okay, but I'm not gonna take it easy on you," she teased.

"I'd expect nothing less from your family."

They walked over to the side, and while everyone resumed their perspective match, most kept one eye on the pair. I wasn't the only one curious about those two. I approached James, and he gave me a flirtatious wink.

"Care to meet your match?"

"Yeah, can you point me in the right direction?" I squinted and looked around.

James laughed as he brought his sword down, clashing with my spear. We fought and practiced our own hand-to-hand combat. I had signed up for kickboxing classes soon after our honeymoon, having a feeling I'd need the skills one day. James went with me for about a year. Then we continued training at home together. We had grown accustomed to fighting each other and pushed one another further than anyone else felt comfortable. At one point we threw down our weapons and sparred without them. The idea that we might lose our weapons during whatever fight awaited us seemed likely, best to be ready.

We practiced getting out of chokeholds when Gabby round housed Xander in the face. He flew backwards stumbling onto his knees, bleeding out his nose. The entire camp went silent as Gabby rushed down next to him almost crying an apology.

They were both on their knees facing each other, him cupping the blood pouring out of his face and she holding his head. She gently helped him up, leading him to the water's edge, cleaning his face and chest.

Something spiked in my chest. It was odd, watching her care for someone as I had cared for her the past eighteen years. She laughed at something he said, and his eyes never left her face as she attended to him.

"Oh boy." James voice felt far away, yet snapped me back to the present. "I wondered there for a minute, but now it just seems inevitable. I wouldn't worry though. With her track record, it'll only last for a month."

"I wouldn't be so sure," I said, not taking my eyes off them. "She's just like me. Before you, I was the same way. It just took me finding you—"

"Yeah, but let's be real. Xander is no *me*." He grinned.

"Oh, he isn't? A mysterious, muscular Door Keeper from another land? Doesn't sound like you at all," I teased.

"But she really doesn't like him does she? She always rolls her eyes and says how weird he is."

"Weird and exotic toe the same line. He's also patient and persistent just like you. He's not going to give up easily."

"You think he likes her?"

"I think he may have begun this journey because of who I am, but he is still here because of her. So, yes. I absolutely think he does." They made their way back towards us, Gabby gesturing wildly and Xander eyeing her carefully with a slight smile.

"Well, I think it might be time that I have my turn sparring with him, just so he knows what kind of father he's dealing with." James gave me a knowing look as he stomped off towards his daughter and the Hiem.

I chuckled watching him continue to be the same adoring, wonderful father he's been to Gabby over the last eight years. Then without warning my head swam, and my knees buckled. My vision blurred, and I fell into the all-consuming blackness.

THE FALL.

Eden

I came to slowly and with trepidation. Nervous energy and feelings of uncertainty radiated through me, and I didn't like it. I unwillingly opened my eyes in Rosalina's apartment. I sat up and looked around. There was no one else there or any of my things anywhere. Standing, I eased my way through the apartment, attempting not to make a sound. I had this deep sense in my gut that I wasn't supposed to be here. This wasn't supposed to be happening.

I walked through the living room into the kitchen and saw her. Sitting at the table, hands folded on the yellow flowered plastic tablecloth, was Rosalina. The light flooded in the large picture window, particles of dust floating in and out of the light. Her blonde and gray hair was haloed in the sun. She turned her eyes toward me and smiled.

"Eden. I'm so glad you're here."

She patted the place in front of her on the table. "Come, sit."

"Where is *here*? I know we can't really be here. I'm trapped in Asylum."

She sighed wearily. "I know, but I'm afraid I won't make it until you return."

I looked at my friend unwilling to accept what she said.

"I asked Mae to bring us here, instead of your father's house. I don't want you to see me like I am. I wanted to say goodbye here—right here, where we changed each other's lives. How I hope you will always remember me."

I reached my hand and grasped her fragile one in mine.

"No, Rosalina. You can't go yet. We're almost home." Tears filled my eyes.

"We both knew this dream would eventually come. I'm sorry I couldn't hold on longer."

"Rosalina, please." The tears spilled down my cheeks. "I'm not ready to say goodbye."

"We never are, amore." She looked at me, her own tears beginning to flow. "You and Gabby—your friendship and trust has been such a gift. You will never know what having you in my life has meant to me." She choked on a sob.

"Please let me be with you. I want to be with you at the end."

"No love, let's stay here. That's not how I want you to remember me."

"Rosalina. You were there to bring me into your world—" My heart thumped and burned in my chest, unsure if I could say it. "Let me be with you when you leave mine."

Our eyes were locked, tears streaming down our faces, our hands clutched so tight our knuckles were white.

"Very well. Help me lie down."

I rose, gingerly laying her back as our surroundings melted into her bedroom in my father's house. Her hair had thinned since our departure, her facial features sallow. Her hand shook as she held mine, convulsing under her determination to hold on.

"Please tell Gabby and James I love them."

"I will. I promise." A tear fell off my face onto her arm. I gently wiped it away. "Thank you for finding me that day. Thank you for telling me the truth. Thank you for giving me this incredible life."

"Oh Eden, I had nothing to do with the life you have. Your destiny is so much bigger than me or anything I did for you. It began with *her,* both of ours did."

"Will you give her a hug for me?" I smiled through the deep wrenching pain in my gut, picturing my mother greeting Rosalina with open arms.

"You think heaven crosses worlds?" she asked, barely able to muster a smile.

"It sure as hell better," I answered.

Her eyes closed, and the smile finally reached her lips.

"I'm going to miss you," I whispered and kissed her wet cheek.

"I love you, Eden."

"I love you, Rosalina."

"In every world . . . " She barely finished before breathing her last.

"In every world." Letting myself be engulfed in grief, I rested my forehead on her unmoving chest, my own shaking uncontrollably.

A hand gently touched my back. Feeling hope swell within, I knew it was my Aunt Mae.

"Thank you, Mae," I whispered through my sobs. "Thank you for letting me be here."

"She was there for you when we could not be. We owe her everything," she said quietly. "We will wait for the ceremony until you return. Be safe my darling. Take your time, and I'll send you back when you're ready."

I nodded and retreated into my sorrow. Even knowing this day would come didn't ease its horrific sting. My friend and my confidant was gone. My irreplaceable Rosalina. Her body still warm, I longed for a way to save her. To somehow breath life back into her. As much as I wanted to fight it, the heavy realization hit me that death was not something I could fight and win.

THE GREAT SADNESS.

Gabby

Seeing Mom laying on the ground unconscious was unbearable. I'd never seen her simply pass out before, and it was incredibly unnerving. Dad picked her up and laid her down in the tree tent. We stayed in there with her, waiting while everyone else stayed outside.

Tears slowly crept down her face through her closed eyelids.

"She's dreaming," Dad realized.

"But why would she throw herself into a dream so randomly, standing in the middle of the beach?"

"Someone else must have thrown her into one. It must be Mae. But I don't know why Mae would pull her . . . " He trailed off, his eyes slowly reaching mine and hovering there until he closed them and sighed.

"Rosalina," he said simply.

"What? I don't understand."

At my words Mom woke up, tears streaming down her face. Dad grabbed her hand and wiped them away. I loved my dad for many reasons, not the least of which was how much he loved my mom.

"I'm so sorry, Eden," he whispered.

"Mom, what happened?" My anxiety grew. "What's wrong with Rosie?"

She sat up and took my hands. "Rosalina was very sick. That's why we brought her to Caelum. It was one of her last wishes."

"Was?" The word caught in my throat.

"I'm sorry, baby. She just passed away." Pain twisted her face.

"Wait, what? I don't understand." But the truth was I did understand. I immediately replayed the last conversation I'd had with Rosie before we left, and I was kidnapped. She was telling me goodbye. I closed my eyes and pictured her still laying in bed, telling me how much she loved me and how proud she was of me.

"Sogno bene il mio amore," she had whispered. *Dream well, my love.*

"Fino a quando ci incontreremo di nuovo, amica," I'd answered. *Until we meet again, friend.*

I slumped into my mother, feeling the full weight of her words. My Rosie was dead. The three of us cuddled up under a blanket wordless for I'm not sure how long. Maybe hours. I thought about the first time I went to Italy and met Rosie, our long talks on Skype when I was mad at my mom. Spending summers with her while my parents traveled. Her visits to Georgia to spend time with the four of us. The four of us. I ached to be with JJ, wishing so desperately he was here, so we could be together. No, I wished the three of us were out of this God-forsaken world with crazy ancient things roaming around. I wanted my family whole, and I wanted us home.

Knowing my parents were allowing me to feel and grieve however I needed to, for as long as I needed to, I let the emotions flow until they ran out. I straightened slowly and wiped my face.

"I miss JJ. I want to go home."

"Okay," Mom pulled my hair over my shoulder. "We are here for whatever you need."

"I know, and don't worry. I'm going to have a ton of questions about why you didn't tell me about Rosie later. But for now, let's just concentrate on getting the heck outta here." I sniffed.

"You got it." Dad got up and left the tent.

Mom stood and helped me up. We made our way out of the tent to find that Nanik had returned. Everyone was gathered around her hearing her account of the meeting with General Sapp. Her voice entered my head before we approached.

"Everything is set. The good news is that he already knew that you had entered Asylum and was nervous of your presence here. Apparently word spread through Iskrem of your journey and made it's way to him. My confirmation of that fact only reinforced my, well Namy's allegiance to him. He is making arrangements to hide Gabrielle in Palus and wants to meet in four days to make the trade."

"Palus?" Marek interjected. "I wasn't expecting that. I assumed we'd meet at the Iskrem door."

"It makes sense though. Palus is where he feels most comfortable. It's also less likely for Aslak to learn he had her," Xander added.

"It is normally a three day journey to the door, but if we fly, it should take half that time. We should leave immediately so we have time to prepare."

"Fly?" I spoke up for the first time.

"Oh, yeah, girl, we fly in Asylum." Charlie grinned. Marek slapped him on the back of the head.

"Don't act like you've flown here. The only time you've flown was on Strix's back bleeding out and unconscious."

I grimaced at the memory of Charlie injured. Turning to walk back to collect my things, Charlie jogged up beside me. "Hey, I'm sorry about Rosie. I didn't know she was sick either. Apparently she didn't want any of us to know. I'm here for you, if you need to talk."

"Thanks Bruncle." I half smiled at him, grateful that his presence always seemed to lift my spirits. Then I punched him in the arm. "What is it with you and those crazy nymphs? Your eyes go all googly when they walk by."

"I can't help it. I think I'm in love." He put his hand over his heart dramatically. "You've got to admit—they are something special." He smiled longingly at Nanik undoing our tree tent and causing the trees to grow straight up.

"They are something alright." I raised an eyebrow.

"Speaking of love, don't think I haven't noticed how you've come around to the future King of the Hiems." He nodded towards Xander.

"Aw, come on Charlie. You know he's not my type."

"What? Royalty, Door Keeper, and not to mention he has awesome hair. I'd kill for those dreads."

I laughed freely for the first time in weeks. "Thanks Charlie, I needed a good laugh."

"Fine, laugh away. Laugh all the way over to your partner to soar romantically in the clouds on a white flying stallion." He wiggled his eyebrows as Xander beckoned me to our horse.

"Shut up," I muttered under my breath as I tried not to notice the muscles flexing on Xander's back as he loaded the horse with our gear.

THE FLIGHT.

Gabby

"Remember the last time we flew together?" Xander shouted, the wind whipping his words back to me holding onto him.

"Yup, although I'm pretty sure I was mad at you at the time."

"Have you forgiven me yet?" His chest flexed under my arms as he readjusted his grip on the horse's mane.

"Yeah, I guess so. So much has happened, it seems stupid to be mad about something like that."

"Good." He paused. "And was I right?"

"About what?"

"Have I earned your trust?" He turned his head slightly to the side.

"Yes—and my friendship."

He smiled and faced forward again.

"I appreciate you staying around and helping my parents."

"I am not just here for them."

His response stirred something in me, but I didn't want to press it, so I changed the subject.

"Do you trust the nymphs?"

"Yes. But no one blames you for not. What you have been through is more than enough reason to doubt. But I promise, I would never gamble with your life. And if I did not trust them, then I would not be going along with this plan."

"How can you be sure? About them?"

"Well, it seems their interests align with ours at the moment. They want to leave Asylum as much as we do. Selfishness is a great motivator. It is in their best interest to work with us. In truth, Namy was a fool to ever think Sapp would honor their agreement and let them return to Palus. The sloths are why they had to leave in the first place. So, we are their best chance. They will not betray us."

"I wish I had your confidence sometimes."

"It is alright. I have enough for us both."

"Xander, did you just make a joke?" I laughed.

"My attempt at one, perhaps."

I chuckled, and then changed the subject again. "I'm worried about Charlie. I don't like how he's so gaga over them."

"Are you jealous?"

"Jealous!? Heck-to-the-no. I just don't want to see him get hurt."

"In most tribes, you and Charlie would be an obvious match. Have you never felt that way?" He looked over his shoulder giving me his profile view again.

"Um, no! That's gross, no way. That has never been on the table."

"What table?"

"Never mind. It's just an expression."

"Well, I don't think it would be, as you say 'gross,' for you and Charlie to be together."

"Well, you've never lived with him."

Xander's body released a quick exhale of breath under my grasp and shook ever so slightly.

"Did you just *laugh*?"

"I do not laugh." His profile exposed a smile.

"You did, the ever serious, future King of the Hiems, just laughed!" I cackled, enjoying teasing him.

"Alright, perhaps I did." He readjusted his grip again. "I am just saying, it seems like you and Charlie love each other. Why not be matched together?"

"I do love Charlie, second only to my parents and JJ. I love him and care for him like a brother. And that might be the way marriage works in Iskrem, but for me, I want to be *in* love with someone. I want to miss them when they are not around and want to spend every waking minute with them. There needs to be a spark, a connection. I want to long for them to be close and for them to be willing to do anything to be with me."

"Like cross worlds?" He looked back to me, the silver shining bright around his large black pupils.

"Are we still talking about Charlie?" My breath caught.

His eyes moved down to my mouth, then back up.

"I think you know I'm not." I noticed his full lips for the first time, willing my eyes back to his.

"Xander—"

Lightening crashed suddenly ahead of us. I hadn't noticed the dark and ominous clouds filling in from most directions, lost in our conversation. Mom and Dad's horse slowed to fly beside us.

"We're not to far from the door. We're gonna go for it!" Dad yelled over the wind.

Xander nodded briskly and grabbed my arm, pulling me tighter into his back. He gently squeezed and yelled, "Hold on tight."

I peaked around Xander to see the wall of heavy rain up ahead. One by one, my family and friends disappeared into the blankets of water falling from the clouds. I squeezed my eyes shut and waited for the downpour.

One second I was dry and the next, soaked to the bone. Practically like I was back in the underwater cave with Caylio. I went to readjust my arms, but Xander's skin was too slippery to get a good grip, so I just grabbed my other wrist and held on for dear life. Thunder boomed through my head and lightening flashed through my closed eyelids.

My heart pounded in my chest, and I became acutely aware of Xander's heart beating slow and steady into my wrist pushed up against his chest. Steady and calm as always. I focused on his rhythm and tried to slow my breathing to lower my own to match his. Within a minute, my own heartbeat slowed, and concentrating on it helped me forget the chaos flying around us.

Xander tapped my leg to get my attention. "We're heading lower, hold on!" I barely heard him over the crashing thunder and rain beating down on us. Ducking my head into his back, the horse tilted underneath us, and the wind shifted. Our hips simultaneously shifted to match the angle of the drop. I opened my eyes for the briefest of seconds to see Wanda and Marek flying next to us. It took everything inside of me not to lose my composure and grip on Xander. Wanda's face was a wild mixture of terror and joy. She was definitely screaming, but I honestly couldn't tell if she thought she was going to die, or was having the ride of her life.

I had to close my eyes to refocus on the task at hand, but the look on her face was burned into my memory forever.

I thought I had an awesome life before I learned the truth. I had amazing friends and a great family. Prom was on the horizon. I was about to graduate and begin my life as an adult. I looked forward to my future past high school. I couldn't wait for the adventures that lay ahead. I thought I had a world of opportunities then. But now I knew, I had no freaking idea what true adventure was.

THE READY AND SET.

Eden

We had been on the mountain for a day, and the rain still fell in sheets outside the cave. Everyone tried sleeping, but the intensity of the lightening and thunder made it difficult. At least it gave us plenty of time to strategize and run scenarios. Thankfully, because the nymphs came through this door, granted centuries ago, they new what lay on the other side.

"The mountain is steep and quite treacherous, so the first of our kind eroded pathways around and up the mountain. The sloths eventually began building a city, but once they realized how difficult it was to maneuver the mountain, they gave up, leaving the foundations and walls intact. This section of the mountain is our best defense. The problem is getting there," Nanik said stoically.

Namy continued, *"The door is located on the north side of the mountain, and there is only a small and rather narrow pathway leading to the abandoned city. Crossing worlds will not be our problem. Nanik and I will take care of that. But getting down the mountain will be the challenge."*

"Don't worry, ladies. The men and I will take care of that." Charlie grinned.

Gabby rolled her eyes. "Um, Charlie you didn't fare so well last time you faced Sapp."

"I was blind-sided! That totally wasn't fair. This time I'm ready for the fight." He shoved his magazine into his Glock.

"And we're together. There are nine of us. We can handle a few sloths." James turned his attention to Charlie. "Make sure your safety is on."

That night, I ran the gamut of my usual barrage of latest dreams. The oval hatch door on the ocean floor, losing JJ on the dark set of spiral stairs, Gabby crying reading the letter, and finally the fire surrounding me and being unwilling to abandon whatever it was I protected. Just as the fire enveloped my torso, I startled awake.

The cave was dark, only a single lantern casting ominous shadows on the walls. The rain had slowed, providing a melodic sound that had gratefully put everyone to sleep. Everyone but Xander.

He rested his back on the cave wall opposite of me. His eyes bore into mine curiously.

"Nightmare," I mouthed.

He nodded once in understanding. Then he looked deeper into the cave and nodded asking me to follow. I slowly crept up, careful not to step on James or Gabby as I made my way over the sleeping bodies toward Xander. We walked only a small ways deeper into the cave, so we remained in the light.

"I am afraid after tomorrow we will not get a chance to talk, and there are still some things I need to share with you." Xander's eyes were hard. "There is something I should show you, from my past. Would you mind using your gift to watch it?"

"I'm not sure it works that way."

"I assure you, it does. If I open my mind to you and replay the memory, you will also be able to see it."

"How do you know that?" I questioned.

"My gift is being able to determine and understand the gifts of the people around me. It's how I knew about JJ's gift, and about yours and Gabrielle's," I wondered why I'd never thought to ask him his gift before. Perhaps because it wasn't so apparent he had one.

"Okay, so what do you want to show me?"

"Here." He held out his hand. I put mine into his as he raised it to his face. My eyes involuntarily closed, as a scene materialized around me.

The cold crept into my bones, and I knew immediately we were in Iskrem. A warm fire burned in the center of a large clearing, snow covered trees and large tented houses scattered around. A dozen Hiem children sat around the fire, laughing and playing with each other. Their snow-white hair danced around loose as a few of the children ran in circles. They suddenly all sat, quiet and patient, as an old hunched figure, covered in animal skin, approached the fire. Her downturned, coal black eyes and leathery, wrinkled skin revealed her age. White braided dreads fell down her back, only a foot from touching the snow-covered ground. The silence in the air was palpable as she stopped in front of the fire, looking around at the children.

Her voice was deep and ancient, capturing the children's attention as soon as she spoke.

"Long ago, before you or your parents, or your parent's parents were born, there was a time when The Tree of Light bloomed. Each and every branch contained seven magical purple flowers, and each flower contained seeds. These seeds were the very important seeds that gave the Stags the power to grow trees and the wisdom and knowledge of all the worlds." The children oohed and aahed. The old woman tiptoed around the fire. "The flowers grew from the light of Caelum's, our mother world, two suns. But when the Great War broke out between our people, the door was shut and never re-opened. For too many years, the door has remained closed. Unable to grow flowers, the tree has been seedless for generations." She stopped suddenly and raised her arms in the air.

"But one day, there will be one who carries the Mark. The Mark of the Tree of Light. The one who carries it will reopen the doors to allow the Tree to bloom once again. Unfortunately, at the ultimate price." She lowered her arms and bent down eye level with the children. "In order for the door to remain open, the Mark will have to burn and wither until no more."

My eyes focused in on one of the smaller children with shorter dread locks and a slight silver rim around his black irises. My waking dream zoomed in slowly getting lost in his coal eyes, as I found myself back in the present staring into the adult version of the Hiem from my vision.

I stood before Xander, hand still on his face, sadness radiating from his eyes. My hand dropped, suddenly understanding.

"The legend," I choked.

The dream of the fire.

The reason I would leave my family. I was protecting the Tree.

I was going to have to die.

The letter Gabby read in the dream, it was me telling her goodbye.

I understood it all now.

My mom sacrificed her life to save mine.

And now I needed to sacrifice mine, to save my daughter's, and the worlds.

Looking at Xander, I didn't have to ask why he didn't tell me sooner. His feelings for Gabby made this even more complicated.

"I'm so sorry, Eden." His face contorted. "I never imagined when I started this journey with you that I would come to care so strongly for you and your family."

"Thank you for telling me the truth now, Xander. It will allow me to do what I need to moving forward." I paused and looked at him with determination, desperately trying to hold myself together. "Obviously, we need to keep this between us."

"Of course," he said knowingly. "But I want you to know you are not alone. I will do whatever you need, whatever you ask of me." He bowed low.

"Thank you. But first we need get out of this horrible world so we can go home. I have a friend to bury."

We walked in silence back towards everyone sleeping. I lay back down in my spot between James and Gabby. As I settled in, Gabby rolled over and curled into me. I wrapped my arm around her as she snuggled her head into the crux of my arm.

Tears stung my eyes once again. I was getting used to the sensation.

But, she was worth it.

She and JJ were always worth it.

Laying my head back the full weight of Rosalina's death and the truth hit me hard. I gave the tears the permission they needed to flow freely. I would see Rosalina soon. I would see my mother soon.

But not tomorrow.

Tomorrow, I was taking my family home.

THE GO.

Eden

Everyone was in position. Namy stood holding her hooded and bound abductee in front of the huge side-by-side doors. The doors opened from the center and created a space large enough for any known animal to pass. The two figures standing in front of them looked dwarfed by their enormous size. The rest of us spread out on both sides, waiting for our cue, weapons ready.

The doors both slowly crept open, only a few feet, allowing for communication. Thankfully, we heard Namy's side of the conversation in our heads.

Where is General Sapp?

A low sloth's grumble followed.

I do not appreciate the terms being changed. I did not want to leave the world without my sister.

More growling.

He is saying Sapp is waiting at the base of the mountain, and I am supposed to follow him to make the trade, she voiced quickly. *He is alone, I feel this is our chance.*

Nanik answered her, *Pass through, and we will be right behind you.*

Namy walked into Palus first, pulling her smaller counterpart behind her. Not being comfortable with us being separated, even for a moment, I darted out of my hiding place towards the doors. A large branch the size of my torso rushed along side me and through the doors, blocking them from being able to close. A growl permeated through the opening as the sloth tried over and over to shut the portal. Nanik expanded the branch to give us enough space to escape from Asylum. By the time all of us had squeezed through, Namy was crumbled on the ground, and the sloth had a giant blade against the throat of the hooded figure. She kicked and flailed, but was no match for the sloth's strength.

Oh my God, this wasn't happening.

James had his gun drawn, but didn't want to shoot her by accident. I attempted to throw the sloth in a dream state, but was unable to enter his subconscious. As my mind raced for anything to save her, a vine fell down from the mountain cliff face above, wrapped around the sloths neck, under his metal helmet, and lifted him just off the ground enough to make him drop her and his weapon, as he attempted to save his own life.

She slumped to the ground, gasping. I ran over and pulled her away from the hanging, choking sloth. As soon as we were clear, James fired his gun at the beast's chest three times.

I yanked her hood off.

"Helvete, that was too close. No, really, take your time next time," Wanda cursed.

I sighed. "You did great. Thank you, Wanda."

"Well, just know that is the last time I'm playing hero. Even with my gift, I don't think it suits me."

"I wouldn't be so sure Wanda. I think it suits you just fine." Marek walked over and helped hoist her up. "Thanks for taking one for the team."

"Ah, yes, well. I do what I can." She blushed.

"Why didn't you just throw him in a dream state Eden?" Marek handed me my weapon.

"I tried, but it wasn't working."

By the time we checked that the sloth was officially dead, Namy was awake, and nursing a headache. We were ready to make our way down the mountain. Moving slowly along the winding path, it started to drizzle, making the already green, thick jungled mountains around us feel even more dangerous. Steeply pointed, tree covered, peaks jutted into the sky in all directions. In fact, we were so high up, there was cloud cover under us, making us unable to see any flat pieces of land at all. This was definitely a part of Palus I'd never seen, in dream or real life. Once we rounded to the other side of the mountain, the pass opened up into the abandoned, unfinished city that the nymphs described to us.

Rows of narrow strips of flat land were cut out of the mountain to allow for stone structures to be erected. It looked like only some foundations and walls had been built. Yet, dozens of walls on various levels had been started. Everything felt highly unsafe perched on the side of the mountain. No wonder the sloths gave up on it. One wrong move and you were plummeting to your death.

Gabby walked up beside me, donning her Valen chain mail that Caylio had made for her. She looked stunning with her hair braided and carrying Ava's weapon. She had gold tattoos painted over her arms and half her face. Apparently Shay had snuck a jar of her gold paint into Gabby's bag, and this morning the twins painted her up for good luck. Despite her youth, she looked like she could rule a world.

"This place gives me the creeps." She shuddered and looked around warily.

"I feel uneasy myself. Let's get down this mountain as quickly as we can. I want to know what is waiting for us at the bottom."

I am afraid you will not have to wait long.

I looked to the twin in my line of sight. Her eyes glanced up onto the ridges above us. I followed her gaze.

Slowly, sloths emerged from behind almost each and every stonewall.

He must have anticipated my betrayal.

No matter which direction I turned, more and more sloths revealed themselves. The nine of us pushed our backs together facing out in all directions weapons drawn.

"I see at least a dozen this way."

"Damn, I only have fourteen bullets left."

"I count twenty."

"Ten my way."

"I can't even count how many I see above us."

"I still have a full magazine."

"Hell, they're below us too."

"We're trapped."

"Dritt."

"Stop cursing in Norwegian, Wanda. At least give us the satisfaction of cursing along with you in English," Charlie grumbled.

"Okay, fine. Shit."

"Yes, thank you. I totally agree," Charlie spat.

"Namy, Nanik, are you with us?" I asked, still unsure as to whether or not to trust the nymphs.

Yes, we want our world back. These creatures have turned it in on itself. While we can and will not kill, we will help incapacitate them. You however, are free to do whatever is necessary. We are with you to the end.

Unsure which twin answered me, and really not caring, I mustered every ounce of courage available.

"Gabby, remember what I said about your gift. Use it, but be ready to fight. Boys, manage your bullets. Everyone, I know we are outnumbered, but we have seen our futures, and we are not destined to die here today," I said, trying to convince myself as well.

"Wait, I haven't! I haven't seen my future!" Wanda panicked.

"Stick with me, Wilhelmina. I'll keep you safe," Marek whispered.

"Gabrielle, may I have the honor of fighting along side you?" Xander spoke while keeping his focus on our enemies.

"If you can keep up," she tried to joke, but the tremble in her voice gave away her fear.

James looked over his shoulder down at me. "In every world?"

"In every world," I whispered.

"For Squash," James said softly.

I nodded, remembering his sacrifice so many years ago.

"For Door Keepers everywhere."

And with that, we all ran from the huddle and the battle began.

THE BATTLE.

Gabby

Training definitely helped give me tools and tricks to use during fighting, but I'm not sure there was anything to prepare me for the complete and utter explosion of chaos in battle. Growls, yells, bullets fired, crashing of swords, and slicing of blades erupted in my head. Everywhere I turned, someone I loved or cared about was in peril.

I attempted to focus on just what was in front of me, but it proved difficult. Pieces of my consciousness kept floating to find my mom or dad. The gymnastic moves I'd practiced did a good job for my defense but nothing to actually harm the enemy.

Xander stuck his axe in his opponent's back, just to pull it out and slice the midsection of the sloth behind him. Meanwhile, I jumped out of the way of an approaching sloth whose huge droopy eyes were set on me. He was simply too big. There was no way I could beat him. Harnessing my mind, I attempted to throw him in a dream state when he backhanded me, sending me flying. I landed on my back.

Dang that hurt.

Throwing my enemies into a dream state was much easier when I was expecting it, and they weren't. The chaos of battle wasn't conducive for mind control. I would definitely have to practice more before it would work while fighting.

I brushed the hair out of my face and checked that I wasn't bleeding when his shadow engulfed me. He stood right over me weapon raised. I swung my Grandmother's hook sword, catching him above the ankles and pulled as hard as I could. The sloth dropped his weapon and fell backwards. Before I could jump up, Xander had stabbed him in the chest.

He reached his hand out, pulling me up. Out of my peripheral a wild tangle of vines grabbed sloth after sloth, pushing and tying them to the rock wall behind us.

The nymphs were on our side after all.

Further to my left Charlie fired bullets into an oversized beast, but it wasn't falling or stopping, and he had one approaching from behind. Running as fast as my feet could carry me, I yelled, "Charlie, behind you!" I sliced the ankles of the sloth he was shooting at. After he went down face first, instinct took over, and I jumped on his back, stabbing him in the back with my blade.

Charlie had already taken his down when he turned and looked at me. "Dang, girl. Thanks."

"Anytime!" I yelled while running and jumping onto the ledge of the rock wall above us. Three sloths had backed Marek and Wanda against the cliff, so Xander and I attacked from the back, taking two of them down before they knew what hit them.

Sloths were dropping or being strung upside down in trees everywhere. I didn't see the twins, but knew they had to be close due to the number of moving and swinging branches that flew around us by their willpower.

Down several ridges below us, I spotted Mom and Dad fighting side by side. Dad obviously had already emptied his magazine, because he was using his machete to slice sloth after sloth. Paluns simply dropped in front of my Mom with little to no effort. Apparently, she had been practicing fighting in the subconscious realm. My mind snapped back to what was happening in front of us.

The four of us put our backs together as at least a dozen more sloths fell onto our ridge from the wall above.

I went low to try to take their feet out when one of the sloths blocked and kicked the weapon out of my hand. Marek immediately killed him, but the sloth next to him grabbed me and threw me up on the ridge above. The Valen had protected my midsection and chest, but two of his talons pierced my exposed shoulder. I rolled over clutching it in pain. Hearing something approaching and not wanting to take any chances considering my best weapon was two ridges down, I pulled the smaller knife from my ankle hoister and jumped onto the back of the sloth that threw me.

I stabbed him in the eye with the knife, and an inhuman roar rang in my ears. I jumped down, and one of my comrades took him down the rest of the way.

I tried to find Mom and Dad, but had climbed so many ridges, I wasn't sure where I left them. The wind picked up, cooling the air several degrees. I finally found them down the mountain about four ridges, maybe one hundred yards away.

I jumped down to the next ridge to retrieve my weapon, swinging it to make sure my injured shoulder still worked and prepared myself for the next enemy. Although not much could have prepared me for the monster that rounded the corner. Charlie swore not too far from me having reached the end of his magazine, fighting his own sloth. Xander, Marek, and Wanda were tied up in their own battles on the ridge above me, and my parents were too far to help.

I was on my own.

My mind suddenly raced to the vision JJ had shown me. The Valen, the gold tattoos, this monster of a beast before me. He told me not to be scared, that I was strong and brave, just like Mom. I crouched and grinned like a crazy person.

I had already won.

I yelled my best battle cry and ran towards the giant sloth. His grayish fur was already matted with blood in many areas. This one apparently didn't go down easy. I ducked his swing and went for his ankles, but one slice didn't do the trick. He simply glared down at me and growled. He lifted his enormous axe above his head and brought it down right on top of me.

Throwing my hook blade up, I caught it right on my handle, blade only six inches from my face. I pushed up with all my might, and then leveraging my weight I swung the hook around slicing him right up the middle.

The giant stumbled back then fell like a fallen log. I stood over him, feeling triumphant. Feeling strong. Feeling free.

THE FATED MOMENT.

Eden

"That's our daughter." James looked in awe at Gabby as her hair whipped around her face in the wind.

I'd never seen her look so wild. Or grown. Or regal.

She looked down at us, standing over one of the bigger sloths I'd ever seen, a smile taking up her entire face. She spun her blade and ran towards us, jumping from level to level until she landed on ours.

But before she reached us, a blood curdling shriek tore through the ruins, echoing off the walls, stopping us all in our tracks.

Marek.

James and I ran as fast as we could towards the noise, Gabby way ahead of us. Jumping up the levels every five feet exhausted me, but the adrenaline propelled me as the fear that Marek was in trouble pushed me forward. Every sloth attempting to block us crumpled in a heap as soon as my mind filled theirs with darkness. We rounded a stone corner and tried to take in the scene before us. Xander, Charlie, and Gabby were fighting off half a dozen sloths trying to protect Marek, who faced the stonewall behind them. He looked like he was struggling, but I couldn't see any signs of injury.

"Go to him. I'll help the kids," James yelled and pushed me towards my brother.

I ducked a sloth's swing and fell into the wall, looking up to see why Marek had screamed and why he was struggling.

Wanda had a spear through her chest pinning her into the stones behind her.

"Wanda, stay with me. Don't give up. I'll get you out of here." Panic filled his face.

I moved against the wall, avoiding the fighting around me, to get to Marek and Wanda. She fell in and out of consciousness.

"Wanda!" He yelled in her face when her head fell forward.

"Stop screaming at me, Marek. I'm right here." Her eyes bugged out of her head as she pulled it back up.

Marek laughed through his apparent frustration. "You crazy old Viking. Just stay still."

"Don't have . . . much choice . . . " She fainted again.

Marek's eyes pleaded with me. "We've got to get her off this wall and stop the bleeding." I nodded, noticing the spear had entered closer to her shoulder than I'd originally thought. If we could get her out of here, she might make it.

"One, two, three!" We both pulled, the spear coming out of the wall and Wanda's chest. Marek caught her, and we moved away from the fighting.

"Nanik!" Marek yelled as he carried Wanda to safety.

"*Yes?*" She appeared as if from nowhere.

"I need some large leaves and small vines." Both fell from the trees above in a pile next to Wanda's lifeless body. I held the leaves over her wound as Marek looped the vines around her body, providing pressure and keeping the leaves in place. "Can you take her up, safe in the trees until we can get her home?"

"*Yes, of course.*" Within seconds, a hammock of small vines was lowered into view. Marek laid Wanda in the woven green bed. Her usually scrunched up face was completely relaxed, which did little to ease my nerves.

"She'll be okay. Trust me—she can endure anything." I put a hand on Marek's shoulder as Wanda was hoisted up in the trees by an invisible force.

"Yeah, I know." Marek's mint eyes were watery. "She's too much of a pain in the ass to go quietly."

Our brother/sister moment was interrupted by the arrival of another wave of the enemy. Sapp wasn't a part of this bunch either. I assumed he would want to finish us off first hand. Squash had told us he was prideful. There was no way he wasn't here.

The sloth I currently fought was smaller than the rest, but faster. I had already tried to knock him out with my gift, but it wasn't working on him. He wielded two short handled axes, both double edged, the metal matching his helmet. I gripped Taran's branch like a baseball bat and swung away, knocking one of the axes out of his talons. He reared his remaining axe back and threw it at me with incredible force. With only milliseconds to spare, I pulled the branch across my chest, the axe sticking into it like a piece of firewood. The force knocked me off my feet and onto my back. The sloth roared furiously, running towards me with talons out, weaponless yet with enough fury for fear to rip through me. I tilted my spear end of my weapon up and stuck the branch into the ground for leverage, and before he knew what happened, he'd impaled himself.

James helped me up. "You know, considering how we both came out looking last time we went up against sloths, I'd say we're doing pretty good."

"I think we were a little more prepared this go around," I rested my hands on my knees, attempting to catch my breath. "Sometimes my gift works and sometimes it doesn't. I don't understand why. How many more are left? I feel like we've been fighting forever!"

"There's under twenty left."

"Where is Sapp?" I narrowed my eyes.

"*Mom!*"

James and I both turned to see Gabby two levels below us, alone. A heavily armed sloth approached her, one with a deep jagged scar running through where his eye used to be, although this time most of the scar hid under an ornate helmet.

I'd jumped down both levels before my brain could even register what was happening. Vaguely aware of yells and hollers around me, I barely felt my body as it moved on instinct. I knew there were still over a dozen sloths left fighting above us. The guys were just going to have to take them down.

Sapp was ours.

The sneer on the ancient beast's face caused fury to rip through me. Gabby stood beside me, her brow creased, determination radiating through every facial muscle. Feeling my gaze, she glanced over my shoulder.

"I can't get to his subconscious," I stammered.

"It's okay. We've got this."

I nodded. "You bet we do."

We both faced our opponent and readied our weapons.

Sapp stopped about ten feet ahead of us and swung his axe through the air, howling, snarling, and pounding his fisted claw into the compacted dirt. Gabby and I held our ground, forcing him to make the first move.

He lunged forward. We dove to opposite sides to avoid his swing, each of us slicing our weapons across his back. His tail swung wide, taking our feet out from beneath us. Gabby attempted hooking one of his legs, and pulled, but it seemed he had some sort of leather protection.

Before we got back to our feet, Sapp had already turned, pinning Gabby against the stonewall. She scrambled up against the wall, pulling her knife from her ankle sheath. I jumped up, ran at full force towards the monster, running up his hunched back, throwing Taran's branch around the sloth's neck and used my strength to choke him.

Sapp reached up, attempting to grab me, his giant talons ripping across my back. Pain shot through every ounce of my body, but I refused to let go. When he realized that wasn't working he abandoned Gabby, pushing me up against the stonewall, the hard stone scrubbing my now open wounds. Every pebble sent waves of nausea until I couldn't take it any more, and finally crumpled to the ground. Sapp stood over me in triumph and lifted his weapon when Gabby stabbed the knife into his shoulder, he stumbled back, and I scrambled out from his line of sight.

"Mom." Gabby bent down to me. "Are you okay?"

"I just need a minute . . . " I braced myself and fought the urge to burst into tears.

Gabby was up and luring the giant beast away from me. Injured and feeling powerless, I could only watch as she blocked, kicked, flipped, and fought the General alone. Darkness crept at the edge of my vision. Any energy I had waned, my thoughts incoherent.

"Gabby . . . " I whispered.

She must have felt my calling out to her, because she turned towards me at the worst possible moment. Sapp used her momentary lack of unawareness to punch her hard, her lifeless body flew through the air. Her hook sword landed at my feet and her body crumpling in a heap next to me.

"No!"

Every emotion imaginable coursed through me.

My eyes wouldn't leave her until her back rose and dropped ever so slightly. Once I knew she was alive, I turned them to the creature before me.

He simply stood in front of me, sniffing, unable to see me, but nonetheless glaring at me with his one eye. Content to feel my pain. Confident he had finally beaten us.

This monster kidnapped my daughter. He almost killed Charlie and tried to kill Marek. He succeeded in killing Squash. He allowed Aslak access to the worlds. And he was never gonna stop.

He'd been on this path for years and years, following his father's obsession, and I knew, if I didn't stop him, it would never end. Especially now that he had actually crossed worlds.

You are never alone.

My mother's voice floated in my mind as if from far away. I'm never alone. I was surrounded by family and friends, fighting along side me. My family at home, in Caelum waiting for me. So many people counting on me, so many people who loved me.

I fought for them.

Noticing vines slithering their way across the ground behind the General, ready to trap him where he stood, I reached out slowly and gripped the hooked blade that belonged to my mother. Taking a deep breath, I cut my eyes to the monster facing me in satisfaction. If a sloth could smirk, he was. Pulling my feet underneath my body, I straightened with all my remaining strength.

I lifted the sword, feeling every movement in my shredded back. Channeling the pain from my injuries and allowing it to fuel my anger, my adrenaline, I pulled energy from everyone I knew were with me in spirit. My mother, my father, James, Gabby, JJ, Mae, Marek, Charlie, my adoptive family, all the Door Keepers who came before me, and those who would come after.

A smile crept up deep within my gut that slowly made its way to my face, as I realized I had an army behind me.

Nanik, now.

The vines whipped around my enemy's feet, securing him where he stood. I leapt forward twice, towards the oversized monster. Then jumping to my left onto the stonewall, I simultaneously hooked my sword around the sloth's neck. Using the momentum of the wall, I pushed myself off, swinging around, allowing my body weight to do the work. By the time I'd swung all the way around the beast, landing where I'd started, Sapp's head, still in his helmet, had already thumped to the ground.

I shuddered, dropping the handle of the sword, and collapsed next to my daughter.

THE DOOR KEEPER FUNERAL.

Eden

The suns set to our backs, as darker shades of blue and purple filled the sky. The shallow water seemed to glow under our bare feet as we stood around in reverent silence. Other than our immediate family, only Door Keepers were present. A somber, yet hopeful mood hung in the air. This was after all, the first true Door Keeper funeral since even before my mother's passing.

The small, round island was only about fifteen feet in diameter and besides the rectangular stone altar in the center, every square foot was filled with flowers, exotic and colorful. My father, Marek, James, and Charlie carried her in on the door. Following the small path onto the island, they laid her on the stone altar.

My eyes teared as they landed on the beautiful cream colored, cotton dress she wore, simple and elegant. Her matching blondish grey hair flowed around her, adorned with small, intricate flowers. Her hands wrapped around a bushel of lavender, centered on her stomach.

Gabby squeezed my hand next to me. I didn't need to hear the sniffles to feel the grief radiating off her.

"She looks so beautiful," she whispered.

"Yes, she does," was all I could bring myself to say.

Gio was the only one standing on the tiny island with her, while the rest of us stood around in the sea. He glanced down at her lovingly and looked around to those in attendance.

"There are few people in the worlds that have the honor of carrying a key. Only a few of us have the opportunity to guard a door, and be responsible for carrying on the legacy of that calling. Some of us have known this was our destiny since our birth." Gio looked to towards James, Charlie, and Jay. "And some of us were surprised by the unknown." He looked towards myself, then down to Rosalina.

"Rosalina was just such a person. She wasn't born into the Door Keeper life, but it seemed to choose her. Ava chose her.

Rosalina carried a key and it's secret for thirty years, and for that we honor her as an honorary Door Keeper today. This door, the door that will carry her into eternity, is the very door that Rosalina was charged to protect. After all, this is the door that brought Ava into her life, as well as the one that brought Rosalina here, to her death.

I know how many of you cared for Rosalina and I want to give you the opportunity to express your gratitude and say your goodbyes."

I looked around at everyone in attendance. Door Keepers from many worlds had come to pay their respects to the human civilian who kept our secret for so long. Most of these Door Keepers had never crossed worlds, having inherited their title since my mother's death and my father's decree. Only a couple had ever been to Caelum before.

My father walked up the path and stood over Rosalina first.

"I owe more than I could ever express in words to Rosalina. If not for her . . . if not for you." He glanced down at our resting friend. "I would have never met my daughter or my grandchildren." His watery gray eyes met mine. "In guarding the key, Rosalina gave me a gift she didn't even know she was giving me. She gave me a second chance. An opportunity to make up for the wrongs I'd done to my own family and to those in other worlds." He paused, making eye contact with my father-in-law. "Rosalina became my friend, my confidant. I will be forever grateful for what she has done for my family and me. May she now and forever, rest in peace." He leaned down, kissed her forehead, and walked off the island.

One by one, those who knew Rosalina and were indebted to her, paid their respects. Tears were shed, laughter filled the darkening sky, and silence commenced when words would not do. Finally, I knew it was my turn to end the tributes. Walking up the small stone path, my eyes stopped on a clump of Serenbes growing among some sunflowers. Reaching down, I plucked one and after reaching her resting body, tucked it over Rosalina's ear.

"It's amazing. Everything I've come to value, from my husband and children even down to this flower, I owe to Rosalina. I wouldn't even know Serenbes existed without her. And let's be honest, I'd probably never have dated you, fallen in love, and had JJ." I glanced at my husband, holding my son. Tears quickly followed. "Rosalina was there when Mom died. She gave me my life," I choked out.

I closed my eyes and took a deep breath.

"I think it's wonderfully poetic that neither Rosalina nor Ava died in the world in which they were born. They died in each other's. What a beautiful connection. It's almost as though, even in her death, she is allowing us the closure my family never got with my mother. And that was simply Rosalina. She was selfless, thoughtful, and wise. She was my friend. She was very important things to many of us, but above all, in fulfilling a promise made to a dying friend, she unknowingly became a Door Keeper. And today, and every day forth, we honor her."

After squeezing Rosalina's clasped hands, I whispered goodbye.

The fire was lit and the flames rose high within minutes. The heat burned my face with emotions I wasn't sure would ever dissipate, burning them into my mind and heart forever. Everyone stood in silence, the crackling of flames and the subtle waves of the sea as the only soundtrack. My eyes followed the burning embers as they rose slowly into the night's sky, like fireflies.

A sweet soprano voice softly began singing to a haunting Scandinavian tune.

Going home, going home
I'm jus' going home
Quiet like, some still day
I'm jus' going home

It's not far, yes close by
Through an open door
Work all done, care laid by
Going to fear no more

All the friends I knew
I'm going home

Nothing lost, all's gain
No more fret nor pain
No more stumbling on the way
No more longing for the day
Going to roam no more

Morning star lights the way
Restless dream all done
Shadows gone, break of day
Real life, yes, begun

Going home, going home
I'm jus' going home
It's not far, yes close by
Through an open door
I'm jus' going home

Going home, going home

Before Wanda had completed the lovely ballad, Gabby slipped her arm around me and laid her head on my shoulder. A few of her tears dripped down my bare arms. After finishing, Wanda walked over to me and took my hand.

"I'm sorry for your loss." Her eyes contained nothing but compassion. "I didn't know Rosalina, but I respect what she did and that she took care of you and brought you back to where you belong."

"Thank you for the beautiful song, Wanda." Gabby smiled down at her.

"It's from one of my favorite symphonies growing up. I thought it prudent." She bowed her head and left with the other Door Keepers, leaving just the family to collect Rosalina's remains.

"She is full of surprises, that one." James came up behind us, resting his hands on our shoulders. "It was a beautiful memorial. The first true Door Keeper funeral I've ever been to."

"Unfortunately, it's been the first one held in many, many years. A tradition that will resume from here on out." My father exhaled.

"Well, let's just hope we won't need one for awhile." Marek and Charlie joined us.

A knot twisted in my stomach, knowing that mine would most likely be next. I looked up at my father forcing myself back into the moment. "Thank you for allowing her to be cremated with the door. I know it's been Caelum and Earth's door for a long time."

"After everything that has happened, Eden, I'm happy for new beginnings. Not long after you returned those years ago, I commissioned Caelum's Door Maker to begin work on a new one. Although, I must say I didn't imagine this would be the catalyst for us to make the change."

"Unfortunately, it's rarely the joyous times that mold us and force us to makes the changes necessary," Mae said solemnly.

"That would make life easier though now, wouldn't it?" Charlie grimaced.

"It would, indeed." Xander appeared, his long white dreads loose, hanging low down his back. "I'm sorry to intrude on your private moment, but I'm afraid I must be heading back to Iskrem. I have much to learn and determine before we plan our next move against Aslak."

"Yes, of course." I nodded.

Charlie interjected. "I should probably reach out to the twins, now that they are back in Palus. I'm sure they can find us some intel on the Paluns' movements and if Aslak makes an appearance there."

Xander eyed him. "That is a good idea, thank you." He turned his attention back to me. "I'll be waiting for you to reach out when you are ready to move forward, once your business is taken care of."

"Thanks, Xander. It should only be a few weeks for us to go to British Columbia and back home to make sure everything is in order for us to be away for an extended period of time."

"Absolutely, I will see you all soon." He nodded at everyone individually, but it was Gabby who got the brief and rare smile.

"See you later, Xander." She smiled back.

* * * * *

I reached over a pair of folded shirts to grab her dresses and lay them in her bag carefully. She hadn't brought many clothes with her, knowing that Caelun garb would be provided when she arrived. I moved across the room that Rosalina and Gabby had shared to get the rest of her things. Even after the funeral, packing up her stuff felt so final, almost as though once the things she owned were packed up and gone, she would be too.

I glanced down at the chest at the foot of the bed. A beautiful handcrafted urn sat on its center, carved by Caelum's Door Maker. He had made a gorgeous round container carved from a tree only found in Caelum with an intricate rose pattern inlaid from an Earth's olive tree across the top. Earth and Caelum, both worlds always represented.

Moving back towards the bed, I remembered she had told me she had written letters to her daughter and grandchildren. I approached the small desk sitting under the window and pulled out the drawer, so I wouldn't forget to pack them. As I slid the drawer out, my heart fell deep into my stomach, and a wave of dread coursed through me.

The water colored stationary edged with yellow flowers sat neatly in a pile.

The same stationary Gabby had been reading in my dreams.

The letter from me.

As if it had already written itself, I knew what the letter would say. I knew why she would be crying, and I knew why I had to write it. I pulled out the chair and sat before I could change my mind. Pulling out the paper and pen, I spread it across the desk. I had to close my eyes and take a deep breath, knowing this would be one of the hardest things I'd ever have to do.

The emotions already pouring too easily from Rosalina's funeral, I had to choke down a sob as I put pen to paper.

My dearest Gabby . . .

THE BUSINESS VACATION.

Eden

    The wind whipped through my hair as I drove the jeep we rented. I glanced down following the red line on the navigation screen to make sure I didn't miss my turn. They only lived on the other side of the island, but there were still plenty of places to get lost. I finally pulled around the cul-de-sac in front of a quaint little chalet styled cottage.
    Taking a deep breath, I grabbed the urn buckled in my passenger seat, and walked toward the house. Colorful flowers crawled up the sides of the gray, wooden shingled walls. With Rosalina's love for flowers, it was easy to see her handiwork here. The front door swung open as I was half way up the walkway.
    "Hello, what can I do for—" The pretty petite woman stopped short when her eyes examined me. She cocked her head to the side. "I'm sorry—are you . . . ?"
    "Hello Celia. I'm Eden."
    "Forgive me." Her smile held a twinge of sadness as she stepped down the stone steps. "Mom told me so much about you, but I must say, you don't look exactly like I expected."
    "Oh?"
    "You look more like someone she used to tell me stories about when I was a little girl." When her smile reached her eyes, she looked just like Rosalina in the old picture of her and my mother. "It's so nice to finally meet you face to face." We shook

hands, and her eyes fell to the carved sphere I held against my torso.

Understanding and comprehension registered on her face, and I was suddenly incredibly thankful I'd called her as soon as we'd returned to Italy to give her time to process through the grief.

"Is that her?" The tears filled her soft brown eyes.

"Yes." I handed her the urn.

"It's beautiful." She knit her eyebrows together, rubbing her fingertips along the scalloped roses inlaid on the wooden carvings. "It's just perfect."

* * * * *

I walked through the ornate screened door and called out for my family. Only silence met my greeting. Throwing my keys on the counter, I passed into the cheerful little kitchen and peered into the dining room. Trying the living room only to find it empty, a squeal echoed from outside behind the house. I pushed myself through the old-timey back screen door to look on onto the expansive low tide, red-sanded beach stretching out like the shallow seas of Caelum.

When we found this little house on Prince Edward Island, I instantly knew that low tide would be my favorite part of the day, for that very reason. I walked the old wooden plank walkway leading me to the stairs, down to the sand flats sprinkled with pockets of seawater. JJ and Gabby played tag with James, giggling and screaming in delight when caught. Gabby saw me first, called out, and waved. James turned and gave me a furrowed brow, a look he always gave me when he was concerned.

"How did it go?" he asked when I approached.

"It went as well as one could have hoped."

"I think it was nice you brought her to them in person."

"I'm just glad we could at least make a trip out of it. You know, spend some time together before we jump back in to what awaits us in Iskrem." I looked out as my kids ran along and splashed in the pools of water.

James put his arm around me. "Yeah, it's beautiful here. I've always wanted to visit this place. My parents used to talk about this part of Canada all the time."

"Celia told me some places we can take the kids while we're here. Some local beaches to look for crabs and sea glass."

"Sounds good. You know I love you."

I returned his soft gaze. "In every world."

*****

"JJ, hang on dude!" James yelled out to our son as he darted from seashell to sea shell up ahead.

"He loves these beaches." I chuckled. "Probably reminds him of Caelum."

"Probably." James thumb caressed mine. "Why did Gabbs bring her backpack?"

"Ever since the kidnapping, I think she's nervous not to be ready for anything."

He grimaced. "I hate that. I don't want her always worried something bad is going to happen."

"Me either." I stared at our daughter walking slowly between JJ and us. "I don't think it's a bad worry. I think it's just a 'want to be prepared' worry."

"I wonder where she got that from?"

As if sensing we were talking about her, she turned and yelled at us, "What are we supposed to be looking for again? Something Kettle . . . ?"

"Teacup Rock!" I yelled back. "I think we'll know it when we see it."

"I'll take your word for it." She smiled as the wind whipped her hair, blocking her face.

Within a few minutes we stumbled across the large red rock, perched like a teacup on a saucer. The tide was low, allowing us to walk around and take pictures in front of the huge rock's balancing act.

Gabby took a selfie with her phone with the whole family. JJ immediately took off on his next sea adventure and left us attempting to catch up.

"This beach is my favorite so far," Gabby commented. "What's it called again?"

"Thunder Cove. Celia recommended it because not too many tourists come here."

"I haven't seen anyone else in a while." James looked around. "Wait, where's JJ?"

I turned around and didn't see him.

"JJ!" I yelled and heard no reply.

The three of us split up before more words were spoken. I ran out towards the waters edge, my feet hitting the dense, compacted sand. Small footprints sprawled towards and disappeared into the water. The water was shallow for a ways but it didn't stop the panic from rising within me. JJ was a good swimmer, but this was unfamiliar ocean water. Why would he have come out here? I turned around in all directions frantically, searching for a glimpse of him.

As soon as my eyes landed on it, I took off running towards it. A giant grey stoned lighthouse rose high out of the middle of the ocean. Water soaked every inch of me as I ran through the shallow water, desperate to reach JJ before he attempted to reach the lighthouse. The dream I'd had so many times floated through my head like a distant memory. I had seen this happening before, but I couldn't remember how it ended. I couldn't tell how deep the water got, considering it was low tide. I hoped it was shallow enough to be safe.

I vaguely heard someone yelling behind me, but I ignored it, knowing every second counted on my current course. Dread filled my stomach as I got closer and closer, not seeing JJ anywhere. The red top towered above the water, but no light emanated from the perch. Only a flicker of a shadow.

JJ.

THE LIGHTHOUSE.

Eden

Thinking of him alone at the top of the lighthouse sent my mind reeling. How had he gotten up there already? I pushed my legs faster. They slowed the deeper the water got. I finally reached the base of the stone and circled it to find metal rungs cemented into the rock. I scrambled up the ladder before a wave crashed into me. I reached the ledge that circled around the lighthouse until I found the door inside. I pushed the door open to enter a dark space with only a little light slicing through the open door behind me. A dark rod iron spiral staircase sat on the opposite side of the circular space and raced up them. About ten steps up I jumped when her voice echoed around me.

"Mom!"

"Gabby, go get your dad. JJ's at the top."

"He's right behind me. I'm coming with you!" Her voiced bounced with every skipped step.

We climbed and climbed until we saw a light above us. My feet carried me upwards even as every muscle in my body screamed at me. A squeal echoed through the circular shaft we rose through. After reaching the platform, Gabby and I tore in opposite directions only to both stop dead in our tracks.

There, perched high on an old dusty box, stood JJ with his arms outstretched against the huge window, laughing in delight.

"JJ!" I half sighed in relief and yelled in immense anger.

"Momma!" JJ turned with the largest smile on his face I'd ever seen. But as soon as he saw the look on our faces, it crumbled.

"I'm sorry. Don't be mad." His eyes immediately teared up. "I'm so sorry."

I ran over and grabbed him, squeezing him tight.

"JJ, this is so dangerous. You should never go off by yourself."

"I'm sorry, but the ocean is so big." He wiped my tears.

"I know the ocean is big, but you scared us all."

James tore into the landing and fell to his knees in relief when he saw JJ in my arms.

"I'm sorry, Daddy. The ocean is so big. Very deep."

"JJ, you know better than to leave without telling us," James got out in between gulps of air.

"Please don't be mad. I can't help it."

"Yes you can. You can help it. Please don't go anywhere alone again."

"But I'm not alone. My family is here."

"Yeah, *now*!" Gabby looked at me with a face that almost made me laugh if adrenaline wasn't still coursing through me.

"Look, the ocean is big." JJ pointed to a door on the far end of the circular room.

"Honey, why do you keep saying that?" I brushed his brown curls out of his eyes. James got up and walked over to the door.

"The ocean is deep," he said again.

"JJ, the ocean is shallow right now, it's low tide." Gabby looked at him blankly.

"Eden." James' tone got my attention immediately.

"Here, take your brother." I handed JJ to Gabby. I walked over to James, and he looked at me hard, his eyes filled with recognition.

"Look."

I followed his gaze, and it took me a moment for my brain to register what I was seeing. A small unassuming lock and knob on the extremely average wooden door. It was completely normal except for the bronzish gold metal the keyhole was made of.

Looking back up into James face I whispered, "A Door Keeper lock? Have you ever heard of a door here?"

"No, I haven't."

"I don't have my key."

"I do." I startled as Gabby's voice perked up behind me.

"Why do you have it?" I looked blankly at my daughter.

"After what we've been through, why would you go anywhere without it?" She raised her eyebrows.

I reached out and took the key from her outstretched hand. Inserting and turning it proved our theory correct. This was a Door. I slowly opened it, having no idea what we'd see on the other side. The only thing that waited on the other side was complete blackness. No feeling of energy or anything out of the ordinary, I slipped through the door without opening it all the way.

My bare feet felt the metal grate beneath me and I saw another spiral staircase, this one leading down.

"It's not another world, but it seems to open to another part of the lighthouse. Gabbs, you don't happen to have a flashlight in that pack of yours, do you?" I called over my shoulder.

"You bet."

A flashlight nudged my side a second later. After turning it on, I slowly made my way down the metal staircase, the sound of the ocean growing louder the further I descended. Knowing my family crept down behind me, I warned them when I reached the bottom.

I stood on a narrow scaffolding that ran the circumference of the lighthouse. Peering down carefully over the side into the middle and pitch-black darkness below, the flashlight glistened on the watery depths.

"Is that the ocean?" James reached the bottom of the stairs and onto the round platform.

"I guess so, but why? Why is the lighthouse hollow?" I asked, not expecting an answer. I ran the flashlight along the stone rounded walls for anything out of the ordinary. The light landed on a large red switch. I hesitated only a second before I flipped it on. The entire vertical stone tunnel glowed with red light. Old school red light bulbs incased in metal hung on different levels of the hole, lighting up the entire interior. Collectively, the four of us leaned over the railing to notice another metal ladder leading down, into the water. The red lights also continued down, below the water line around ten feet below the waters surface.

The red water glowed eerily below us, as it lapped against the interior of the lighthouse.

"What is that?" Gabby pointed and squinted her eyes. A metal glistened in the water, looking like it was set in the stone rock below.

"I don't know what that is, but I sure recognize that."

James pointed to a bronze mask hanging on the wall.

A breathing apparatus that looked a lot like the one Gabby had been given by Calyio.

"Guys, this one's just like mine." Gabby picked it up, inspecting it. Her eyes glistened as she looked at us.

JJ broke the silence that had filled the empty space.

"The ocean is big, very, very deep." His eyes were wide and expectant. "Momma and Gabby are explorers."

"Buddy, you think we should explore the big and deep ocean?"

"Yes, definitely a good idea!" He smiled his toothy grin.

"I think it's a *great* idea." Gabby shoved the breathing apparatus at me and pulled out another from her pack.

"You packed that thing too?" James asked surprised.

"Look at where we are Dad and what we are doing. Are you really asking me that right now?" She pulled the mask over her head.

"Okay, if you both are doing this, promise me you'll go down, take a look, then come right back up. No funny business."

"We wouldn't dream of it, Dad."

"That's seriously not funny." He glared at our daughter.

"We'll be right back. I promise. We're not going anywhere." I put my hand on his arm.

Gabby and I lowered ourselves down the ladder carefully, the mask feeling a bit uncomfortable up my nose. I reached the water first and pushed back towards the center of the circle to let Gabby down. As soon as she was submerged, we went underwater. The first gulp of air through the mask felt wrong, but with every breath the oxygen to my lungs came easier and with less effort.

I swam down, the salt water stinging my eyes, and found myself face to face with a huge oval hatch. It was at least six feet tall, made of the Door Maker's metal material. Rivets and bolts rose along the edges and three large circles were engraved down the center of the hatch. The top circle was a series of circles interconnected, forming one larger circle. The lower one looked more like a vent, but encased within a glass material that seemed to cover it. The middle was a round wheel, with a perfect keyhole in its center.

This was a door. And before my brain had even put the pieces together I knew it was to the lost world, the world where the door's metal originated from, and the world Calyio came from, where Valen was harvested.

This was the lost Door.

I looked to Gabby, and she nodded. She pulled the key out from around her neck and handed it to me. We swam towards the door and grabbed on to a piece of the hatch to secure ourselves.

Inserting the key, the wheel clicked as though it was free to turn. We wedged our feet against the stonewall to get leverage and turned the wheel to the submarine door. It groaned in protest with every inch. It took us a good solid minute of turning before we heard the clinking of metal, signaling the unlocking mechanisms. Pushing our feet against the stones, we pulled with all our might. The groaning and creaking of the Valen increased with each bit of progress.

Within seconds of the door opening, warm sweet water filled the space salt water had previously occupied, and kelp tickled our bare legs. Gabby and I gazed completely mesmerized into the lost world no human had seen in over half a millennium.

At that moment, I knew JJ was more in tune with the worlds than any of us knew possible. At that moment, I understood that every dream, every foreshadowing glimpse had led us here. Even Rosalina's death and her daughter moving to this island on the other side of the planet, was predestined. At this moment, fate was in control, and no matter what we did, no matter what choices I made, I wasn't going to be able to escape mine.

THE EPILOGUE.

My dearest Gabby,
    Somebody said that it couldn't be done.
But you with a chuckle replied, That maybe it couldn't,
    but you would be one,
    that wouldn't say so till you tried.
So you buckled right in with a trace of a grin
    on your face if you worried, you hid it.
    And you started to sing
as you tackled the thing, that couldn't be done,
    and you did it.
There are thousands to tell you it can not be done.
    There are thousands to prophesy failure.
There are thousands to point out to you one by one,
    the dangers that wait to assail you.
But just buckle right in, with a bit of a grin,
    just take off your coat and go do it.
Just start to sing, as you tackle the thing,
    that can not be done, and you'll do it.

    One of my greatest joys in my life was saying this poem with you every night. Hearing your tiny voice sing the words always filled me with hope for our future. I pray these words do the same for you today as you look forward to what is to come.

    Gabby, I am so sorry. I'm sorry for every unfulfilled promise. I'm sorry for every way that I may have failed you. But most of all, I am sorry that I can't be there for you today of all days.

There is no way I can put into words how much I love you. Those three little words can't fully convey the adoration, pride, or gratefulness I feel for you. I adore your fun loving spirit and ability to brighten a room simply by entering it. I love your infectious laugh and how giddy you get when you stay up too late. Even how you used to cut your eyes at me when your Dad or I embarrassed you when you were in middle school. How your eyes sparkle when you tell a joke.

I am so incredibly proud of the woman you have become. You are so brave, fearless, kind, and selfless. I saw the bravery and fearlessness in you even as a child, that look of determination you got on your face before trying a new skill in gymnastics. The same look you wore before we faced Sapp on that cliff in Palus. The same look I'm sure you're wearing right now.

I am most grateful for your kind heart and selflessness. You are an amazing older sister to JJ, always willing to put his needs above your own. I can't count the number of nights you read to him before bed, constantly giving in to his "one more time, please, Gabbs!" Your willingness to bear with us through his tantrums and teachable moments proves that you will take good care of him now that I'm gone.

Both JJ and your dad will need your strength moving forward. But please, never be afraid to be vulnerable, especially to those closest to you. That includes your family as well as those you choose for your inner circle. Admitting your weaknesses allows those around you to truly love you, to truly accept you, flaws and all. And those are the best, most lasting relationships. Please never forget that.

I desperately need you to know that you gave me everything I could I have ever wanted in life, before I became a Door Keeper and every moment since.

I wouldn't have traded you and JJ, or your futures, for anything, and that is why I had to die. I realized that just as Ava died to give me the life I needed to raise you, I had to sacrifice myself to give you the life you were called to live.

And my sweetest Gabby, you have been called to live an incredible and important life. I want you to know that I do not regret a single thing. Rosalina reminded me that all things serve a purpose, even death. Take the lessons given in hardships and grief and let them teach you only the things they can—perseverance, gratitude, and courage.

No matter how difficult the circumstance, however tough your situation, you will survive. And knowing you, my love, you will not only survive, but you'll find your joy again. Never forget to be grateful for the little things. That is one thing I've learned from my life, to enjoy and be thankful for it all. The good and the bad, because it all teaches you, molds you, makes you who you are.

And if you are anything Gabby, you are the physical manifestation of happiness. Your ability to bring joy into any situation is a gift you received from Ava. I hope that it is passed onto your daughter one day. I may have stumbled upon my only true regret. One of the few things I'll never get to see or experience. You will be the most amazing mother . . .

Although I am not here with you physically, you know enough of our family to know we are never truly gone. Even death cannot separate us, because the dream world is eternal. And just remember, whenever you are scared or afraid, need some encouragement, or even just miss me, I'm only a dream away. I love you, Gabbs.

Forever yours,
Mom

Eden and Gabby's story will conclude in
THE DOOR CLOSES

ACKNOWLEDGMENTS

Of course the first person I want to thank is my incredible husband, Andy. You have given me one of the most amazing gifts, the freedom to pursue my passions. Thank you for every word of encouragement, plot suggestion, and piece of advice. But above all, thanks for inspiring one of my most favorite characters. You are my real life James, in every world.

Peyton, I adore you, plain and simple. You are one of the biggest joys in my life. Your laughter, sense of humor, talent, and discipline floor me every single day. You are such a ginormous part of these books, and I'm so grateful for your enthusiasm about them. Thank you for loving me and letting me be a part of your life.

Eli, my perfect little man, who is almost as tall as me now. I can't tell you what a joy it was to write JJ. To be able to think back to when you were small and capture some of my most favorite moments was such a gift. I'm so thrilled that your character made its debut in this book, and I can't wait to see where he goes. Your kind heart, gentle soul, and unbridled enthusiasm about what you love make you remarkable. I love you, little man.

Mom and Dad, I can't thank you enough for raising me in such a way that prepped me to follow my dreams. When I think back to my childhood, you encouraged me to do my best, use my imagination, and always celebrated my wins no matter how small. Thank you for believing in The Door Keeper Trilogy and being such a huge support in this entire process.

To the rest of my family, thank you for always being there for me and for inspiring some of the coolest characters ever.

Next, I have to thank my Beta Readers. The insanely amazing ladies who helped me hone this story. I couldn't ask for a more wonderful group of ladies to go through this process with. I trust you with Eden and Gabby and appreciate all of your amazing feedback and advice.

Bonnie. BEENIE. My book buddy. We've already walked through so much together, and it's been wonderfully unexpected to continue through writing, publishing, and promoting books together. Thank you for always being one of the first people I call with an idea or good news.

Tara. Girlfriend. Our friendship has weathered different continents, countries, babies, illness, hairstyles and crazy colors, churches, and many different jobs. I don't think it's a coincidence that we both landed with writing. Of course our paths would merge back together, and I couldn't be more thrilled.

Natalie. Oh, my sweet, D. We have journeyed through some amazing and insane things side by side. I can never thank you enough for walking with me through this process. Thank you for coming over and talking me down while I rotated from laughter to crying over edits for The Door Keeper. That was a moment I'll never forget.

Maureen. You have been such a long time, dependable friend, my favorite to reconnect with after any amount of absence. Because it never feels that way. We always pick back up with ease, always feeling like yesterday when we hung out last, and we always end up laughing. You consistently blow me away with your talent, wisdom, and vulnerability. I appreciate you so dang much.

Jessica. Stewie and Steen forever. You will forever hold a unique and important place in my heart for the large part you played in me getting here. Although we are no longer on the same path and seeing each other all of the time, you are a permanent fixture in my life. It still blows me away that you printed off TLD for your notes. I will keep it forever. :)

Jordan. You may have been later to The Door Keeper game than the rest of these ladies, but you have more than made up for it with your encouragement, enthusiasm, and ridiculous party throwing skills. You are an amazing friend who really understands what it looks like to lift up those around you. You are incredible, and I'm honored that you have chosen me as a friend.

To my super talented cover designer, Brittney. You took a crude drawing and turned it into a masterpiece. I couldn't have done it without you, and I appreciate your putting up with the many pestering texts on my end.

I believe my editor deserves the most apologies, however. Kim, you were so patient with me and really pushed this story to the next level. I appreciate your willingness to have conversations and to encourage me as you corrected. Between my love for sentence fragments and my incessant need to make my characters smile, you consistently and gently nudged in the right direction. I aways felt your belief in my work, which is more than any writer could ask from their editor. You are simply the best.

Shout out to the lady golf cart cop on Fripp Island who forever solidified my friendship with six girlfriends. Wherever you are, we never intended to pay that $200 ticket for breaking the "common sense while driving a golf cart" law that didn't actually exist. You gave us something to laugh about for the next three years. Wanda forever.

To you, my dear reader. Thank you for taking the time to read this story. Thank you for loving Eden and Gabby as I do and for investing in this book series. I appreciate every purchase, every review, every word of encouragement, and every email. You guys make this process a heck of a whole lot more fun, and I'm forever indebted.

And to wrap this all up, a never ending thanks to my Abba above. I am here, at this very precious moment in my life, because of you and all of your goodness. Paul says in Ephesians that you are capable of immeasurably more than we can fathom. You have already stretched the confines of what I thought was possible, and it's hard to imagine much more. But I don't doubt you. And I don't doubt your goodness. Thank you, Abba. Thank you for everything that led me here. I am now and forever, yours.

STEEN JONES

Steen was born and raised in Woodstock, Georgia. While only recently discovering her passion for writing, she's always been an artist and a storyteller. After owning a social enterprise for five years, and raising two children with special needs, Steen decided to pursue a story idea that gripped her many years ago and The Door Keeper Trilogy was born.

When she's not writing, you can find her reading in her treehouse, painting, cuddling with her two dogs, or baking. Steen loves binge watching TV shows with her husband and spending time with her two incredible children in their backyard pool.

For more information about Steen, please contact at the following sites:
- Website: thedoorkeepertrilogy.com
- Email: steen@thedoorkeepertrilogy.com
- Instagram: @steenjonesauthor
- Facebook: facebook.com/steenjonesauthor